D1324321

SIR THOMAS MALORY

King Arthur and his Knights

also edited by R. T. Davies

Samuel Johnson: Selected Writings
Medieval English Lyrics: A Critical Anthology

Geoffrey Chaucer: The Prologue to the Canterbury Tales
(published by G. G. Harrap)

SIR THOMAS MALORY

King Arthur and his Knights

a selection from what has been known as
Le Morte Darthur, made and edited by
R. T. DAVIES

FABER & FABER
3 Queen Square London

First published in 1967 by
Faber and Faber Limited
3 Queen Square London W.C.1
First published in this edition 1976
Printed in Great Britain by
Robert MacLehose and Company Limited
Printers to the University of Glasgow

ISBN 0 571 11106 8

For
Betty Sheldon

Contents

ॐ&

Acknowledgements

My thanks are due to the Warden and Fellows of Winchester College who readily allowed me to use their manuscript of Malory, and to the Fellows' Librarian, Mr. J. M. G. Blakiston, and the Archivist, Mr. P. J. Gwyn, who were most friendly and hospitable. Professor C. F. Bühler, Keeper of the Printed Books in the Pierpont Morgan Library, promptly answered my questions. Of my colleagues in the University of Liverpool, from whom I continually learn so much in ways too many to mention, Mr. N. F. Blake and Mr. G. O. Rees, in particular, helped with some points of detail, and Mr. B. F. Nellist discussed the book with me as it grew and, with characteristic generosity of time and learning, criticized it thoroughly in its first draft. To him, especially, I am particularly grateful. To all my colleagues in the Department of English Literature I am grateful for their making it possible for me to enjoy a term free from teaching in which to get on with this book. I should like to thank, also, Miss M. Burton and Mrs. I. Wright, of our Department of English, who have valiantly converted my manuscript into type, the staff of the Harold Cohen Library and of the Arts Reading Room for their efficiency and kindness, and the University of Liverpool, itself, which made me a grant towards my expenses. Finally, may I say how much I appreciate the tact and patience of my publishers, particularly of Mr. Alan Pringle, and the vision and understanding which makes them wish to make medieval literature more widely read.

Introduction

This book of Sir Thomas Malory's makes real a world of knights and ladies, castles, adventures and enchantment, which is picturesque and remote from our own. But among its woods and hermits and gay pavilions there fall in love and into misfortune, there hate, heroically endure and laugh, men and women much like ourselves. In both these respects, the 'romantic' and the 'perennial', this book can please the modern reader immediately.

Written, however, some five hundred years ago, it has features that show it to belong peculiarly to certain medieval literary traditions. Though Malory never applies the word 'romance' to his own work and only uses it at all of his sources in Book Two, his book resembles, in several respects, other medieval works that go by that name. If it is a verbal art form at all, like 'epic' or 'satire', the romance is no easier than they are to define. Works that called themselves romances had been composed during at least three centuries by Malory's time, so that it is not surprising to find in them a diversity that might suggest (as it does in three centuries of modern novels) that here was little by way of a recognizable genre at all. Perhaps, however, the romance may be said to have been a narrative fiction about knights and ladies who were impelled by love or religion or a desire for hazardous adventure or for a fight. In an Arthurian romance it was at the court of King Arthur, the granter of boons, that a knight's adventures began and to which he both returned and sent those he vanquished. Knights of Malory's own day were not 'errant', and expectantly questing, just as swords no more floated miraculously down rivers then than now. Knights errant and the marvellous, which was so dear to the medieval heart and certainly not peculiar to romances, may, then, perhaps, be called characteristic features of this verbal art form.

The world of the romances was highly idealized but what was idealized was often the everyday. Battles between men-at-arms in the fifteenth century were as much blood and skilled butchery as in Malory, as much the clang and crunch of metal on metal. In Alnwick or in Bamborough Castle, during the Wars of the Roses, a contemporary Sir Launcelot could just as well have inspected the 'estures'. Moreover, medieval romances treated the supernatural and the fantastic as matter-of-fact with practical consequences, and Malory's unselfconscious mention of the twenty thousand pounds Guenevere spent on the search for Launcelot, while uncharacteristic of French romances, is no bit of exceptional 'materialism', peculiar to a mercenary author, but altogether characteristic of the literary tradition of chivalry in English.

The structure of a number of thirteenth- and fourteenth-century French romances may also be regarded as characteristic although not essential. In them, encounters are typically by chance, and action often proceeds adventitiously. An example will be found in Malory's Book Three where several stories, one might say, interlace. Such interlacing pleases because it mixes immediate inconsequentiality, which relaxes, and diverse and abundant matter, which refreshes, with the comfortable reassurance of eventual return and the promise of further development after no matter how long or complex an interval. On the bigger scale, Malory's whole book is richly diverse and comprises many themes and characters some of which interweave irregularly throughout. To enter his book is to enter just such a wood as his Launcelot might and to wander, variously delighted and enthralled by its teeming adventures.

For many of us, medieval prose romance is Malory. And yet Professor Vinaver has shown that in Malory many of these characteristic romance features are very much reduced, and Book Three itself, for all I have said about it as a sample of romance form, is an instance of this reduction: the story line has been simplified in that it consists of selected short episodes which were very far apart in the many pages of the probable French source. It seems likely that this was by Malory's deliberate design. But this is uncertain because in no case do we know exactly which text Malory used for his translation, so that we cannot be sure he did not find what look like his innovations in an unknown source. With this major reservation, we may say, however, that it is in Books Seven and Eight that Malory's artistic genius is most apparent. Here the romance mode of interlacing many stories has been entirely superseded by the more Aristotelian and more modern mode of a unity of action or theme, to which everything is, in the end, subordinate.

Malory's French sources—the French books mentioned by him and Caxton—were, the experts tell us, very largely prose developments of thirteenth-century prose romances. For Malory's last book, however, it has been argued that the sources were an English stanzaic poem, *Le Morte Arthur*, and a French one, the *Mort Artu*. On the other hand, for Book Four and that part of Book Seven concerned with the healing of Sir Urry, no source is known. Book Two derives from an alliterative English poem, the *Morte Arthure*, (and has not only in its action, sentiment and dialogue the primitive vigour and crudity of its source but, in many instances, its very wording, emphatic, monosyllabic and consonantal).

Even such a quick glance at some of his likely sources supports the view that Malory assembled in his book a unique collection of heterogeneous Arthurian materials. There is no other Arthurian book like it. And of that literary tradition in which it was said earlier that he was working it can now be conveniently said that it was not one of form only, but also of content. It is of traditional tales that Malory's is an original retelling, rearrangement and reinterpretation.

Before more can be said about this it will be helpful to digress for a paragraph or two. There are two versions of his work extant. They are a printed text and one in manuscript. It was in 1485, the year of the Battle of Bosworth and of the accession of Henry VII (who was to call his eldest son, Arthur, in 1486), that William Caxton, England's first printer, published his edition. He edited his copy, as he tells us on page 250, dividing it into books and chapters, providing a preface and epilogue, and, presumably, shortening my Book Two, which is twice the length of his version. Only two copies of this edition remain, one in the John Rylands Library in Manchester and one in the Pierpont Morgan Library in New York. Until recently our knowledge of what Malory wrote depended on these two printed books and it was in terms of Caxton's books and chapters that reference was made to it. I have, therefore, reproduced these in square brackets in this select edition rather as is the practice in modern editions of the Bible, the chapters and verses of which were also imposed by an editor.

Caxton's editing, however, was partly based on divisions he found in his copy. This we know because of the evidence available since 1934 when Mr. W. F. Oakeshott discovered in the Library of Winchester College a version of Malory in manuscript. Experts date it about 1480. The beginnings of some of Caxton's books correspond with its chief divisions, and of many of his chapters with the one hundred and six red initial letters that occur not very systematically throughout it. My organization of the work into eight sections is based on the chief divisions of the Winchester MS., and in this I follow most scholars since the practice was begun by Professor Vinaver in the first edition of Malory to be derived from that manuscript in 1947. It is most likely that Caxton's printing and the Winchester MS. are independent of each other and are at least copies of copies of what Malory wrote.

Several of the books in the manuscript have tailpieces which are absent from Caxton's printing. The first of these, on page 58, at the end of Book One, begins, 'Here ends this tale': it reads as if Malory certainly had in mind a continuation of his work, were it possible to find further copy, and conceived of what he was doing in terms of tales or books; it also connects with the following Book which takes up in its opening paragraph the concluding reference to the coming to court of Launcelot and Tristram. Malory has linked the two tales or books together in terms of a time sequence—what happens in Book Two takes place after that in Book One—and in terms of two of his chief characters—much of what happens after this point is about Launcelot and Tristram.

Each Book, except Book Four, is linked with those before and after it in this sort of way and there can, therefore, be no other order for the tales than this. Despite the absence of this obvious linking, Book Four, Sir Gareth's Tale, is integral because no knight is more intimate with Launcelot than he who is almost as good a knight as Launcelot himself, by whom he was knighted. Moreover, with Tristram and Lamorak, and like Launcelot at the last, he is opposed to Gawain whom he regards as 'vengeable'. The justice with which he does so regard him is proved with cruel irony when it is his death which is the ground of Gawain's making that final war on Launcelot which destroys them all.

There are some other links between the Books such as Merlin's warning to Arthur that Guenevere will not be faithful to him (p. 49), the forecast that Launcelot will save

Guenevere from the fire (p. 62), and Galahad's achievement of the sword that was Balin's (pp. 46 and 47). It might be thought that such predictions contributed to a sense that destiny is being fulfilled, but that is not, however, one of Malory's conspicuous or vital themes. He makes little of it.

Although we do not know what title, if any, Malory intended his work to have, Caxton, in his Epilogue, showed that he regarded what he had printed as one book, about King Arthur and his knights, and, in the tailpiece of the last Book, it can scarcely be any other than Malory himself who refers to this work as 'the whole book of King Arthur and of his noble knights', and envisages our reading from its 'beginning' to its 'ending'. The work comprises, then, eight principal 'books' or 'tales' – terms which are used indifferently and which are used also of constituent stories within these larger divisions (pp. 30, 61, 79) – in each case demarcated by such direct comment at the beginning or end as will be found on pages 58, 61, 79, 80, 166, 205, 249, e.g. 'Here follows Sir Gareth's Tale of Orkney,' and proves to have as its general subject the origin, diverse flowering and fall of an exemplary king, Arthur, and of his knights, and, in particular, of Sir Launcelot.

There are, of course, many and gross imperfections and weaknesses of structure and unity. Although Book Five, of Tristram, keys into the Book that follows it, it is the one Book of them all that might make one wonder if Malory had not intended each Book to be separate to an extent that has caused Professor Vinaver to call his edition *The Works of Malory*. For one thing, it is by no means obvious how its events are related chronologically to those in other Books. But the wonder is not so much that there are defects in general cohesion, as that there is so much cohesion as there is. Chaucer above all, but also, for example, Gower and the poet of *Sir Gawain and the Green Knight*, had, some three-quarters of a century earlier, created works in verse conspicuous for their sophisticated unity. But the vast body of diverse Arthurian lore which Malory tackled has been aptly compared by C. S. Lewis to a great medieval church in which its various parts are of various periods and whatever unity there is is not that of any one artist. We should have been much helped had Malory revised his earlier Books (which there is very little to suggest he did) let alone re-written them as a novelist would in the light of what he had achieved in the last two, and with the kind of skill he had by practice then acquired. He might have fetched out and developed more thoroughly themes that are undoubtedly present and stimulate the attentive reader, but which, despite the amount of selection and arrangement which comparison with his sources suggests he made, still fail to stand out distinctly. There is, for example, the feud between, on the one hand, King Lot and his sons, Gawain, Gaheris and Aggravaine, and, on the other, King Pellinore and his sons, Lamorak, Agglovale and Percival. This theme includes the connection of the death of Lamorak with that of Tristram, in so much as both were slain treacherously (pp. 200–1, 215).

Malory's style is remarkable for its time in this kind of literature. We do not know whether he was acquainted with English religious homiletic writing, which enjoyed a tradition continuous from Pre-Norman Conquest to Tudor England, and with other prose narratives of the fifteenth century, such as the didactic preachers' stories of the *Gesta Romanorum* and the *Golden Legend*, or the instructive guide-book, *Mandeville's Travels*. Such works as these were less ambitious but, like his, generally translations, sometimes from French. There are certainly other likenesses between some of this prose and Malory's, but so, too, there are between his literary artefact and, for example, the unpretentious, everyday letters of the time. A number remain and are, presumably, written much as they would have been spoken. The major stylistic difference between Book Two, with its alliterative English source, and the other Books, together with Malory's capacity to accommodate such diverse matter as bloody battles, human passion and the appearances of the Grail, suggest that his chameleon genius took its colour from his sources and immediate purposes. Vocabulary and syntax are generally simple, the one comprising chiefly native English words and the other being loosely articulated with 'and's' and 'so's' and 'but's'. His style is basically unsophisticated, direct, concrete, colourful and vigorous, like English speech and never far from it. It might be hazarded that it was for this reason that Malory's dialogue is outstandingly good, were it not that dialogue is good also in English writers more obviously within a literary tradition, such as Chaucer and the poet of *Sir Gawain and the Green Knight*.

On almost every page some passage arrests and moves and reveals Malory's genius as an imaginative writer. Since medieval artists are so often to be seen as didactic or artificial, he is, perhaps, nearer to John Keats, and to Keats's 'Man of Achievement', than might have been expected, in that he has a capacity for entering into a variety of characters and situations and living them out on the page for their own sake and not to make a point or to instruct or to decorate or even to contribute to a greater artistic whole. Though many of the characters are not differentiated at all, Pellinore, Dinadan, Guenevere, Palomydes, Bors, to mention a few, all have distinctive personalities. But they are not, of course, all Malory's peculiar creation: as usual it is not easy to distinguish the traditional and the new. Certainly, on the one hand, multiplicity of invention is characteristically medieval as many an illuminated manuscript or carving in stone or wood will testify, while, on the other, Malory does not always develop fully the potential of his diverse figures. In reading him, however, we may, at one time, be laughing at some of the extravagances of the chivalric attitude and at another sympathizing with it even when it prompts the loyal rescue of a woman who has been frequently distrustful and petulant. Even at the last Guenevere will say to Launcelot as he vows to live the life of penance and prayer, 'I may never believe you.' And, unkind as this may seem, she has some justice on her side for, with creative percipience of the kind I am here indicating, Malory has Launcelot then request a last kiss!

It was the diversity of Malory's work and its power to please which Caxton remarked in his Preface: 'herein may be seen noble chivalry, courtesy, humanity, friendliness, hardiness, love, friendship, cowardice, murder, hate, virtue and sin. . . . And for to pass the time this book shall be pleasant to read in.' Caxton also expected it to serve a moral purpose, but whether, in this, he had interpreted Malory aright is a matter for discussion. Equally, the extent to which, on the one hand, the author wrote with a preconceived moral design and with his principles fully formed, or, on the other, found his moral values as he met the exigencies of translating and retelling the tales under the immediate compulsion of his imagination, is a question to be asked not only of Malory's work but of that of any creative artist. Were the latter the case it might account, for example, for the several, not obviously connected, causes given for the breaking up of the Round Table—the quest of the Sankgreall (pp. 129, 146, 149), the work of Fortune (p. 226), the adultery of Launcelot and Guenevere (p. 240), the ill-will of Aggravaine and Mordred (pp. 206, 208, 223), and Arthur's permitting a situation in which he and Launcelot are divided (pp. 218, 230).

Nevertheless, throughout the immense diversity of the whole book there is implicitly affirmed and variously explored the value of a noble way of life appropriate to 'worshipful' men and women. It is one of the factors unifying the work. Prowess shows itself the first characteristic of a knight, that is to say, his valour, physical strength and combative skill. He keeps faith and is honest. He is merciful and he courteously serves women. Guile, treachery and cowardice are consistently rejected.

Very occasionally Malory makes an overt statement about the 'worshipful way'. For example, on pp. 176–7, in a passage for which no source is known, saying that worshipful men and women will always love one more than another, he distinguishes between love 'in King Arthur's days' and 'love nowadays', and, calling the old-fashioned love 'virtuous', so makes his own characteristically impulsive and simple reconciliation of romantic love and Christianity. Marriage is never mentioned, but this love is loyal to one person, stable, steady and continent, and, in this sense, so righteous that he can say of the adulterous Guenevere, whose love was 'virtuous', that she 'had a good end', that is, died in a state of grace. In fact, of course, Guenevere's final state of grace is achieved by her rejection of love in the practice of penance and prayer: she becomes a religious, and everyone marvels how 'virtuously' she is 'changed'. Moreover, Malory blurs the nature of her intimacy with Launcelot at the moment of her being finally surprised in her room with her lover, saying he does not know whether they were in bed together or not. It is this sort of opacity with which we are so often presented in trying to interpret Malory. But his success in making warmly real and desirable to us the relationship between his lovers implicitly affirms the worth he feels there is in it: it is part of the worshipful way that Launcelot follows which is neither ignoble, like King Mark's way, nor holy, like Sir Galahad's, but the way for a country gentleman and a horsed soldier who has not renounced this mutable and sinful world as a monk but, as the best knight 'of a sinful man', strives to make of the world and the flesh something noble. Indeed, such is the quality of the life he lives 'in the world' that, when he leaves it to seek the Grail, he is able to achieve almost as much spiritually as one who has always rejected it, Galahad the greatest Grail knight himself.

These are the sort of guarded considerations one is led to make about what Malory may have found he was saying with developing authority and consistency in his corpus, or series, of Arthurian tales. It was not something merely topical, growing, perhaps, out of the wars and politics of his time. It is a measure of his greatness that, if knightly armour and hermits' cells are to us picturesque archaisms, what Malory describes going on inside them is as relevant to us today as it ever was. It is a further measure of his greatness that it was not until the eighteenth century that England knew again prose narrative of such stature.

We cannot be certain, however, who was this artist called Sir Thomas Malory in both versions of his work. In the Winchester MS., at the end of my Book One, he is called a 'knight prisoner', and, in Caxton's edition, at the end of my Book Eight, as he prays for 'good deliverance', he reports that he has ended his book in 1469–70, that is, during the Wars of the Roses. Though there are records of other Malorys, only one Sir Thomas Malory is known at this time, and though there is no evidence of his being a prisoner in 1469–70, earlier he was in jail several times, and, when he died in 1471, he was buried near to the prison of Newgate. This Sir Thomas came of an old Warwickshire family, was married, fought in the wars, served as an M.P., and lived on his estates. It is an unresolved paradox, however, which cannot be lightly set aside, that, though there is no record of his conviction, he was variously charged with robbery, cattle-raiding, extortion and rape. But, supposing that it was this Sir Thomas who wrote these chivalric Tales, it would not be the first time that great and even edifying art came from a life apparently small and even disreputable, while it is not at all unlikely that, just as a Launcelot, a Gawain and a Guenevere could be exquisitely penitent, so could a Thomas

Malory, one who was, perhaps, no less than his hero, Launcelot, 'unstable'.*

Caxton tells us in his Preface that it was his doubts about the historicity of Arthur that inhibited his printing a book about him. This is, in itself, an interesting fact in an age which some might have thought ready to accept any fascinating legend as true, on authority, and particularly a legend so alive in popular imagination.

Though Caxton's standards in matters of historical evidence were, even so, inferior to our own, what early evidence exists suggests that it is not impossible that the figure of Malory's Arthur has some slight foundation in history. He may have been an outstanding leader of the British against the invading Saxons in late 5c. or early 6c. Nennius, in his *Historia Brittonum* of the early 9c., mentions such an Arthur and also a battle he won at Mons Badonis. To this battle there is also a reference made in the middle of 6c., much nearer to its likely date, by Gildas in his *De Excidio Britanniae*. But Gildas does not mention Arthur. The name of Arthur, however, scarcely to be found in Britain before, occurs four or five times in late 6c. and early 7c., which may suggest that parents were calling their children after a national figure of a generation or two earlier.

What may, then, have been a historical hero must very soon have become a figure of Celtic folk-lore: perhaps an actual Hercules may have been joined with a Hercules of myth. Certainly in the 11c. Welsh story of Culhwch and Olwen, which can be read in a collection of tales called by Lady Guest *The Mabinogion* and which is translated in the Everyman series, Arthur is the mighty King of far-flung

---

*A book discussing a second Sir Thomas Malory, who was a Yorkshireman of Hutton and Studley, has come to my notice only as this edition goes to press: William Matthews, *The Ill-Framed Knight*.

dominions, ruling a court of warriors in a faery world and performing fantastic adventures.

In 12c., Geoffrey of Monmouth, in his *Historia Regum Britanniae*, set Arthur as an imperial conqueror in a Norman court. Here for the first time are Merlin, Arthur's birth-story, Mordred's treachery and the crucial connection of love between the sexes with chivalric achievement. Geoffrey was done into French in mid 12c. by Wace who introduced the Round Table.

In part from Wace and in part more immediately from Celtic sources Chrétien de Troyes, in later 12c., drew that 'Matter of Britain' which was the subject of his seminal romances. In him the element of refined love developed and in him the Sankgreall first appeared. Prose cycles of Arthurian romances, in 13c., owed much to Chrétien, and it is developments of these, referred to by him as the French book, that Malory used as his major source.

I have taken my text, primarily, from a microfilm copy of the Winchester MS. and have examined the MS. itself for particular points. The beginning and end are missing, as I have indicated in the textual notes, and these I have taken from H. O. Sommer's *Le Morte Darthur: the original edition of William Caxton* (London, 1889), which reproduces the copy in the John Rylands Library, Manchester. The last pages of this printed copy are also missing and have been replaced by transcripts made by Whittaker from the copy in the Pierpont Morgan Library. Where the transcript is wrong I have, of course, accepted the reading in the American copy.

Emendations are shown as follows: [ ] = omitted in Winchester MS. but reads thus in Caxton (unless there is a note explaining); ⟨ ⟩ = omitted in Winchester MS. and supplied by me, generally to help make the sense clearer to the modern reader rather than to restore what I surmise to be what Malory wrote. (Sometimes there is a comment in a note.)

The division into Books I have explained on p. 17. Book titles are mine unless they are in inverted commas when they will be found somewhere in the MS. The selection I have made comprises about one sixth of Malory's whole work.

I have introduced modern punctuation and use of capitals, paragraph division and arrangement of speech. I have silently substituted modern forms of some verbs and pronouns, use of some prepositions and spellings of some words: e.g. for 'they *been*' I read 'they *are*', for *flamand, flaming*, for *ye, you*, for 'take him *to* your prisoner', '*as* your prisoner', for *encheve*, *achieve*, for *sin, since*, etc. I have tried to standardize spelling throughout. In general my object has been to remove as discreetly as I could whatever, for the non-specialist, is merely quaint or off-putting or unnecessarily obscure, without in any way seriously altering the text from a literary point of view. Some will wish I had done more, some much less.

The glossary is meant to give, as briefly as possible, the meanings of difficult words. Please note that, though the present-day meaning is not given, this may sometimes be the meaning of the word. Please note, also, that, though many words in the text have present-day spellings, they do not have present-day meanings, but those in the glossary.

King Arthur and his Knights

Caxton's Preface

After that I had accomplished and finished divers histories as well of contemplation as of other historial and worldly acts of great conquerors and princes, and also certain books of examples and doctrine, many noble and divers gentlemen of this realm of England came and demanded me many and ofttimes wherefore that I have not do made and imprinted the noble history of the Sankgreall and of the most renowned Christian king, first and chief of the three best Christian, and worthy, King Arthur, which ought most to be remembered among us Englishmen before all other Christian kings.

For it is notoirly known through the universal world that there are nine worthy and the best that ever were, that is to wit, three paynims, three Jews and three Christian men. As for the paynims, they were before the Incarnation of Christ, which were named, the first, Hector of Troy, of whom the history is common both in ballad and in prose, the second, Alexander the Great, and the third, Julius Caesar, Emperor of Rome, of whom the histories are well-known and had. And as for the three Jews which also were before the Incarnation of our Lord—of whom the first was Duke Joshua, which brought the children of Israel into the Land of Behest, the second, David, King of Jerusalem, and the third, Judas Maccabaeus—of these three the Bible rehearses all their noble histories and acts. And sith the said Incarnation have been three noble Christian men installed and admitted through the universal world into the number of the nine best and worthy: of whom was first the noble Arthur, whose noble acts I purpose to write in this present book here following; the second was Charlemagne, or Charles the Great, of whom the history is had in many places, both in French and English; and the third and last was Godfrey of Boulogne, of whose acts and life I made a book unto the excellent prince and king of noble memory, King Edward the Fourth.

The said noble gentlemen instantly required me to imprint the history of the said noble king and conqueror, King Arthur, and of his knights, with the history of the Sankgreall and of the death and ending of the said Arthur, affirming that I ought rather to imprint his acts and noble feats than of Godfrey of Boulogne or any of the other eight, considering that he was a man born within this realm and King and Emperor of the same, and that there are in French divers and many noble volumes of his acts, and also of his knights.

To whom I answered that divers men hold opinion that there was no such Arthur and that all such books as are made of him are but feigned and fables, because that some chronicles make of him no mention nor remember him nothing, nor of his knights.

Whereto they answered – and one in special said – that in him that should say or think that there was never such a king called Arthur might well be aretted great folly and blindness, for he said that there were many evidences of the contrary. First, you may see his sepulchre in the monastery of Glastonbury, and also, in *Polychronicon*, in the fifth book, the sixth chapter, and in the seventh book, the twenty-third chapter, where his body was buried and after found and translated into the said monastery. You shall see also in the history of

28

Boccaccio, in his book *De Casu Principum*, part of his noble acts and also of his fall. Also Geoffrey, in his Brutish book, recounts his life. And in divers places of England many remembrances are yet of him and shall remain perpetually, and also of his knights: first, in the Abbey of Westminster, at Saint Edward's shrine, remains the print of his seal in red wax, enclosed in beryl, in which is written, 'Patricius Arthurus Brittaniae Galliae Germaniae Daciae Imperator'; item, in the castle of Dover you may see Gawain's skull and Cradock's mantle; at Winchester, the Round Table; in other places, Launcelot's sword and many other things.

Then, all these things considered, there can no man reasonably gainsay but there was a King of this land named Arthur. For in all places, Christian and heathen, he is reputed and taken for one of the nine worthy, and the first of the three Christian men. And also he is more spoken of beyond the sea, more books made of his noble acts, than there are in England, as well in Dutch, Italian, Spanish and Greekish, as in French. And yet of record remain in witness of him in Wales, in the town of Camelot, the great stones and marvellous works of iron lying under the ground, and royal vaults, which divers now living have seen. Wherefore it is a marvel why he is no more renowned in his own country, save only it accords to the word of God which says that no man is accepted for a prophet in his own country.

Then, all these things foresaid alleged, I could not well deny but that there was such a noble king named Arthur and reputed one of the nine worthy, and first and chief of the Christian men. And many noble volumes are made of him and of his noble knights in French, which I have seen and read beyond the sea, which are not had in our maternal tongue. But in Welsh are many and also in French, and some in English, but nowhere nigh all. Wherefore such as have late been drawn out briefly into English I have, after the simple cunning that God has sent to me, under the favour and correction of all noble lords and gentlemen, enprised to imprint a book of the noble histories of the said King Arthur and of certain of his knights, after a copy unto me delivered, which copy Sir Thomas Malory did take out of certain books of French and reduced it into English.

And I, according to my copy, have done set it in imprint to the intent that noble men may see and learn the noble acts of chivalry, the gentle and virtuous deeds that some knights used in those days, by which they came to honour, and how they that were vicious were punished and oft put to shame and rebuke; humbly beseeching all noble lords and ladies, with all other estates, of what estate or degree they are of, that shall see and read in this said book and work, that they take the good and honest acts in their remembrance, and to follow the same, wherein they shall find many joyous and pleasant histories and noble and renowned acts of humanity, gentleness and chivalries. For herein may be seen noble chivalry, courtesy, humanity, friendliness, hardiness, love, friendship, cowardice, murder, hate, virtue and sin. Do after the good and leave the evil and it shall bring you to good fame and renown!

And for to pass the time this book shall be pleasant to read in. But for to give faith and believe that all is true that is contained herein, you are at your liberty. But all is written for our doctrine and for to beware that we fall not to vice nor sin but to exercise and follow virtue, by which we may come and attain to good fame and renown in this life, and, after this short and transitory life, to come unto everlasting bliss in Heaven—the which he grant us that reigns in Heaven, the Blessed Trinity. Amen.

Book One

King Arthur's Early Days

[I.1] It befell in the days of Uther Pendragon, when he was King of all England and so reigned, that there was a mighty duke in Cornwall that held war against him long time, and the duke was called the Duke of Tintagel. And so by means King Uther sent for this Duke, charging him to bring his wife with him, for she was called a fair lady and a passing wise, and her name was called Igrayne.

So when the Duke and his wife were come unto the King, by the means of great lords they were accorded both. The King liked and loved this lady well, and he made them great cheer out of measure and desired to have lain by her, but she was a passing good woman and would not assent unto the King. And then she told the Duke, her husband, and said, 'I suppose that we were sent for that I should be dishonoured. Wherefore, husband, I counsel you that we depart from hence suddenly, that we may ride all night unto our own castle.'

And, in like wise as she said, so they departed, that neither the King nor none of his Council were aware of their departing. As soon as King Uther knew of their departing so suddenly he was wonderly wroth. Then he called to him his privy Council and told them of the sudden departing of the Duke and his wife. Then they advised the King to send for

the Duke and his wife by a great charge: 'And if he will not
come at your summons, then may you do your best. Then
have you cause to make mighty war upon him.'

So that was done and the messengers had their answers –
and that was this, shortly, that neither he nor his wife would
not come to him. Then was the King wonderly wroth. And
then the King sent him plain word again and bade him be
ready and stuff him and garnish him, for within forty days he
would fetch him out of the biggest castle that he has.

When the Duke had this warning, anon he went and furnished and garnished two strong castles of his of the which
the one hight Tintagel and the other castle hight Terrabil.
So his wife, Dame Igrayne, he put in the castle of Tintagel
and himself he put in the castle of Terrabil, the which had
many issues and posterns out. Then in all haste came Uther
with a great host and laid a siege about the castle of Terrabil,
and there he pitched many pavilions. And there was great
war made on both parts and much people slain.

Then for pure anger and for great love of fair Igrayne the
King Uther fell sick. So came to the King Uther Sir Ulfius,
a noble knight, and asked the King why he was sick.

'I shall tell thee,' said the King. 'I am sick for anger and
for love of fair Igrayne, that I may not be whole.'

'Well, my lord,' said Sir Ulfius, 'I shall seek Merlin and
he shall do you remedy that your heart shall be pleased.'

So Ulfius departed and by adventure he met Merlin in a
beggar's array. And there Merlin asked Ulfius whom he
sought, and he said he had little ado to tell him.

'Well,' said Merlin, 'I know whom thou seekest, for thou
seekest Merlin. Therefore seek no further for I am he. And
if King Uther will well reward me and be sworn unto me to
fulfil my desire, that shall be his honour and profit more than
mine, for I shall cause him to have all his desire.'

'All this will I undertake,' said Ulfius, 'that there shall be
nothing reasonable but thou shalt have thy desire.'

'Well,' said Merlin, 'he shall have his intent and desire. And therefore,' said Merlin, 'ride on your way, for I will not be long behind.'

[I.2] Then Ulfius was glad and rode on more than a pace till that he came to King Uther Pendragon and told him he had met with Merlin.

'Where is he?' said the King.

'Sir,' said Ulfius, 'he will not dwell long.'

Therewithal Ulfius was aware where Merlin stood at the porch of the pavilion's door, and then Merlin was bound to come to the King. When King Uther saw him he said he was welcome.

'Sir,' said Merlin, 'I know all your heart every deal. So you will be sworn unto me, as you are a true king anointed, to fulfil my desire, you shall have your desire.' Then the King was sworn upon the four Evangelists.

'Sir,' said Merlin, 'this is my desire: the first night that you shall lie by Igrayne you shall get a child on her; and, when that is born, that it shall be delivered to me for to nourish thereas I will have it, for it shall be your worship and the child's avail as mickle as the child is worth.'

'I will well,' said the King, 'as thou wilt have it.'

'Now make you ready,' said Merlin. 'This night you shall lie with Igrayne in the castle of Tintagel. And you shall be like the Duke, her husband, Ulfius shall be like Sir Brastias, a knight of the Duke's, and I will be like a knight that hight Sir Jordanus, a knight of the Duke's. But wait you make not many questions with her nor her men, but say you are diseased, and so hie you to bed and rise not on the morn till I come to you, for the Castle of Tintagel is but ten miles hence.'

So this was done as they devised. But the Duke of Tintagel espied how the King rode from the siege of Terrabil. And therefore that night he issued out of the castle at a postern for to have distressed the King's host, and so through his

33

own issue the Duke himself was slain ere ever the King came
to the castle of Tintagel. So after the death of the Duke, King
Uther lay with Igrayne more than three hours after his death,
and begot on her that night Arthur. And, ere day came,
Merlin came to the King and bade him make him ready, and
so he kissed the Lady Igrayne and departed in all haste. But
when the Lady heard tell of the Duke, her husband, and by
all record he was dead ere ever King Uther came to her, then
she marvelled who that might be that lay with her in likeness
of her lord. So she mourned privily and held her peace.

Then all the barons by one assent prayed the King of
accord betwixt the Lady Igrayne and him. The King gave
them leave, for fain would he have been accorded with her.
So the King put all the trust in Ulfius to entreat between
them. So by the entreaty at the last the King and she met
together.

'Now will we do well,' said Ulfius. 'Our King is a lusty
knight and wifeless, and my lady Igrayne is a passing fair
lady. It were great joy unto us all and it might please the
King to make her his queen.'

Unto that they all well accorded and moved it to the King.
And anon, like a lusty knight, he assented thereto with good
will, and so in all haste they were married in a morning with
great mirth and joy.

And King Lot of Lothian and of Orkney then wedded
Morgause that was Gawain's mother, and King Nentres of
the land of Garlot wedded Elayne. All this was done at the
request of King Uther. And the third sister, Morgan le Fay
was put to school in a nunnery, and there she learned so
much that she was a great clerk of necromancy. And, after,
she was wedded to King Uriens of the land of Gore that was
Sir Uwaine le Blaunche Mains' father.

[I.3, 4, 5] Then Queen Igrayne waxed daily greater and
greater. So it befell, after, within half a year, as King Uther
lay by his queen, he asked her, by the faith she owed to him,

whose was the child within her body. Then was she sore
abashed to give answer. 'Dismay you not,' said the King, 'but
tell me the truth, and I shall love you the better, by the faith
of my body.'

'Sir,' said she, 'I shall tell you the truth. The same night
that my lord was dead, the hour of his death, as his knights
record, there came into my castle of Tintagel a man like my
lord in speech and in countenance, and two knights with him
in likeness of his two knights, Brastias and Jordanus. And so
I went unto bed with him as I ought to do with my lord. And
the same night, as I shall answer unto God, this child was
begotten upon me.'

'That is truth,' said the King, 'as you say, for it was I myself that came in the likeness. And, therefore, dismay you
not, for I am father to the child.' And there he told her all
the cause how it was by Merlin's counsel. Then the Queen
made great joy when she knew who was the father of her
child.

Soon came Merlin unto the King and said, 'Sir, you must
purvey you for the nourishing of your child.'

'As thou wilt,' said the King, 'be it.'

'Well,' said Merlin, 'I know a lord of yours in this land
that is a passing true man and a faithful, and he shall have
the nourishing of your child. And his name is Sir Ector, and
he is a lord of fair livelode in many parts in England and
Wales. And this lord, Sir Ector, let him be sent for for to
come and speak with you, and desire him yourself, as he
loves you, that he will put his own child to nourishing to
another woman and that his wife nourish yours. And when
the child is born let it be delivered to me at yonder privy
postern, unchristened.'

So, like as Merlin devised, it was done. And when Sir
Ector was come he made fiaunce to the King for to nourish
the child like as the King desired, and there the King granted
Sir Ector great rewards. Then when the Lady was delivered

the King commanded two knights and two ladies to take the child bound in a cloth of gold, 'and that you deliver him to what poor man you meet at the postern gate of the castle'. So the child was delivered unto Merlin, and so he bore it forth unto Sir Ector and made an holy man to christen him and named him Arthur. And so Sir Ector's wife nourished him with her own pap.

Then, within two years, King Uther fell sick of a great malady. And, in the meanwhile, his enemies usurped upon him and did a great battle upon his men and slew many of his people.

'Sir,' said Merlin, 'you may not lie so as you do, for you must to the field though you ride on an horse-litter. For you shall never have the better of your enemies but if your person be there, and then shall you have the victory.'

So it was done as Merlin had devised, and they carried the King forth in an horse-litter with a great host toward his enemies, and at St. Albans there met with the King a great host of the north. And that day Sir Ulfius and Sir Brastias did great deeds of arms, and King Uther's men overcame the northern battle and slew many people and put the remnant to flight. And then the King returned unto London and made great joy of his victory.

And then he fell passing sore sick so that three days and three nights he was speechless. Wherefore all the barons made great sorrow and asked Merlin what counsel were best.

'There nis none other remedy,' said Merlin, 'but God will have his will. But look you all barons be before King Uther tomorn, and God and I shall make him to speak.'

So on the morn all the barons with Merlin came before the King. Then Merlin said aloud unto King Uther, 'Sir, shall your son, Arthur, be King, after your days, of this realm with all the appertinence?'

Then Uther Pendragon turned him and said in hearing of them all, 'I give him God's blessing and mine and bid him pray for my soul, and righteously and worshipfully that he claim the crown upon forfeiture of my blessing.'

And therewith he yielded up the ghost. And then was he interred as longed to a king: wherefore the Queen, fair Igrayne, made great sorrow, and all the barons.

Then stood the realm in great jeopardy long while, for every lord that was mighty of men made him strong, and many weened to have been King. Then Merlin went to the Archbishop of Canterbury and counselled him for to send for all the lords of the realm and all the gentlemen-of-arms that they should to London come by Christmas upon pain of cursing, and for this cause, that Jesu, that was born on that night, that he would, of his great mercy, show some miracle, as he was come to be King of mankind, for to show some miracle who should be rightwis King of this realm. So the Archbishop by the advice of Merlin sent for all the lords and gentlemen-of-arms that they should come by Christmas even unto London, and many of them made them clean of their life that their prayer might be the more acceptable unto God.

So in the greatest church of London – whether it were Paul's or not the French book makes no mention – all the estates were, long ere day, in the church for to pray. And when matins and the first mass was done there was seen in the churchyard, against the High Altar, a great stone four square, like unto a marble stone, and in midst thereof was like an anvil of steel a foot on high, and therein stuck a fair sword, naked, by the point. And letters there were written in gold about the sword that said thus: 'Whoso pulls out this sword from this stone and anvil is rightwis King born of all England.' Then the people marvelled and told it to the Archbishop.

'I command,' said the Archbishop, 'that you keep you within your church and pray unto God still, that no man touch the sword till the High Mass be all done.'

So when all masses were done, all the lords went to behold the stone and the sword. And when they saw the scripture, some essayed, such as would have been King, but none might stir the sword nor move it.

'He is not here,' said the Archbishop, 'that shall achieve the sword, but, doubt not, God will make him known. But this is my counsel,' said the Archbishop, 'that we let purvey ten knights, men of good fame, and they to keep this sword.'

So it was ordained. And then there was made a cry that every man should essay that would for to win the sword. And upon New Year's Day the barons let make a jousts and a tournament that all knights that would joust or tourney there might play. And all this was ordained for to keep the lords together and the commons, for the Archbishop trusted that God would make him known that should win the sword.

So upon New Year's Day when the service was done the barons rode unto the field, some to joust and some to tourney. And so it happed that Sir Ector, that had great livelode about London, rode unto the jousts, and with him rode Sir Kay, his son, and young Arthur, that was his nourished brother. And Sir Kay was made knight at All Hallowmas before. So as they rode to the joustsward Sir Kay had lost his sword for he had left it at his father's lodging. And so he prayed young Arthur for to ride for his sword.

'I will well,' said Arthur, and rode fast after the sword.

And when he came home the lady and all were out to see the jousting. Then was Arthur wroth and said to himself, 'I will ride to the churchyard and take the sword with me that sticks in the stone, for my brother, Sir Kay, shall not be without a sword this day!'

So when he came to the churchyard Sir Arthur alighted and tied his horse to the stile. And so he went to the tent and found no knights there for they were at jousting. And so he handled the sword by the handles and lightly and fiercely pulled it out of the stone, and took his horse and rode his way until he came to his brother, Sir Kay, and delivered him the sword.

And as soon as Sir Kay saw the sword he wist well it was the sword from the stone, and so he rode to his father, Sir Ector, and said, 'Sir, lo! here is the sword of the stone, wherefore I must be King of this land.'

When Sir Ector beheld the sword he returned again and came to the church, and there they alighted all three and went into the church. And anon he made Sir Kay to swear upon a book how he came to that sword.

'Sir,' said Sir Kay, 'by my brother, Arthur, for he brought it to me.'

'How got you this sword?' said Sir Ector to Arthur.

'Sir, I will tell you. When I came home for my brother's sword, I found nobody at home to deliver me his sword, and so I thought my brother, Sir Kay, should not be swordless, and so I came hither eagerly and pulled it out of the stone without any pain.'

'Found you any knights about this sword?' said Sir Ector.

'Nay,' said Arthur.

'Now,' said Sir Ector to Arthur, 'I understand you must be King of this land.'

'Wherefore I?' said Arthur, 'and for what cause?'

'Sir,' said Ector, 'for God will have it so, for there should never man have drawn out this sword but he that shall be rightwis King of this land. Now let me see whether you can put the sword thereas it was and pull it out again.'

'That is no maystry,' said Arthur, and so he put it in the stone. Therewithal Sir Ector essayed to pull out the sword and failed.

[I.6] 'Now essay,' said Sir Ector unto Sir Kay. And anon he pulled at the sword with all his might, but it would not be.

'Now shall you essay,' said Sir Ector to Arthur.

'I will well,' said Arthur, and pulled it out easily.

And therewithal Sir Ector kneeled down to the earth, and Sir Kay.

'Alas!' said Arthur, 'mine own dear father and brother, why kneel you to me?'

'Nay! nay! my lord, Arthur, it is not so. I was never your father nor of your blood, but I wot well you are of an higher blood than I weened you were.' And then Sir Ector told him all how he was betaken him for to nourish him and by whose commandment and by Merlin's deliverance. Then Arthur made great dole when he understood that Sir Ector was not his father.

'Sir,' said Ector unto Arthur, 'will you be my good and gracious lord when you are King?'

'Else were I to blame,' said Arthur, 'for you are the man in the world that I am most beholding to, and my good lady and mother your wife, that as well as her own hath fostered me and kept. And if ever it be God's will that I be King as you say, you shall desire of me what I may do and I shall not fail you. God forbid I should fail you!'

'Sir,' said Sir Ector, 'I will ask no more of you but that you will make my son, your foster-brother, Sir Kay, seneschal of all your lands.'

'That shall be done,' said Arthur, 'and more, by the faith of my body—that never man shall have that office but he, while he and I live.'

Therewithal they went unto the Archbishop and told him how the sword was achieved and by whom. And on Twelfth Day all the barons came thither and to essay to take the sword, who that would essay. But there before them all there might none take it out but Arthur. Wherefore there were many lords wroth and said it was great shame unto them all and the realm to be overgoverned with a boy of no high blood born. And so they fell out at that time that it was put off till Candlemas, and then all the barons should meet there again. But always the ten knights were ordained to watch the sword day and night, and so they set a pavilion over the stone and the sword, and five always watched.

So at Candlemas many more great lords came thither for to have won the sword, but there might none prevail. And right as Arthur did at Christmas he did at Candlemas, and pulled out the sword easily, whereof the barons were sore agrieved and put it off in delay till the high feast of Easter. And as Arthur sped before, so did he at Easter. Yet there were some of the great lords had indignation that Arthur should be King, and put it off in a delay till the feast of Pentecost. Then the Archbishop of Canterbury, by Merlin's providence, let purvey then of the best knights that they might get, and such knights as Uther Pendragon loved best and most trusted in his days. And such knights were put about Arthur as Sir Bawdewyn of Bretayn, Sir Kay, Sir Ulfius, Sir Brastias: all these with many others were always about Arthur day and night till the feast of Pentecost.

[I.7] And at the feast of Pentecost all manner of men essayed to pull at the sword, that would essay, but none might prevail but Arthur, and he pulled it out before all the lords and commons that were there. Wherefore all the commons cried at once: 'We will have Arthur unto our King! We will put him no more in delay, for we all see that it is God's will that he shall be our King, and who that holds against it we will slay him.'

And therewithal they kneeled at once, both rich and poor, and cried Arthur mercy because they had delayed him so long. And Arthur forgave them and took the sword between both his hands and offered it upon the altar where the Archbishop was, and so was he made knight by the best man that was there.

And so anon was the coronation made, and there was he sworn unto his lords and the commons for to be a true king, to stand with true justice from thenceforth the days of this life. Also then he made all lords that held of the crown to come in

and to do service as they ought to do. And many complaints
were made unto Sir Arthur of great wrongs that were done
since the death of King Uther, of many lands that were
bereaved lords, knights, ladies and gentlemen: wherefore
King Arthur made the lands to be given again unto them
that ought them. . . .

Arthur wars with rebel kings and lords, including King Lot, who
refuse as King a 'beardless boy that was come of low blood'. Arthur
himself learns that Uther and Igrayne were his parents only after
he has begotten Mordred, incestuously, on Morgause, Igrayne's
daughter by the previous marriage, and therefore his half-sister.
(Morgause is the mother of Gawain, Gareth, Gaheris and Aggravaine, and the wife of King Lot.) Later, Arthur is about to die at the
hands of a knight in a joust.

[I.24] . . . And therewith Merlin cast an enchantment on
the knight that he fell to the earth in a great sleep. Then
Merlin took up King Arthur and rode forth on the knight's
horse.

'Alas!' said Arthur, 'what hast thou done, Merlin? Hast
thou slain this good knight by thy crafts? For there lives not
so worshipful a knight as he was. For I had lever than the
stint of my land a year that he were alive.'

'Care you not,' said Merlin, 'for he is wholer than you: he
is but asleep and will awake within this hour. I told you,' said
Merlin, 'what a knight he was. Now here had you been slain
had I not been. Also there lives not a bigger knight than he
is one. And after this he shall do you good service. And his
name is King Pellinore, and he shall have two sons that shall
be passing good men as any living: save one in this world
they shall have no fellows for prowess and for good living,
and their names shall be Percival and Sir Lamorak of Wales.
And he shall tell you the name of your own son, begotten of
your sister, that shall be the destruction of all this realm.'

[I.25] Right so the King and he departed and went unto

an hermitage, and there was a good man and a great leech. So the hermit searched the King's wounds and gave him good salves. And so the King was there three days, and then were his wounds well amended that he might ride and go, and so departed.

And as they rode King Arthur said, 'I have no sword.'

'No force!' said Merlin. 'Hereby is a sword that shall be yours, and I may.'

So they rode till they came to a lake that was a fair water and broad. And in the midst Arthur was aware of an arm clothed in white samite that held a fair sword in that hand.

'Lo!' said Merlin. 'Yonder is the sword that I spoke of.'

So with that they saw a damsel going upon the lake.

['What damsel is that?' said Arthur.

'That is the Lady of the Lake,'] said Merlin. 'There is a great rock and therein is as fair a palace as any on earth and richly besene. And this damsel will come to you anon, and then speak you fair to her that she may give you that sword.'

So anon came this damsel to Arthur and salewed him and he her again.

'Damsel,' said Arthur, 'what sword is that yonder that the arm holds above the water? I would it were mine, for I have no sword.'

'Sir Arthur,' said the damsel, 'that sword is mine, and, if you will give me a gift when I ask it you, you shall have it.'

'By my faith,' said Arthur, 'I will give you what gift that you will ask!'

'Well,' said the damsel, 'go you into yonder barge and row yourself to the sword and take it and the scabbard with you. And I will ask my gift when I see my time.'

So King Arthur and Merlin alighted and tied their horses unto two trees, and so they went into the barge. And when they came to the sword that the hand held then King Arthur took it up by the handles and bore it with him, and

the arm and the hand went under the water. And so he came
unto the land and rode forth. . . .

> The gift which the Lady of the Lake eventually asks (maintaining
> that he slew her brother) is the head of Balin, a knight from
> Northumberland in Arthur's prison. But Balin beheads her, dis-
> closing she caused his mother's death, and is banished his court by
> Arthur. Balin kills Launceor who rides after him, and, seeing it,
> Launceor's lover kills herself. Merlin blames Balin, 'for thou
> mightest have saved her', and goes on: 'because of the death of that
> lady thou shalt strike a stroke most dolorous that ever man struck
> . . . for thou shalt hurt the truest knight . . . and through that stroke
> three kingdoms shall be brought into great poverty, misery and
> wretchedness twelve years. And the knight shall not be whole of
> that wound many years.'
>
> Balin and his brother, Balan, defeat one of the rebel kings, Royns
> of Wales, and Pellinore kills King Lot. (It is forecast that 'Sir
> Gawain shall revenge his father's death on King Pellinore.')

[II.14] . . . Then they rode three or four days and never
met with adventure. And so by fortune they were lodged
with a gentleman. And as they sat at supper Balin heard one
complain grievously by him in a chamber.

'What is this noise?' said Balin.

'For sooth,' said his host, 'I will tell you. I was but late at
a jousting and there I jousted with a knight that is brother
unto King Pellam, and twice I smote him down. And then
he promised to quite me on my best friend. And so he
wounded thus my son that cannot be whole till I have of that
knight's blood. And he rides all invisible but I know not
his name.'

'Ah!' said Balin, 'I know that knight's name, which is
Garlond, and he has slain two knights of mine in the same
manner. Therefore I had lever meet with that knight than
all the gold in this realm for the despite he has done me.'

'Well,' said his host, 'I shall tell you how. King Pellam of
Lystenoyse has made do cry in all the country a great feast

that shall be within these twenty days, and no knight may come there but he bring his wife with him or his paramour. And that, your enemy and mine, you shall see that day.'

'Then I promise you,' said Balin, 'part of his blood to heal your son withal.'

'Then we will be forward tomorn,' said he.

So on the morn they rode all three toward King Pellam, and they had fifteen days' journey ere they came thither. And that same day began the great feast. And so they alighted and stabled their horses and went into the castle, but Balin's host might [not] be let in because he had no lady. But Balin was well received and brought unto a chamber and unarmed him. And there was brought him robes to his pleasure, and would have had Balin leave his sword behind him.

'Nay,' said Balin, 'that will I not, for it is the custom of my country a knight always to keep his weapon with him. Or else,' said he, 'I will depart as I am.'

Then they gave him leave with his sword, and so he went into the castle and was among knights of worship and his lady before him. So after this Balin asked a knight and said, 'Is there not a knight in this court which his name is Garlond?'

'Yes, sir, yonder he goes, the knight with the black face, for he is the marvelest knight that is now living. And he destroys many good knights, for he goes invisible.'

'Well,' said Balin, 'is that he?' Then Balin advised him long and thought: 'If I slay him here I shall not escape. And if I leave him now, peradventure I shall never meet with him again at such a steven, and much harm he will do, and he live.'

And therewith this Garlond espied that Balin visaged him, so he came and slapped him on the face with the back of his hand and said, 'Knight, why beholdest thou me so? For shame, eat thy meat and do that thou came for!'

'Thou sayest sooth,' said Balin. 'This is not the first spite that thou hast done me, and therefore I will do that I came

45

for,' and rose him up fiercely and clove his head to the shoulders.

'Now give me your truncheon,' said Balin [to his lady], 'that he slew your knight with.'

And anon she gave it him, for always she bore the truncheon with her. And therewith Balin smote him through the body and said openly, 'With that truncheon thou slewest a good knight, and now it sticks in thy body.'

Then Balin called unto his host and said, 'Now may we fetch blood enough to heal your son withal!'

[II.15] So anon all the knights rose from the table for to set on Balin. And King Pellam himself arose up fiercely and said, 'Knight, why hast thou slain my brother? Thou shalt die therefore ere thou depart.'

'Well,' said Balin, 'do it yourself.'

'Yes,' said King Pellam, 'there shall no man have ado with thee but I myself, for the love of my brother.'

Then King Pellam [caught in his hand] a grim weapon and smote eagerly at Balin, but he put his sword betwixt his head and the stroke and therewith his sword brast in sunder. And when Balin was weaponless he ran into a chamber for to seek a weapon, [and so] from chamber to chamber, and no weapon could he find. And always King Pellam followed after him. And at the last he entered into a chamber [that] was marvellously dight and rich and a bed arrayed with cloth of gold, the richest that might be, and one lying therein, and thereby stood a table of clean gold. And upon the table stood a marvellous spear strangely wrought.

So when Balin saw the spear he got it in his hand and turned to King Pellam and felled him and smote him passingly sore with that spear, that King Pellam [fell] down in a swoon. And therewith the castle broke roof and walls and fell down to the earth. And Balin fell down and might not stir hand nor foot, and for the most party of that castle was dead through the dolorous stroke.

Right so lay King Pellam and Balin three days. [II.16]
Then Merlin came thither and took up Balin and got him
a good horse, for his was dead, and bade him void out of
that country.

'Sir, I would have my damsel,' said Balin.

'Lo!' said Merlin, 'where she lies dead.'

And King Pellam lay so many years sore wounded and
might never be whole till that Galahad the Haute Prince
healed him in the quest of the Sankgreall. For in that place
was part of the blood of our Lord Jesu Christ which Joseph
of Aramathea brought into this land. And there himself [lay]
in that rich bed. And that was the spear which Longeus
smote our Lord with to the heart. And King Pellam was
nigh of Joseph's kin, and that was the most worshipfullest
man alive in those days, and great pity it was of his hurt, for
through that stroke it turned to great dole, tray and tene.

Then departed Balin from Merlin, 'for,' he said, 'never in
this world we part neither meet no more'. So he rode forth
through the fair countries and cities and found the people
dead slain on every side, and all that ever were alive cried
and said:

'Ah! Balin, thou hast done and caused great vengeance in
these countries! For the dolorous stroke thou gave unto
King Pellam these three countries are destroyed. And doubt
not but the vengeance will fall on thee at the last!' ...

Previously, before the arrival of the Lady of the Lake (p. 44),
Balin had succeeded, where all the other knights failed, in drawing
a sword carried by a damsel who said it could be drawn only by 'a
clean knight without villainy and of gentle strain on father's side and
on mother's side'. When Balin insisted on keeping the sword she
warned him that 'you shall slay with that sword the best friend that
you have'.

After wounding King Pellam, Balin happens to exchange his own
shield for another, so that his brother, Balan, does not recognize him
when they meet and both fight together in fatal ignorance, Balin

47

using the fated sword. Merlin prophesies, when they die, 'there shall never man handle this sword but the best knight of the world, and that shall be Sir Launcelot or else Galahad, his son. And Launcelot with his sword shall slay the man in the world that he loves best, that shall be Sir Gawain.' He then fixes the sword upright in marble so that—we are told in anticipation—it eventually floats down river to Camelot ('in English called Winchester') to be achieved by Galahad.

[III.1] In the beginning of Arthur, after he was chosen King by adventure and by grace, for the most party of the barons knew not he was Uther Pendragon's son but as Merlin made it openly known, but yet many kings and lords held him great war for that cause. But well Arthur overcame them all. The most party days of his life he was ruled by the counsel of Merlin. So it fell on a time King Arthur said unto Merlin, 'My barons will let me have no rest but needs I must take a wife, and I would none take but by thy counsel and advice.'

'It is well done,' said Merlin, 'that you take a wife, for a man of your bounty and nobless should not be without a wife. Now is there any,' said Merlin, 'that you love more than another?'

'Yea!' said King Arthur. 'I love Guenevere, the King's daughter of Lodegrean, of the land of Camelerd, the which holds in his house the Table Round that you told me he had it of my father, Uther. And this damsel is the most valiant and fairest that I know living, or yet that ever I could find.'

'Certes,' said Merlin, 'as of her beauty and fairness she is one of the fairest alive. But, and you loved her not so well as you do, I should find you a damsel of beauty and of goodness that should like you and please you, and your heart were not set. But thereas man's heart is set he will be loath to return.'

'That is truth,' said King Arthur.

But Merlin warned the King covertly that Guenevere was

48

not wholesome for him to take to wife, for he warned him that Launcelot should love her and she him again, and so he turned his tale to the adventures of the Sankgreall.

Then Merlin desired of the King for to have men with him that should enquire of Guenevere, and so the King granted him. And so Merlin went forth unto King Lodegrean of Camelerd and told him of the desire of the King that he would have unto his wife Guenevere, his daughter.

'That is to me,' said King Lodegrean, 'the best tidings that ever I heard, that so worthy a king, of prowess and nobless, will wed my daughter. And as for my lands, I would give it him if I wist it might please him, but he has lands enough—he needs none. But I shall send him a gift that shall please him much more, for I shall give him the Table Round which Uther, his father, gave me. And when it is full complete there is an hundred knights and fifty. And as for an hundred good knights, I have myself: but I want fifty, for so many have been slain in my days.'

And so King Lodegrean delivered his daughter, Guenevere, unto Merlin, and the Table Round with the hundred knights. And so they rode freshly with great royalty, what by water and by land, till that they came nigh unto London.

[III.2] When King Arthur heard of the coming of Queen Guenevere and the hundred knights with the Table Round, then King Arthur made great joy for her coming and that rich present, and said openly, 'This fair lady is passingly welcome to me for I have loved her long, and therefore there is nothing so lief to me. And these knights with the Table Round please me more than right great riches.'

And in all haste the King let ordain for the marriage and the coronation in the most honourablest wise that could be devised. 'Now, Merlin,' said King Arthur, 'go thou and espy me in all this land fifty knights which be of most prowess and worship.'

So within short time Merlin had found such knights that

should fulfil twenty and eight knights, but no more would he find. Then the Bishop of Canterbury was fetched and he blessed the seges with great royalty and devotion and there set the eight and twenty knights in their seges. And when this was done Merlin said, 'Fair sirs, you must all arise and come to King Arthur for to do him homage: he will the better be in will to maintain you.'

And so they arose and did their homage. And when they were gone Merlin found in every sege letters of gold that told the knights' names that had sat there. . . .

> Arthur knights Gawain and Torre, who is discovered not to be the son of Aries, the cow-herd, but the illegitimate son of King Pellinore. Pellinore arouses Gawain's envy when he is honoured in Arthur's court so that Gawain proposes to Gaheris, his brother, that they should kill him, 'for he slew our father, King Lot.'

[III.5] Then was this feast made ready and the King was wedded at Camelot unto Dame Guenevere in the church of St. Stephen's with great solemnity. Then as every man was set as his degree asked, Merlin went to all the knights of the Round Table and bade them sit still—'that none of you remove, for you shall see a strange and a marvellous adventure'.

Right so as they sat there came running in a white hart into the hall and a white brachet next him, and thirty couple of black running-hounds came after with a great cry. And the hart went about the Round Table, and as he went by the side-boards the brachet ever bit him by the buttock and pulled on a piece, wherethrough the hart leapt a great leap and overthrew a knight that sat at the side-board. And therewith the knight arose and took up the brachet and so went forth out of the hall and took his horse and rode his way with the brachet.

Right so came in the lady on a white palfrey and cried aloud unto King Arthur and said, 'Sir, suffer me not to have this despite, for the brachet is mine that the knight has led away!'

'I may not do therewith,' said the King.

So with this there came a knight riding all armed on a great horse and took the lady away with force with him, and ever she cried and made great dole. So when she was gone the King was glad, for she made such a noise.

'Nay!' said Merlin, 'you may not leave it so, this adventure, so lightly, for these adventures must be brought to an end or else it will be disworship to you and to your feast.'

'I will,' said the King, 'that all be done by your advice.' Then he let call Sir Gawain for he must bring again the white hart.

'Also, sir, you must let call Sir Torre, for he must bring again the brachet and the knight, or else slay him. Also let call King Pellinore, for he must bring again the lady and the knight or else slay him. And these three knights shall do marvellous adventures ere they come again.'

Then were they called all three as it is rehearsed before and every of them took their charge and armed them surely. But Sir Gawain had the first request and therefore we will begin at him and so forth to these others.

Here begins the first battle that ever Sir Gawain did after he was made knight. . . .

[III.7] Then Sir Gawain and Gaheris followed after [the white hart and let slip at the hart three couple of greyhounds. And so they chased the hart into a castle and in the chief place of the castle they slew the hart]. Right so there came a knight out of a chamber with a sword drawn in his hand and slew two of the greyhounds even in the sight of Sir Gawain, and the remnant he chased with his sword out of the castle. And when he came again he said, 'Ah! my white hart, me repents that thou art dead, for my sovereign lady gave thee to me, and evil have I kept thee, and thy death shall be evil bought, and I live.'

And anon he went into his chamber and armed him and came out fiercely. And there he met with Sir Gawain and he said, 'Why have you slain my hounds? I would that you had wroken your anger upon me rather than upon a dumb beast.'

'Thou sayest truth,' said the knight. 'I have avenged me on thy hounds and so I will on thee ere thou go.'

Then Sir Gawain alighted on foot and dressed his shield and struck together mightily and clove their shields and stooned their helms and broke their hauberks, that their blood thirled down to their feet. So at the last Sir Gawain smote so hard that the knight fell to the earth, and then he cried mercy and yielded him and besought him, as he was a gentle knight, to save his life.

'Thou shalt die,' said Sir Gawain, 'for slaying of my hounds.'

'I will make amends,' said the knight, 'to my power.'

But Sir Gawain would no mercy have, but unlaced his helm to have stricken off his head. Right so came his lady out of a chamber and fell over him, and so he smote off her head by misfortune.

'Alas,' said Gaheris, 'that is foul and shamefully done, for that shame shall never from you. Also you should give mercy unto them that ask mercy, for a knight without mercy is without worship.'

So Sir Gawain was sore astoned of the death of this fair lady that he wist not what he did and said unto the knight, 'Arise! I will give thee mercy.'

'Nay! nay!' said the knight, 'I take no force of thy mercy now, for thou hast slain with villainy my love and my lady that I loved best of all earthly things.'

'Me sore repents it,' said Sir Gawain, 'for I meant the stroke unto thee. But now thou shalt go unto King Arthur and tell him of thine adventure and how thou art overcome by the knight that went in the quest of the white hart.'

'I take no force,' said the knight, 'whether I live or die.'

But at the last, for fear of death, he swore to go unto King Arthur, and he made him to bear the one greyhound before him on his horse and the other behind him.

'What is your name,' said Sir Gawain, 'ere we depart?'

'My name is,' said the knight, 'Blamoure of the Maryse.'

And so he departed toward Camelot. [III.8] And Sir Gawain went unto the castle and made him ready to lie there all night, and would have unarmed him.

'What will you do?' said Gaheris. 'Will you unarm you in this country? You may think you have many foes in this country.'

He had no sooner said the word but there came in four knights well armed and assailed Sir Gawain hard and said unto him: 'Thou new-made knight, thou hast shamed thy knighthood, for a knight without mercy is dishonoured. Also thou hast slain a fair lady to thy great shame unto the world's end, and, doubt thee not, thou shalt have great need of mercy ere thou depart from us.'

And therewith one of them smote Sir Gawain a great stroke that nigh he fell to the earth. And Gaheris smote him again sore. And so they were assailed on the one side and on the other, that Sir Gawain and Gaheris were in jeopardy of their lives. And one with a bow, an archer, smote Sir Gawain through the arm that it grieved him wonderly sore.

And as they should have been slain there came four fair ladies and besought the knights of grace for Sir Gawain. And goodly at the request of these ladies they gave Sir Gawain and Gaheris their lives and made them to yield them as prisoners. Then Sir Gawain and Gaheris made great dole.

'Alas,' said Sir Gawain, 'mine arm grieves me sore that I am like to be maimed,' and so made his complaint piteously.

So early on the morn there came to Sir Gawain one of the four ladies that had heard his complaint and said, 'Sir knight! what cheer?'

'Not good!'

'Why so? It is your own default,' said the lady, 'for you have done passing foul for the slaying of this lady, the which will be great villainy unto you. But be you not of King Arthur's?' said the lady.

'Yes, truly,' said Sir Gawain.

'What is your name?' said [the] lady, 'for you must tell ere you pass.'

'Fair lady, my name is Sir Gawain, the King's son, Lot of Orkney, and my mother is King Arthur's sister.'

'Then are you nephew unto the King,' said the lady. 'Well!' said the lady, 'I shall so speak for you that you shall have [conduct] to go unto King Arthur for his love.'

And so she departed and told the four knights how the prisoner was King Arthur's nephew, 'and his name is Sir Gawain, King Lot's son of Orkney.'

So they gave him leave and took him the hart's head with him because it was in the quest. And then they delivered him under this promise, that he should bear the dead lady with him in this manner: the head of her was hanged about his neck and the whole body of her before him on his horse's mane.

Right so he rode forth unto Camelot. And, anon as he was come, Merlin did make King Arthur that Sir Gawain was sworn to tell of his adventure and how he slew the lady and how he would give no mercy unto the knight, wherethrough the lady was slain. Then the King and the Queen were greatly displeased with Sir Gawain for the slaying of the lady, and there, by ordinance of the Queen, there was set a quest of ladies upon Sir Gawain, and they judged him for ever while he lived to be with all ladies and to fight for their quarrels, and ever that he should be courteous and never to refuse mercy to him that asks mercy. Thus was Sir Gawain sworn upon the four Evangelists that he should never be against lady nor gentlewoman but if he fight for a lady and his adversary fights for another.

And thus ends the adventure of Sir Gawain that he did at the marriage of Arthur. . . .

[III.15] Thus, when the quest was done of the white hart, the which followed Sir Gawain, and the quest of the brachet, which followed Sir Torre, King Pellinore's son, and the quest of the lady that the knight took away, which at that time followed King Pellinore: then the King established all the knights and gave them riches and lands; and charged them never to do outrage nor murder and always to flee treason and to give mercy unto him that asks mercy, upon pain of forfeiture [of their] worship and lordship of King Arthur for evermore; and always to do ladies, damsels and gentlewomen and widows [succour]—strengthen them in their rights and never to enforce them, upon pain of death. Also that no man take no battles in a wrongful quarrel for no love nor for no world's goods. So unto this were all knights sworn of the Table Round, both old and young, and every year so were they sworn at the high feast of Pentecost.

[IV.1] So after these quests of Sir Gawain, Sir Torre and King Pellinore, then it befell that Merlin fell in dotage on the damsel that King Pellinore brought to court, and she was one of the damsels of the Lady of the Lake that hight Nineve. But Merlin would not let her have no rest but always he would be with her. And ever she made Merlin good cheer till she had learned of him all manner of things that she desired: and he was assotted upon her that he might not be from her.

So on a time he told to King Arthur that he should not endure long, but, for all his crafts, he should be put into the earth quick. And so he told the King many things that should befall, but always he warned the King to keep well his sword and the scabbard, [for he told him how the sword and the scabbard] should be stolen by a woman from him that he most trusted. Also he told King Arthur that he should miss him, 'and yet had you lever than all your lands have me again'.

'Ah!' said the King, 'since you know of your evil adventure, purvey for it and put it away by your crafts, that misadventure.'

'Nay!' said Merlin, 'it will not be.'

He departed from the King and within a while the Damsel of the Lake departed and Merlin went with her evermore wheresoever she yode. And oftentimes Merlin would have had her privily away by his subtle crafts. Then she made him to swear that he should never do none enchantment upon her if he would have his will, and so he swore. Then she and Merlin went over the sea unto the land of Benwick thereas King Ban was King that had great war against King Claudas.

And there Merlin spoke with King Ban's wife, a fair lady and a good. Her name was Elayne. And there he saw young Launcelot. And there the Queen made great sorrow for the mortal war that King Claudas made on her lands.

'Take none heaviness,' said Merlin, 'for this same child, young Launcelot, shall, within this twenty year, revenge you on King Claudas that all Christendom shall speak of it, and this same child shall be the most man of worship of the world. And his first name is Galahad, that know I well,' said Merlin, 'and, since, you have confirmed him Launcelot.'

'That is truth,' said the Queen. 'His name was first Galahad. Ah! Merlin,' said the Queen, 'shall I live to see my son such a man of prowess?'

'Yea! hardely, lady, on my peril you shall see it, and live many winters after!'

Then, soon after, the lady and Merlin departed. And by ways he showed her many wonders and so came into Cornwall. And always he lay about to have her maidenhood and she was ever passing weary of him and would have been delivered of him, for she was afraid of him for cause he was a devil's son and she could not be shift of him by no means. And so one a time Merlin did show her in a rock whereas was a great wonder, and wrought by enchantment, that went under a great stone. So by her subtle working she made Merlin to go under that stone to let her wit of the marvels there: but she wrought so there for him that he came never out for all the craft he could do, and so she departed and left Merlin. . . .

[IV.5] So as Sir Bagdemagus rode to see many adventures so it happed him to come to the rock thereas the Lady of the Lake had put Merlin under the stone, and there he heard him make a great dole. Wherefore Sir Bagdemagus would have helped him and went unto the great stone, and it was so heavy that an hundred men might not lift it up. When Merlin wist that he was there he bade him leave his labour for all was in vain, for he might never be helped but by her that put him there.

And so Bagdemagus departed and did many adventures and proved, after, a full good knight, and came again to the court and was made knight of the Round Table. So on the morn there befell new tidings and many other adventures.

Morgan le Fay, Arthur's half-sister, is prevented by her son Uwaine from killing Uriens, her husband. Arthur banishes Uwaine from his court since his mother and he scheme against him, and Gawain decides to keep his cousin company. He promises Pelleas to win for him the love of Ettarde, but instead, with treachery, wins it temporarily for himself. Ettarde finally dies of sorrow, enchanted into a love for Pelleas which he now refuses to return – 'and Pelleas loved never after Sir Gawain but as he spared him for the love of the King. . . .'

[IV.29] . . . So Sir Tristram many days after fought with Sir Marhalt in an island. And there they did a great battle but, [at] the last, Sir Tristram slew him. So Sir Tristram was so wounded that unneth he might recover, and lay at a nunnery half a year.

And Sir Pelleas was a worshipful knight and was one of the four that achieved the Sankgreall. And the Damsel of the Lake made by her means that never he had ado with Sir Launcelot du Lake, for where Sir Launcelot was at any jousts or at any tournament she would not suffer him to be there that day but if it were on the side of Sir Launcelot.

Here ends this tale, as the French book says, from the marriage of King Uther unto King Arthur that reigned after him and did many battles. And this book ends whereas Sir Launcelot and Sir Tristram come to court. Who that will make any more let him seek other books of King Arthur or of Sir Launcelot or Sir Tristram: for this was drawn by a knight prisoner, Sir Thomas Malory, that God send him good recovery. Amen.

Explicit.

Book Two

'The tale of the noble King Arthur that was Emperor himself'

[V] It befell when King Arthur had wedded Queen Guenevere and fulfilled the Round Table, and so after his marvellous knights and he had vanquished the most part of his enemies, then soon after came Sir Launcelot du Lake unto the court, and Sir Tristram came that time also.

And then so it befell that the Emperor of Rome, Lucius, sent unto Arthur messengers commanding him to pay his trewage that his ancestors have paid before him. When King Arthur wist what they meant he looked up with his grey eyes and angered at the messengers passing sore. . . .

King Arthur refuses to pay tribute and sets out with his knights to fight the Emperor who is advancing against him. 'And Sir Tristram at that time beleft with King Mark of Cornwall for the love of La Beall Isode, wherefore Sir Launcelot was passing wroth.' Arrived in Normandy King Arthur is told of a marauding giant at St. Michael's Mount whom he seeks to destroy.

. . . Then the King yode up to the crest of the crag and then he comforted himself with the cold wind. And then he yode forth by two well-streams and there he finds two fires flaming full high, and at that one fire he found a careful widow wringing her hands, sitting on a grave that was new-marked. Then Arthur salewed her, and she him again, and asked her why she sat sorrowing.

59

'Alas!' she said, 'careful knight! Thou carpes over loud! Yon is a werlow will destroy us both. I hold thee unhappy. What dost thou on this mountain? Though here were such fifty you were too feeble for to match him all at once. Whereto bearest thou armour? It may thee little avail, for he needs none other weapon but his bare fist. Here is a duchess dead, the fairest that lived. He has murdered that mild ⟨one⟩ without any mercy. He forced her by filth of himself and so, after, slit her unto the navel.'

'Dame,' said the King, 'I come from the Conqueror, Sir Arthur, for to treat with the tyrant for his liege people.'

'Fy! on such tretise,' she said then, 'for he sets nought by the King neither by no man else. But, and thou have brought Arthur's wife, Dame Guenevere, he will be more blither of her than thou haddest given him halfondele France. And, but if thou have brought her, press him not too nigh. Look what he has done unto fifteen kings: he has made him a coat full of precious stones and the borders thereof is the beards ⟨of⟩ fifteen kings, and they were of the greatest blood that dured on earth. Other farme had he none of fifteen realms. This present ⟨which⟩ was sent him to, this last Christmas, they sent him in faith for saving of their people. And for Arthur's wife he lodges him here, for he hath more treasure than ever had Arthur or any of his elders. And now thou shalt find him at supper with six knave children, and there he has made pickle and powder with many precious wines, and three fair maidens, that turn the broach, that bide to go to his bed, for they three shall be dead within four hours, ere the filth is fulfilled that his flesh asks.'

'Well!' said Arthur, 'I will fulfil my message for all your grim words.'

'Then fare thou to yonder fire that flames so high, and there thou shalt find him sikerly for sooth.'

Then he passed forth to the crest of the hill and saw where he sat at his supper alone, gnawing on a limb of a large man.

And there he beekes his broad lendes by the bright fire and breechless him seems. And three damsels turned three broachs and thereon was twelve children but late born, and they were broached in manner like birds. When the King beheld that sight his heart was nigh bleeding for sorrow. Then he hailsed him with angerful words:

'Now he that all wields give thee sorrow, thief, there thou sittest, for thou art the foulest freike that ever was formed, and fiendly thou feedest thee, the devil have thy soul! And by what cause, thou carle, hast thou killed these Christian children? Thou hast made many martyrs by murdering of these lands. Therefore thou shalt have thy meed through Michael that owns this mount. And, also, why hast thou slain this fair duchess? Therefore, dress thee, dog's son! for thou shalt die this day through the dint of my hands.'

Then the glutton gloored and greved full foul. He had teeth like a greyhound: he was the foulest wight that ever man saw, and there was never such one formed on earth, for there was never devil in hell more horriblier made, for he was from the head to the foot five fathom long and large. And therewith sturdily he started upon his legs and caught a club in his hand all of clean iron. Then he swaps at the King with that kyd weapon. He crushed down with the club the coronal down to the cold earth. The King covered him with his shield and reaches a box even-infourmed in the midst of his forehead, that the slipped blade unto the brain reaches.

Yet he shapes at Sir Arthur, but the King shunts a little and reaches him a dint high upon the haunch and there he swaps his genitrottes in sunder. Then he roared and brayed. . . .

King Arthur destroys the giant after further fierce fighting, and later defeats the Roman army, himself killing the Emperor. He is crowned Emperor by the Pope and returns to England. 'And here follows after many noble tales of Sir Launcelot du Lake.'

61

Book Three

'Noble tales of Sir Launcelot'

[VI.1] Soon after that King Arthur was come from Rome into England, then all the knights of the Round Table resorted unto the King and made many jousts and tournaments. And some there were, that were but knights, increased in arms and worship, that passed all other of their fellows in prowess and noble deeds, and that was well proved on many.

But in especial it was proved on Sir Launcelot du Lake, for in all tournaments, jousts and deeds of arms, both for life and death, he passed all other knights, and at no time was he overcome but if it were by treason or enchantment. So this Sir Launcelot increased so marvellously in worship and honour, therefore he is the first knight that the French book makes mention of after King Arthur came from Rome. Wherefore Queen Guenevere had him in great favour above all other knights, and so he loved the Queen again above all other ladies days of his life, and for her he did many deeds of arms and saved her from the fire through his noble chivalry.

Thus Sir Launcelot rested him long with play and game. And then he thought himself to prove in strange adventures and bade his nephew, Sir Lionel, for to make him ready, 'for we must go seek adventures'. So they mounted on their horses, armed at all rights, and rode into a deep forest and so into a plain.

So the weather was hot about noon and Sir Launcelot had great lust to sleep. Then Sir Lionel espied a great apple-tree that stood by a hedge and said, 'Sir, yonder is a fair shadow: there may we rest us and our horses.'

'It is truth,' said Sir Launcelot, 'for this seven year I was not so sleepy as I am now.'

So there they alighted and tied their horses unto sundry trees, and Sir Launcelot laid him down under this apple-tree and his helmet under his head. And Sir Lionel waked whilst he slept. So Sir Launcelot slept passing fast.

And in the meanwhile came there three knights riding, as fast fleeing as they might ride, and there followed them three but one knight. And when Sir Lionel him saw he thought he saw never so great a knight neither so well-faring a man and well apparelled unto all rights. So within a while this strong knight had overtaken one of the three knights and there he smote him to the cold earth that he lay still. And then he rode unto the second knight and smote him so that man and horse fell down. And so straight unto the third knight and smote him behind his horse's arse a spear-length. And then he alighted down and reined his horse on the bridle and bound all three knights fast with the reins of their own bridles.

When Sir Lionel had seen him do thus he thought to essay him, and made him ready, and privily he took his horse and thought not for to awake Sir Launcelot, and so mounted upon his horse and overtook the strong knight. He bade him turn, and so he turned and smote Sir Lionel so hard that horse and man he bore to the earth. And so he alighted down and bound him fast and threw him overthwart his own horse as he had served the other three and so rode with them till he came to his own castle. Then he unarmed them and beat them with thorns all naked and, after, put them in deep prison where were many more knights that made great dole.

[VI.2] So when Sir Ector de Maris wist that Sir Launcelot was passed out of the court to seek adventures he was wroth with himself and made him ready to seek Sir Launcelot. And as he had ridden long in a great forest he met with a man was like a forester.

'Fair fellow,' said Sir Ector, 'dost thou know this country or any adventures that are [here nigh-hand]?'

'Sir,' said the forester, 'this country know I well. And hereby within this mile is a strong manor and well-dyked, and by that manor on the left hand there is a fair ford for horse to drink of and over that ford there grows a fair tree. And thereon hang many fair shields that wielded sometime good knights, and at the [bole] of the tree hangs a basin of copper and latten. And strike upon that basin with the butt of thy spear three times and soon after thou shalt hear new tidings: and else hast thou the fairest [grace] that ever had knight this many years that passed through this forest.'

'Gramercy,' said Sir Ector, and departed, and came unto this tree and saw many fair shields, and, among them all, he saw his brother's shield, Sir Lionel, and many more that he knew that were of his fellows of the Round Table, the which grieved his heart, and ⟨he⟩ promised to revenge his brother. Then, anon, Sir Ector beat on the basin as he were wood and then he gave his horse drink at the ford.

And there came a knight behind him and bade him come out of the water and make him ready. Sir Ector turned him shortly and in feawtir cast his spear, and smote the other knight a great buffet that his horse turned twice about.

'That was well done,' said the strong knight, 'and knightly thou has stricken me.' And therewith he rushed his horse on Sir Ector and caught him under his right arm and bore him clean out of the saddle, and so rode with him away into his castle and threw him down in middle of the floor.

Then this said Tarquin said unto Sir Ector, 'For thou

hast done this day more unto me than any knight did this twelve year, now will I grant thee thy life, so thou wilt be sworn to be my true prisoner.'

'Nay!' said Sir Ector, 'that will I never promise thee but that I will do mine advantage.'

'That me repents,' said Sir Tarquin. Then he gan unarm him and beat him with thorns all naked and, sithen, put him down into a deep dungeon, and there he knew many of his fellows.

But when Sir Ector saw Sir Lionel then made he great sorrow. 'Alas! brother,' said Sir Ector, 'how may this be? And where is my brother, Sir Launcelot?'

'Fair brother, I left him asleep, when that I from him yode, under an apple-tree, and what is become of him I cannot tell you.'

'Alas!' said the prisoners, 'but if Sir Launcelot help us we shall never be delivered, for we know now no knight that is able to match with our master Tarquin.'

[VI.3] Now leave we these knights prisoners and speak we of Sir Launcelot du Lake that lies under the apple-tree sleeping. About the noon so there came by him four queens of a great estate, and, for the heat should not nigh them, there rode four knights about them and bore a cloth of green silk on four spears betwixt them and the sun. And the queens rode on four white mules.

Thus, as they rode, they heard a great horse beside them grimly neigh. Then they looked and were aware of a sleeping knight lay all armed under an apple-tree. And, anon as they looked on his face, they knew well it was Sir Launcelot, and began to strive for that knight, and every ⟨one⟩ of them said they would have him to her love.

'We shall not strive,' said Morgan le Fay, that was King Arthur's sister. 'I shall put an enchantment upon him that he shall not awake of all this seven hours, and then I will lead him away unto my castle. And when he is surely within my

65

hold I shall take the enchantment from him, and then let him
choose which of us he will have unto paramour.'

So this enchantment was cast upon Sir Launcelot, and
then they laid him upon his shield and bore him so on horseback betwixt two knights and brought him unto the Castle
Chariot. And there they laid him in a chamber cold and at
night they sent unto him a fair damsel with his supper ready
dight. By that the enchantment was passed. And when she
came she salewed him and asked him what cheer.

'I cannot say, fair damsel,' said Sir Launcelot, 'for I wot
not how I came into this castle but it be by enchantment.'

'Sir,' said she, 'you must make good cheer. And if you are
such a knight as is said you are, I shall tell you more tomorn
by prime of the day.'

'Gramercy, fair damsel,' said Sir Launcelot, 'for your
good will.'

And so she departed, and there he lay all that night without any comfort. And on the morn early come these four
queens passingly well besene, and all they bidding him good
morn and he them again.

'Sir knight,' the four queens said, 'thou must understand
thou art our prisoner and we know thee well that thou art
Sir Launcelot du Lake, King Ban's son. And because ⟨of⟩
that we understand your worthiness, that thou art the noblest
knight living, and also we know well there can no lady have
thy love but one, and that is Queen Guenevere, and now
thou shalt her love lose for ever and she thine. For it behoves
thee now to choose one of us four, for I am Queen Morgan
le Fay, Queen of the land of Gore, and here is the Queen of
North Wales, and the Queen of Estland, and the Queen of
the Out Isles. Now choose one of us, which that thou wilt
have to thy paramour, or else to die in this prison.'

'This is an hard case,' said Sir Launcelot, 'that either I
must die or to choose one of you. Yet had I lever die in this
prison with worship than to have one of you to my paramour,

magre mind head. And therefore you are answered: I will
none of you, for you are false enchanters. And as for my
lady, Dame Guenevere, were I at my liberty as I was, I
would prove it on yours that she is the truest lady unto her
lord living.'

'Well,' said the Queens, 'is this your answer—that you
will refuse us?'

'Yea! on my life!' said Sir Launcelot. 'Refused you are
by me.'

So they departed and left him there alone that made great
sorrow.

[VI.4] So after that noon came the damsel unto him with
his dinner and asked him what cheer.

'Truly, damsel,' said Sir Launcelot, 'never so ill.'

'Sir,' she said, 'that me repents, but, and you will be ruled
by me, I shall help you out of this distress, and you shall have
no shame nor villainy, so that you will [hold] my promise.'

'Fair damsel, I grant you. But sore I am of these Queens'
crafts afraid, for they have destroyed many a good knight.'

'Sir,' said she, 'that is sooth, and for the renown and
bounty that they hear of you they will have your love. And,
sir, they say your name is Sir Launcelot du Lake, the flower
of knights, and they are passing wroth with you that you
have refused them. But, sir, and you would promise me to
help my father on Tuesday next coming, that has made a
tournament betwixt him and the King of North Wales—for
the last Tuesday past my father lost the field through three
knights of Arthur's court—and if you will be there on
Tuesday next coming and help my father, and ⟨then⟩
tomorn by prime, by the grace of God, I shall deliver you
clean.'

'Now, fair damsel,' said Sir Launcelot, 'tell me your
father's name and then shall I give you an answer.'

'Sir knight,' she said, 'my father's name is King Bagdemagus, that was foul rebuked at the last tournament.'

'I know your father well,' said Sir Launcelot, 'for a noble king and a good knight, and, by the faith of my body, your father shall have my service and you both at that [day].'

'Sir,' she said, 'gramercy, and tomorn look you are ready betimes and I shall deliver you, and take you your armour, your horse, shield and spear. And hereby, within this ten mile, is an abbey of white monks and there I pray you to abide me and thither shall I bring my father unto you.'

'And all this shall be done,' said Sir Launcelot, 'as I am true knight.'

And so she departed and came on the morn early and found him ready. Then she brought him out of twelve locks and took him his armour and his own horse, and lightly he saddled him and took his spear in his hand and so rode forth and said, 'Damsel, I shall not fail, by the grace of God!'

And so he rode into a great forest all that day and never could find no highway. And so the night fell on him, and then was he aware in a slade of a pavilion of red sendel. 'By my faith,' said Sir Launcelot, 'in that pavilion will I lodge all this night.'

And so he there alighted down and tied his horse to the pavilion and there he unarmed him. And there he found a bed and laid him therein and fell asleep sadly.

[VI.5] Then within an hour there came that knight that ought the pavilion. He weened that his leman had lain in that bed and so he laid him adown by Sir Launcelot and took him in his arms and began to kiss him. And when Sir Launcelot felt a rough beard kissing him he started out of the bed lightly and the other knight after him. And either of them got their swords in their hands and out at the pavilion door went the knight of the pavilion and Sir Launcelot followed him. And there by a little slade Sir Launcelot wounded him sore, nigh unto the death. And then he yielded him to Sir Launcelot, and so he granted him, so that he would tell him why he came into the bed.

'Sir,' said the knight, 'the pavilion is mine own. And as this night I had assigned my lady to have slept with her, and now I am likely to die of this wound.'

'That me repents,' said Sir Launcelot, 'of your hurt, but I was adread of treason for I was late beguiled. And, therefore, come on your way into your pavilion, and take your rest, and, as I suppose, I shall staunch your blood.' And so they went both into the pavilion and, anon, Sir Launcelot staunched his blood.

Therewithal came the knight's lady that was a passing fair lady. And when [she] espied that her lord, Belleus, was sore wounded she cried out on Sir Launcelot and made great dole out of measure.

'Peace! my lady and my love,' said Sir Belleus, 'for this knight is a good man and a knight of adventures.' And there he told her all the case how he was wounded: 'And when that I yielded me unto him he left me goodly and has staunched my blood.'

'Sir,' said the lady, 'I require thee, tell me what knight thou art and what is your name.'

'Fair lady,' he said, 'my name is Sir Launcelot du Lake.'

'So me thought ever by your speech,' said the lady, 'for I have seen you often ere this and I know you better than you ween. But now would you promise me of your courtesy, for the harms that you have done to me and to my lord, Sir Belleus, that, when you come unto King Arthur's court, for to cause him to be made knight of the Round Table? For he is a passing good man-of-arms and a mighty lord of lands of many out isles.'

'Fair lady,' said Sir Launcelot, 'let him come unto the court the next high feast and look you come with him, and I shall do my power. And he prove him doughty of his hands, he shall have his desire.'

So within a while the night passed and the day shone. Then Sir Launcelot armed him and took his horse, and so he was taught to the abbey. [VI.6] And as soon as he came thither the daughter of King Bagdemagus heard a great horse trot on the pavement, and she then arose and yode to a window, and there she saw Sir Launcelot. And, anon, she made men fast to take his horse from him and let lead him into a stable, and himself unto a chamber and unarmed him. And this lady sent him a long gown and came herself and made him good cheer, and she said he was the knight in the world that was most welcome unto her. Then in all haste she sent for her father, Bagdemagus, that was within twelve mile of that abbey, and before even he came with a fair fellowship of knights with him. And when the King was alighted of his horse he yode straight unto Sir Launcelot's chamber, and there he found his daughter. And then the King took him in his arms and either made other good cheer.

Then Sir Launcelot made his complaint unto the King, how he was betrayed, and how he was brother unto Sir Lionel, which was departed from him he wist not where, and how his daughter had delivered him out of prison: 'Therefore, while that I live, I shall do her service and all her kindred.'

'Then am I sure of your help,' said the King, 'on Tuesday next coming?'

'Yea! sir,' said Sir Launcelot, 'I shall not fail you, for so have I promised my lady, your daughter. But, sir, what knights are those of my lord, King Arthur's, that were with the King of North Wales?'

'Sir, it was Sir Madore de la Porte and Sir Mordred and Sir Gahalantine that all forfared my knights, for against them three I, neither none of mine, might bear no strength.'

'Sir,' said Sir Launcelot,' as I hear say, that tournament shall be here within this three mile of this abbey. But, sir, you shall send unto me three knights of yours such as you trust, and look that the three knights have all white shields and no picture on their shields, and you shall send me another of the same suit. And we four will out of a little wood in midst of both parties come, and we shall fall on the front of our enemies and grieve them that we may. And thus shall I not be known what manner of knight I am.'

So they took their rest that night. And this was on the Sunday. And so the King departed and sent unto Sir Launcelot three knights with four white shields. And on the Tuesday they lodged them in a little, leafy wood beside thereas the tournament should be. And there were scaffolds and towers that lords and ladies might behold and give the prize.

Then came into the field the King of North Wales with nine-score helms, and then the three knights of King Arthur's stood by themselves. Then came into the field King Bagdemagus with four-score helms. And then they feawtired their spears and came together with a great dash. And there was slain of knights at the first encounter twelve knights of King Bagdemagus' party and six of the King of North Wales' side and party, and King Bagdemagus' party were far set aside and aback.

[VI.7] With that came in Sir Launcelot and he thrust in with his spear in the thickest of the press. And there he smote down with one spear five knights, and of four of them he broke their backs. And in that throng he smote down the King of North Wales and broke his thigh in that fall. All this doing of Sir Launcelot saw the three knights of Arthur's. 'Yonder is a shrewd geste,' [said Sir Madore de la Porte,] 'therefore have here once at him!' So they encountered and Sir Launcelot bore him down horse and man so that his shoulder went out of joint.

'Now it befalls me,' said Sir Mordred, 'to stir me, for Sir Madore has a sore fall.' And then Sir Launcelot was aware of him and got a spear in his hand and met with him. And Sir Mordred broke his spear upon him and Sir Launcelot gave him such a buffet that the arson of the saddle broke and so he drove over the horse's tail that his helm smote into the earth a foot and more, that nigh his neck was broken. And there he lay long in a swoon.

Then came in Sir Gahalantine with a great spear and Sir Launcelot against him in all that they might drive, that both their spears to-brast even to their hands. And then they flung out with their swords and gave many sore strokes. Then was Sir Launcelot wroth out of measure and then he smote Sir Gahalantine on the helm that his nose, ears and mouth brast out on blood. And therewith his head hung low and with that his horse ran away with him and he fell down to the earth.

Anon therewithal Sir Launcelot got a spear in his hand and, ere ever that spear broke, he bore down to the earth sixteen knights, some horse and man, and some the man and not the horse. And there was none that he hit surely but that he bore none arms that day. And then he got a spear and smote down twelve knights and the most party of them never throve after. And then the knights of the King of North Wales' party would joust no more, and there the gre was given to King Bagdemagus.

So either party departed unto his own and Sir Launcelot rode forth with King Bagdemagus unto his castle. And there he had passing good cheer both with the King and with his daughter, and they proffered him great gifts. And on the morn he took his leave and told the King that he would seek his brother Sir Lionel that went from him when he slept. So he took his horse and betaught them all to God and there he said unto the King's daughter, 'If that you have need any time of my service, I pray you let me have knowledge and I shall not fail you, as I am true knight.'

And so Sir Launcelot departed and by adventure he came into the same forest there he was taking his sleep before, and in the midst of an highway he met a damsel riding on a white palfrey, and there either salewed other. 'Fair damsel,' said

Sir Launcelot, 'know you in this country any adventures near-hand?'

'Sir knight,' said the damsel, 'here are adventures nigh, and thou durst prove them.'

'Why should I not prove?' said Sir Launcelot. 'For for that cause came I hither.'

'Well,' said she, 'thou seemest well to be a good knight, and if thou dare meet with a good knight I shall bring thee where is the best knight and the mightiest that ever thou found, so thou wilt tell me thy name and what knight thou art.'

'Damsel, as for to tell you my name, I take no great force. Truly, my name is Sir Launcelot du Lake.'

'Sir, thou beseems well: here is adventures fast by that fall for thee. For hereby dwells a knight that will not be over-matched by no man I know, but you do overmatch him. And his name is Sir Tarquin. And, as I understand, he has, in his prison, of Arthur's court good knights three-score and four that he hath won with his own hands. But when you have done that journey you shall promise me, as you are a true knight, for to go and help me and other damsels that are distressed daily with a false knight.'

'All your intent, damsel, and desire I will fulfil, so you will bring me unto this knight.'

'Now, fair knight, come on your way!'

And so she brought him unto the ford and the tree where hung the basin. So Sir Launcelot let his horse drink and sithen he beat on the basin with the butt of his spear till the bottom fell out. And long did he so but he saw no man. Then he rode endlong the gates of that manor nigh half an hour. And then was he aware of a great knight that drove an horse before him, and overthwart the horse lay an armed knight bound. And ever as they came near and near Sir Launcelot thought he should know him. Then was he aware that it was Sir Gaheris, Gawain's brother, a knight of the Table Round.

'Now, fair damsel,' said Sir Launcelot, 'I see yonder a knight fast bound that is a fellow of mine and brother he is unto Sir Gawain. And at the first beginning I promise you, by the leave of God, for to rescue that knight. But if his master sit the better in his saddle, I shall deliver all the prisoners that he has out of danger, for I am sure he has two brethren of mine prisoners with him.'

But by that time that either had seen other they griped their spears unto them. 'Now, fair knight,' said Sir Launcelot, 'put that wounded knight off that horse and let him rest awhile and let us two prove our strengths. For, as it is informed me, thou doest and hast done me great despite, and shame unto knights of the Round Table. And therefore now defend thee!'

'And thou art of [the] Round Table,' said Tarquin, 'I defy thee and all thy fellowship!'

'That is overmuch said,' Sir Launcelot said, 'of thee at this time.'

[VI.8] And then they put their spears in their rests and came together with their horses as fast as they might run. And either smote other in midst of their shields that both their horses' backs brast under them and the knights were both astoned. And, as soon as they might, they avoided their horses and took their shields before them and drew out their swords and came together eagerly, and either gave other many strong strokes, for there might neither shields nor harness hold their strokes.

And so within a while they had both many grim wounds and bled passing grievously. Thus they fared two hours and more, trasing and rasing either other where they might hit any bare place. Then at the last they were breathless both and stood leaning on their swords.

'Now, fellow,' said Sir Tarquin, 'hold thy hand a while, and tell me that I shall ask of thee.'

'Say on!' said Sir Launcelot.

Then Sir Tarquin said, 'Thou art the biggest man that ever I met withal and the best-breathed, and as like one knight that I hate above all other knights. So be it that thou art not he, I will lightly accord with thee, and for thy love I will deliver all the prisoners that I have, that is three-score and four, so thou would tell me thy name. And thou and I will be fellows together and never to fail thee, while that I live.'

'You say well,' said Sir Launcelot, 'but sithen it is so that I have thy friendship and may have, what knight is that that thou hatest above all things?'

'Faithfully,' said Sir Tarquin, 'his name is Sir Launcelot du Lake, for he slew my brother, Sir Carados, at the Dolorous Tower, that was one of the best knights alive. And therefore him I except of all knights, for may I him once meet, the one shall make an end, I make mine avow. And for Sir Launcelot's sake I have slain an hundred good knights and as many I have maimed all utterly that they might never after help themselves, and many have died in prison. And yet have I three-score and four, and all [shall] be delivered, so thou wilt tell me thy name, so be it that thou art not Sir Launcelot.'

'Now see I well,' said Sir Launcelot, 'that such a man I might be, I might have peace, and such a man I might [be], that there should be mortal war betwixt us. And now, Sir knight, at thy request I will that thou wit and know that I am Sir Launcelot du Lake, King Ban's son of Benwick, and very knight of the Table Round. And now I defy thee, and do thy best!'

'Ah!' said Sir Tarquin, 'thou art to me most welcome of any knight, for we shall never depart till the one of us be dead!'

Then they hurtled together as two wild bulls, rushing and lashing with their shields and swords that sometimes they fell both on their noses. Thus they fought still two hours and

more and never would have rest, and Sir Tarquin gave Sir
Launcelot many wounds that all the ground thereas they
fought was all besparkled with blood.

[VI.9] Then, at the last, Sir Tarquin waxed faint and gave
somewhat aback and bore his shield low for weary. That
espied Sir Launcelot and leapt upon him fiercely and got him
by the beaver of his helmet and plucked him down on his
knees and anon he raced off his helm and smote his neck in
sunder. And when Sir Launcelot had done this he yode unto
the damsel and said, 'Damsel, I am ready to go with you
where you will have me, but I have no horse.'

'Fair sir,' said this wounded knight, 'take my horse and
then let me go into this manor and deliver all these prisoners.'

So he took Sir Gaheris' horse and prayed him not to be
grieved.

'Nay, fair lord, I will that you have him at your commandment for you have both saved me and my horse. And
this day I say you are the best knight in the world, for you
have slain this day in my sight the mightiest man and the
best knight except you that ever I saw. But, fair sir,' said Sir
Gaheris, 'I pray you tell me your name.'

'Sir, my name is Sir Launcelot du Lake that ought to help
you of right for King Arthur's sake, and in especial for my
lord, Sir Gawain's sake, your own brother. And when that
you come within yonder manor, I am sure you shall find
there many knights of the Round Table, for I have seen
many of their shields that I know hang on yonder tree.
There is Sir Kay's shield and Sir Galihud's shield and Sir
Bryan de Lystenoyse's shield, and Sir Alyduke's shield,
with many more that I am not now advised of, and Sir
Marhalt's and also my two brethren's shields, Sir Ector de
Maris and Sir Lionel. Wherefore, I pray you, greet them all
from me and say that I bid them to take such stuff there as
they find, that, in any wise, my two brethren go unto the
court and abide me there till that I come, for by the feast of

Pentecost I cast me to be there – for as at this time I must ride with this damsel for to save my promise.'

And so they departed from Gaheris. And Gaheris yode into the manor and there he found a yeoman porter keeping many keys. Then Sir Gaheris threw the porter unto the ground and took the keys from him, and hastily he opened the prison door and there he let all the prisoners out, and every man loosed other of their bonds. And when they saw Sir Gaheris, all they thanked him for they weened that he had slain Sir Tarquin because that he was wounded.

'Not so, sirs,' said Sir Gaheris. 'It was Sir Launcelot that slew him worshipfully with his own hands, and he greets you all well and prays you to haste you to the court. And as unto you, Sir Lionel and Sir Ector de Maris, he prays you to abide him at the court of King Arthur.'

'That shall we not do,' said his brethren. 'We will find him, and we may live.'

'So shall I,' said Sir Kay, 'find him ere I come to the court, as I am true knight.'

Then they sought the house thereas the armour was, and then they armed them. And every knight found his own horse and all that longed unto him. So forthwith there came a forester with four horses laden with fat venison. And anon Sir Kay said, 'Here is good meat for us for one meal, for we had not many a day no good repast.'

And so that venison was roasted, sodden and baked. And so, after supper, some abode there all night. But Sir Lionel and Sir Ector de Maris and Sir Kay rode after Sir Launcelot to find him if they might.

[VI.10] Now turn we to Sir Launcelot that rode with the damsel in a fair highway. 'Sir,' said the damsel, 'here by this way haunts a knight that distresses all ladies and gentlewomen and, at the least, he robs them or lies by them.'

'What?' said Sir Launcelot. 'Is he a thief and a knight? – and a ravisher of women? He does shame unto the Order of

knighthood and contrary unto his oath. It is pity that he
lives! But, fair damsel, you shall ride on, before, yourself, and
I will keep myself in covert. And if that he trouble you or
distress you, I shall be your rescuer and learn him to be
ruled as a knight.'

So this maid rode on by the way a soft ambling pace, and
within a while came out a knight on horseback out of the
wood and his page with him. And there he put the damsel
from her horse, and then she cried. With that came Sir
Launcelot, as fast as he might, till he came to the knight,
saying, 'Ah! false knight and traitor unto knighthood!
Who did learn thee to distress ladies, damsels and gentlewomen?'

When the knight saw Sir Launcelot thus rebuking him he
answered not but drew his sword and rode unto Sir Launcelot. And Sir Launcelot threw his spear from him and drew
his sword and struck him such a buffet on the helmet that he
clove his head and neck unto the throat.

'Now hast thou thy payment that long thou hast deserved.'

'That is truth,' said the damsel, 'for like as Tarquin
watched to distress good knights, so did this knight attend to
destroy and distress ladies, damsels and gentlewomen. And
his name was Sir Perys de Forest Savage.'

'Now, damsel,' said Sir Launcelot, 'will you any more
service of me?'

'Nay, sir,' she said, 'at this time. But Almighty Jesu
preserve you wheresoever you ride or go, for the curtest
knight thou art, and meekest unto all ladies and gentlewomen that now lives. But one thing, Sir knight, me thinks
you lack, you that are a knight wifeless—that you will not
love some maiden or gentlewoman. For I could never hear
say that ever you loved any of no manner of degree, and that
is great pity. But it is noised that you love Queen Guenevere
and that she has ordained by enchantment that you shall
never love none other but her, neither none other damsel nor

lady shall rejoice you. Wherefore there are many in this land, of high estate and low, that make great sorrow.'

'Fair damsel,' said Sir Launcelot, 'I may not warn people to speak of me what it pleases them. But for to be a wedded man, I think it not, for then I must couch with her and leave arms and tournaments, battles and adventures. And as for to say to take my pleasaunce with paramours, that will I refuse, in principal for dread of God, for knights that are adventurous should not be advoutrers nor lecherous, for then they are not happy nor fortunate unto the wars, for either they shall be overcome with a simpler knight than they are themselves or else they shall slay by unhap and their cursedness better men than they are themselves. And so who that uses paramours shall be unhappy and all thing unhappy that is about them.'

And so Sir Launcelot and she departed. And then he rode in a deep forest two days and more and had strait lodging. So on the third day he rode on a long bridge and there started upon him suddenly a passing foul carle. . . .

After recounting more such adventures this Book concludes: 'And so at that time Sir Launcelot had the greatest name of any knight of the world, and most he was honoured of high and low.

'Explicit a noble tale of Sir Launcelot du Lake.'

Book Four

'Sir Gareth's Tale'

❧

Here follows Sir Gareth's Tale of Orkney that was called
Beaumains by Sir Kay.

[VII.1] In Arthur's days, when he held the Round Table
most plenour, it fortuned ⟨that⟩ the King commanded that
the high feast of Pentecost should be held at a city and a
castle in those days that was called Kinke Kenadonne, upon
the sands that marched nigh Wales. So ever the King had a
custom that at the feast of Pentecost, in especial before other
feasts in the year, he would not go that day to meat until that
he had heard or seen of a great marvel. And for that custom
all manner of strange adventures came before Arthur as at
that feast before all other feasts.

And so Sir Gawain, a little before the noon of the day of
Pentecost, espied at a window three men upon horseback and
a dwarf upon foot. And so the three men alighted and the
dwarf kept their horses. And one of the men was higher than
the other twain by a foot and a half. Then Sir Gawain went
unto the King and said, 'Sir, go to your meat, for here at
hand come strange adventures.'

So the King went unto his meat with many other kings.
And there were all the knights of the Round Table, unless
that any were prisoners or slain at encounters. (Then at the
high feast evermore they should be fulfilled, the whole

number of an hundred and fifty, for then was the Round Table fully complished.)

Right so came into the hall two men well besene and richly, and upon their shoulders there leaned the goodliest young man and the fairest that ever they all saw. And he was large and long and broad in the shoulders, well-visaged, and the largest and the fairest hands that ever man saw. But he fared as he might not go nor bear himself but if he leaned upon their shoulders. Anon as the King saw him there was was made peace and room, and right so they yode with him unto the high dais without saying of any words. Then this young much man pulled him aback and easily straight upright, saying,

'The most noble king, King Arthur, God you bless and all your fair fellowship, and in especial the fellowship of the Table Round! And for this cause I come hither, to pray you and require you to give me three gifts, and they shall not be unreasonably asked but that you may worshipfully grant them me, and to you no great hurt nor loss. And the first [done] and gift I will ask now and the other two gifts I will ask this day twelve-month wheresoever you hold your high feast.'

'Now ask you,' said King Arthur, 'and you shall have your asking.'

'Now, sir, this is my petition at this feast, that you will give me meat and drink sufficiently for this twelve-month, and at that day I will ask mine other two gifts.'

'My fair son,' said King Arthur, 'ask better, I counsel thee, for this is but a simple asking. For mine heart gives me to thee greatly that thou art come of men of worship, and greatly my conceit fails me but thou shalt prove a man of right great worship.'

'Sir,' he said, 'thereof be as be may, for I have asked that I will ask at this time.'

'Well,' said the King, 'you shall have meat and drink

enough! I never forbade it my friend nor my foe. But what is thy name, I would wit?'

'Sir, I cannot tell you.'

'That is marvel,' said the King, 'that thou knowest not thy name, and thou art one of the goodliest young men that ever I saw!'

Then the King betook him to Sir Kay the Steward, and charged him that he had of all manner of meats and drinks of the best and also that he had all manner of finding as though he were a lord's son.

'That shall little need,' said Sir Kay, 'to do such cost upon him, for I undertake he is a villain born and never will make man, for, and he had been come of gentlemen, he would have asked horse and armour. But as he is, so he asks. And sithen he hath no name, I shall give him a name which shall be called Beaumains, that is to say, "Fairhands". And into the kitchen I shall bring him and there he shall have fat browes every day, that he shall be as fat at the twelve-month end as a pork hog!'

Right so the two men departed and left him with Sir Kay that scorned and mocked him. [VII.2] Thereat was Sir Gawain wroth. And in especial Sir Launcelot bade Sir Kay leave his mocking – 'for I dare lay my head he shall prove a man of great worship!'

'Let be!' said Sir Kay. 'It may not be by reason, for as he is, so he has asked.'

'Yet, beware!' said Sir Launcelot. 'So you gave the good knight, Brunor, Sir Dinadan's brother, a name, and you called him "La Cote Male Tayle," and that turned you to anger afterward.'

'As for that,' said Sir Kay, 'this shall never prove none such, for Sir Brunor desired ever worship, and this desires ever meat and drink and broth. Upon pain of my life, he was fostered up in some abbey and, howsoever it was, they failed meat and drink and so hither he is come for his sustenance.'

And so Sir Kay bade get him a place and sit down to meat. So Beaumains went to the hall door and set him down among boys and lads, and there he ate sadly. And then Sir Launcelot after meat bade him come to his chamber, and there he should have meat and drink enough, and so did Sir Gawain. But he refused them all for he would do none other but as Sir Kay commanded him for no proffer.

But as touching Sir Gawain, he had reason to proffer him lodging, meat and drink, for that proffer came of his blood, for he was nearer kin to him than he wist of. But that Sir Launcelot did was of his great gentleness and courtesy.

So thus he was put into the kitchen and lay nightly as the kitchen boys did. And so he endured all that twelve-month and never displeased man nor child, but always he was meek and mild. But ever when he saw any jousting of knights, that would he see and he might. And ever Sir Launcelot would give him gold to spend, and clothes, and so did Sir Gawain. And, where there were any maystries doing, thereat would he be, and there might none cast bar nor stone to him by two yards. Then would Sir Kay say, 'How likes you my boy of the kitchen?'

So this passed on till the feast of Whitsuntide, and at that time the King held it at Caerleon in the most royalest wise that might be, like as he did yearly. But the King would no meat eat upon Whitsunday until he heard of some adventures. Then came there a squire unto the King and said, 'Sir, you may go to your meat for here comes a damsel with some strange adventures.'

Then was the King glad and set him down. Right so there came a damsel unto the hall and salewed the King and prayed him for succour.

'For whom?' said the King. 'What is the adventure?'

'Sir,' she said, 'I have a lady of great worship as my sister and she is besieged with a tyrant that she may not out of her

castle. And because here are called the noblest knights of the
world, I come to you for succour.'

'What is your lady called and where dwells she? And who
is he and what is his name that has besieged her?'

'Sir King,' she said, 'as for my lady's name, that shall not
you know for me as at this time, but I let you wit she is a lady
of great worship and of great lands. And as for that tyrant
that besieges her and destroys her lands, he is called the Red
Knight of the Red Laundes.'

'I know him not,' said the King.

'Sir,' said Sir Gawain, 'I know him well, for he is one of
the perilest knights of the world. Men say that he has seven
men's strength and from him I escaped once full hard with
my life.'

'Fair damsel,' said [the] King, 'there are knights here that
would do their power for to rescue your lady, but, because
you will not tell her name nor where she dwells, therefore
none of my knights that here are now shall go with you, by
my will.'

'Then must I seek further,' said the damsel.

[VII.3] So with these words came Beaumains before the
King while the damsel was there, and thus he said, 'Sir King,
God thank you, I have been this twelve-month in your
kitchen and have had my full sustenance. And now I will ask
my other two gifts that are behind.'

'Ask on now, upon my peril,' said the King.

'Sir, this shall be my first gift of the two gifts, that you will
grant me to have this adventure of this damsel, for it belongs
unto me.'

'Thou shalt have it,' said the King. 'I grant it thee.'

'Then, sir, this is that other gift that you shall grant me—
that Sir Launcelot du Lake shall make me knight, for of him
I will be made knight and else of none. And when I am
passed I pray you let him ride after me and make me knight
when I require him.'

'All this shall be done,' said the King.

'Fie on thee!' said the damsel. 'Shall I have none but one that is your kitchen knave?' Then she waxed angry and anon she took her horse.

And with that there came one to Beaumains and told him his horse and armour was come for him, and a dwarf had brought him all things that needed him in the richest wise. Thereat the court had much marvel from whence came all that gear. So when he was armed there was none but few so goodly a man as he was. And right so he came into the hall and took his leave of King Arthur and Sir Gawain and of Sir Launcelot, and prayed him to hie after him. And so he departed and rode after the damsel. [VII.4] But there went many after to behold how well he was horsed and trapped in cloth of gold, but he had neither spear nor shield. Then Sir Kay said all openly in the hall, 'I will ride after my boy of the kitchen to wit whether he will know me for his better.'

'Yet,' said Sir Launcelot and Sir Gawain, 'abide at home.'

So Sir Kay made him ready and took his horse and his spear and rode after him. And right as Beaumains overtook the damsel, right so came Sir Kay and said, 'Beaumains! What, sir, know you not me?'

Then he turned his horse and knew it was Sir Kay that had done all the despite to him as you have heard before. Then said Beaumains, 'Yea! I know you well for an ungentle knight of the court, and therefore beware of me!'

Therewith Sir Kay put his spear in the rest and ran straight upon him. And Beaumains came as fast upon him with his sword, and, with a foin, thrust him through the side that Sir Kay fell down as he had been dead. Then Beaumains alighted down and took Sir Kay's shield and his spear and started upon his own horse and rode his way.

All that saw Sir Launcelot and so did the damsel, and then he bade his dwarf start upon Sir Kay's horse and so he did. By that Sir Launcelot was come, and anon he proffered Sir

Launcelot to joust, and either made them ready and came together so fiercely that either bore other down to the earth, and sore were they bruised. Then Sir Launcelot arose and helped him from his horse, and then Beaumains threw his shield from him and proffered to fight with Sir Launcelot on foot.

So they rushed together like two boars, trasing and traversing and foining the mountenance of an hour. And Sir Launcelot felt him so big that he marvelled of his strength, for he fought more liker a giant than a knight, and his fighting was so passing durable and passing perilous. For Sir Launcelot had so much ado with him that he dread himself to be shamed and said, 'Beaumains, fight not so sore! Your quarrel and mine is not great but we may soon leave off!'

'Truly that is truth,' said Beaumains, 'but it does me good to feel your might. And yet, my lord, I showed not the utterance!'

[VII.5] 'In God's name,' said Sir Launcelot, 'for I promise you, by the faith of my body, I had as much to do as I might have to save myself from you unshamed, and therefore have you no doubt of none earthly knight.'

'Hope you so that I may any while stand a proved knight?'

'Do as you have done to me,' said Sir Launcelot, 'and I shall be your warrant.'

'Then I pray you,' said Beaumains, 'give me the Order of Knighthood.'

'Sir, then must you tell me your name of right, and of what kin you are born.'

'Sir, so that you will not discover me, I shall tell you my name.'

'Nay, sir,' said Sir Launcelot, 'and that I promise you by the faith of my body, until it is openly known.'

Then he said, 'My name is Gareth, and brother unto Sir Gawain of father's side and mother's side.'

'Ah! sir, I am more gladder of you than I was, for ever me thought you should be of great blood and that you came not to the court neither for meat nor drink.'

Then Sir Launcelot gave him the Order of Knighthood. And then Sir Gareth prayed him for to depart and so he to follow the lady. So Sir Launcelot departed from him and came to Sir Kay and made him to be borne home upon his shield. And so he was healed hard with the life. And all men scorned Sir Kay, and in especial Sir Gawain. And Sir Launcelot said that it was not his part to rebuke no young man – 'for full little know you of what birth he is come of and for what cause he came to the court'.

And so we leave of Sir Kay and turn we unto Beaumains. When that he had overtaken the damsel, anon she said, 'What dost thou here? Thou stinkest all of the kitchen! Thy clothes are bawdy of the grease and tallow. What weenest thou?' said the lady '– that I will allow thee for yonder knight that thou killed? Nay, truly, for thou slewest him unhappily and cowardly. Therefore, turn again, thou bawdy kitchen knave! I know thee well, for Sir Kay named thee Beaumains. What art thou but a lusk and a turner of broachs and a ladle-washer?'

'Damsel,' said Sir Beaumains, 'say to me what you will, yet will not I go from you whatsoever you say, for I have undertaken to King Arthur for to achieve your adventure, and so shall I finish it to the end or else I shall die therefore.'

'Fie on thee, kitchen knave! Wilt thou finish mine adventure? Thou shalt anon be met withal that thou wouldest not for all the broth that ever thou supped once to look him in the face.'

'As for that, I shall essay,' said Beaumains. . . .

He perseveres and repeatedly triumphs in combat though repeatedly humiliated by Dame Lyonet. But she eventually acknowledges he must 'be come of gentle blood, for so foul and so shamefully did never woman revile a knight as I have done you, and ever cour-

teously you have suffered me, and that came never but of gentle
blood.'

[VII.15] . . . And upon the morn [Beaumains] and the
damsel Lyonet heard their mass and broke their fast and
then they took their horses and rode throughout a fair forest.
And then they came to a plain and saw where was many
pavilions and tents and a fair castle, and there was much
smoke and great noise. And when they came near the siege
Sir Beaumains espied on great trees, as he rode, how there
hung full goodly armed knights by the neck and their shields
about their necks with their swords and gilt spurs upon their
heels. And so there hung nigh a forty knights shamefully
with full rich arms. Then Sir Beaumains abated his countenance and said, 'What means this?'

'Fair sir,' said the damsel, 'abate not your cheer for all
this sight, for you must courage yourself or else you are all
shent. For all these knights came hither to this siege to
rescue my sister, Dame Lyoness, and, when the Red Knight
of the Red Laundes had overcome them, he put them to this
shameful death without mercy and pity. And in the same
wise he will serve you but if you quit you the better.'

'Now Jesu defend me,' said Sir Beaumains, 'from such
vilans death and shondeship of harms, for rather than I
should so be faren withal I will rather be slain in plain
battle.'

'So were you better,' said the damsel, 'for, trust not! In
him is no courtesy, but all goes to the death or shameful
murder. And that is pity,' said the damsel, 'for he is a full
likely man and a noble knight of prowess and a lord of great
lands and of great possessions.'

'Truly,' said Sir Beaumains, 'he may be well a good
knight, but he uses shameful customs, and it is marvel that
he endures so long that none of the noble knights of my lord
Arthur's have not dealt with him.'

And then they rode unto the dykes and saw them double-dyked with full warly walls, and there was great noise of minstrelsy. And the sea beat upon that one side of the walls where were many ships and mariners' noise with 'hale' and 'how'. And also there was fast by a sycamore tree and thereon hung an horn, the greatest that ever they saw, of an elephant's bone, 'and this Knight of the Red Laundes has hung it up there to this intent that if there come any errant knight he must blow that horn, and then will he make him ready and come to him to do battle. But, sir, pray you,' said the damsel, 'blow you not the horn till it be nigh noon, for now it is about prime, and now increases his might, that, as men say, he has seven men's strength.'

'Ah! fie, for shame, fair damsel! Say you never so more to me, for and he were as good a knight as ever was any, I shall never fail him in his most might, for either I will win worship worshipfully or die knightly in the field.'

And therewith he spurred his horse straight to the sycamore tree and so blew the horn eagerly that all the siege and the castle rang thereof. And then there leapt out many knights out of their tents and pavilions, and they within the castle looked over the walls and out at windows. Then the Red Knight of the Red Laundes armed him hastily and two barons set on his spurs on his heels, and all was blood-red, his armour, spear and shield. And an earl buckled his helm on his head, and then they brought him a red spear and a red steed. And so he rode into a little vale under the castle that all that were in the castle and at the siege might behold the battle.

[VII.16] 'Sir,' said the damsel Lyonet unto Sir Beaumains, 'look you be glad and light, for yonder is your deadly enemy and at yonder window is my lady, my sister Dame Lyoness.'

'Where?' said Beaumains.

'Yonder,' said the damsel, and pointed with her finger.

'That is truth,' said Beaumains, 'she seems afar the fairest lady that ever I looked upon, and, truly,' he said, 'I ask no better quarrel than now for to do battle, for truly she shall be my lady and for her will I fight.'

And ever he looked up to the window with glad countenance, and this lady, Dame Lyoness, made curtsy to him down to the earth, holding up both her hands. With that the Red Knight called unto Beaumains and said, 'Sir Knight, leave thy beholding and look on me, I counsel thee, for, I warn thee well, she is my lady and for her I have done many strong battles!'

'If thou so have done,' said Beaumains, 'me seems it was but waste labour, for she loves none of thy fellowship, and thou to love that loves not thee is but great folly. For, and I understood that she were not right glad of my coming, I would be advised ere I did battle for her. But I understand by the sieging of this castle she may forbear thy fellowship. And therefore, wit thou well, thou Red Knight, I love her and will rescue her, or else to die therefore.'

'Sayest thou that?' said the Red Knight. 'Me seems thou oughtest of reason to beware by yonder knights that thou sawest hang on yonder trees!'

'Fie, for shame!' said Beaumains, 'that ever thou shouldest say so or do so evil, for, in that, thou shamest thyself and all knighthood, and thou mayest be sure there will no lady love thee that knows thee and thy wicked customs. And now thou weenest that the sight of those hanged knights should fear me? Nay, truly, not so! That shameful sight causes me to have courage and hardiness against thee much more than I would have against thee and thou were a well-ruled knight!'

'Make thee ready,' said the Red Knight, 'and talk no more with me.'

Then they put their spears in the rest and came together with all the might that they had both, and either smote other in the midst of their shields that the paytrels, sursingles and cruppers brast and fell to the earth, both, and the reins of their bridles in their hands. And so they lay a great while sore astoned, that all that were in the castle and in the siege weened their necks had been brast.

Then many a stranger and other said that the strange knight was a big man and a noble jouster, 'for ere now we saw never no knight match the Red Knight of the Red Laundes'. Thus they said both within and without.

Then lightly and deliverly they avoided their horses and put their shields before them and drew their swords and ran together like two fierce lions, and either gave other such two buffets upon their helms that they reeled backward, both, two strides. And then they recovered, both, and hewed great pieces of other's harness and their shields, that a great part fell in the fields.

[VII.17] And then thus they fought till it was past noon and never would stint till at the last they lacked wind, both, and then they stood wagging, staggering, panting, blowing and bleeding, that all that beheld them for the most part wept for pity. So when they had rested them a while they yode to battle again, trasing, traversing, foining and rasing as two boars. And at some time they took their bere as it had been two rams, and hurled together that some time they fell grovelling to the earth, and at some time they were so amated that either took other's sword in the stead of his own.

And thus they endured till evensong that there was none that beheld them might know whether was like to win the battle. And their armour was so forhewen that men might see their naked sides, and in other places they were naked, but ever the naked places they did defend. And the Red Knight was a wily knight in fighting and that taught Beaumains to be wise, but he abought it full sore ere he did espy his fighting.

And thus by assent of them both they granted either other to rest, and so they set them down upon two molehills there beside the fighting place and either of them unlaced other

91

helms and took the cold wind, for either of their pages was
fast by them to come when they called them to unlace their
harness and to set them on again at their commandment.
And then Sir Beaumains, when his helm was off, he looked
up to the window and there he saw the fair lady, Dame
Lyoness, and she made him such countenance that his heart
waxed light and jolly. And therewith he bade the Red
Knight of the Red Laundes make him ready, 'and let us do
our battle to the utterance'.

'I will well,' said the knight.

And then they laced on their helms and avoided their
pages and yode together and fought freshly. But the Red
Knight of the Red Laundes waited him at an overthwart and
smote him that his sword fell out of his hand. And yet he
gave him another buffet upon the helm that he fell grovelling
to the earth, and the Red Knight fell over him for to hold
him down.

Then cried the Maiden Lyonet on hight and said, 'Ah!
Sir Beaumains. Where is thy courage become? Alas! my
lady, my sister, beholds thee and she shrieks and weeps so
that it makes mine heart heavy.'

When Sir Beaumains heard her say so he abraided up
with a great might and got him upon his feet and lightly he
leapt to his sword and griped it in his hand and doubled his
pace unto the Red Knight, and there they fought a new
battle together. But Sir Beaumains then doubled his strokes
and smote so thick that his sword fell out of his hand. And
then he smote him on the helm that he fell to the earth, and
Sir Beaumains fell upon him and unlaced his helm to have
slain him. And then he yielded him and asked mercy and
said with a loud voice, 'Ah! noble knight, I yield me to thy
mercy!'

Then Sir Beaumains bethought him on his knights that
he had made to be hanged shamefully, and then he said, 'I
may not with my worship to save thy life for the shameful

[deaths] that thou hast caused many full good knights to die.'

'Sir,' said the Red Knight, 'hold your hand! and you shall know the causes why I put them to so shameful a death.'

'Say on!' said Sir Beaumains.

'Sir, I loved once a lady fair and she had her brethren slain and she told me it was Sir Launcelot du Lake or else Sir Gawain. And she prayed me, as I loved her heartily, that I would make her a promise by the faith of my knighthood for to labour in arms daily until that I had met with one of them, and all that I might overcome I should put them to vilans death. And so I assured her to do all the villainy unto Arthur's knights, and that I should take vengeance upon all these knights. And, sir, now I will tell thee that every day my strength increases till noon until I have seven men's strength.'

[VII.18] Then came there many earls and barons and noble knights and prayed that knight to save his life, 'and take him as your prisoner'. And all they fell upon their knees and prayed him of mercy that he would save his life. 'And, sir,' they all said, 'it were fairer of him to take homage and fealty and let him hold his lands of you than for to slay him, for by his death you shall have none advantage, and his misdeeds that he ⟨has⟩ done may not be undone. And therefore make you amends for all parties, and we all will become your men and do you homage and fealty.'

'Fair lords,' said Beaumains, 'wit you well I am full loath to slay this knight, nevertheless he has done passing ill and shamefully. But insomuch ⟨that⟩ all that he did was at a lady's request I blame him the less, and so for your sake I will release him that he shall have his life, upon this covenant—that he go into this castle and yield him to the lady, and, if she will forgive and quite him, I will well with this he make her amends of all the trespass that he has done against her and her lands. And also, when that is done, that he go unto the court of King Arthur, and that he ask Sir Launcelot mercy and Sir Gawain for the evil will he has had against them.'

'Sir,' said the Red Knight, 'all this will I do as you command me, and siker assurance and borrows you shall have.'

So when the assurance was made he made his homage and fealty, and all the earls and barons with him. And then the maiden Lyonet came to Sir Beaumains and unarmed him and searched his wounds and staunched the blood, and in like wise she did to the Red Knight of the Red Laundes. And there they sojourned ten days in their tents. And ever the Red Knight made all his lords and servants to do all the pleasure unto Sir Beaumains that they might do.

And so within a while the Red Knight yode unto the castle and put him in her grace, and so she received him upon sufficient surety so that all her hurts were well restored of all that she could complain. And then he departed unto the court of King Arthur, and there openly the Red Knight put himself in the mercy of Sir Launcelot and of Sir Gawain, and there he told openly how he was overcome and by whom and also he told all the battles from the beginning to the ending.

'Jesu, mercy!' said King Arthur and Sir Gawain. 'We marvel much of what blood he is come, for here is a noble knight!'

'Have you no marvel,' said Sir Launcelot, 'for you shall right well know that he is come of full noble blood, and, as for his might and hardiness, there are but full few now living that is so mighty as he is and of so noble prowess.'

'It seems by you,' said King Arthur, 'that you know his name and from whence he came.'

'I suppose I do so,' said Sir Launcelot, 'or else I would not have given him the high Order of Knighthood. But he gave me such charge at that time that I will never discover him until he require me or else it is known openly by some other.'

[VII.19] Now turn we unto Sir Beaumains that desired Dame Lyonet that he might see her lady.

'Sir,' she said, 'I would you saw her fain.'

Then Sir Beaumains all armed took his horse and his spear and rode straight unto the castle. And when he came to the gate he found there men armed, and pulled up the drawbridge and drew the portcullis. Then he marvelled why they would not suffer him to enter. And then he looked up to a window and there he saw fair Dame Lyoness that said on hight, 'Go thy way, Sir Beaumains, for as yet thou shalt not have wholly my love unto the time that thou be called one of the number of the worthy knights. And, therefore, go and labour in worship this twelve-month, and then you shall hear new tidings.'

'Alas! fair lady,' said Sir Beaumains, 'I have not deserved that you should show me this strangeness. And I had weened I should have had right good cheer with you, and unto my power I have deserved thanks. And well I am sure I have bought your love with part of the best blood within my body.'

'Fair, courteous knight,' said Dame Lyoness, 'be not displeased neither be not overhasty, for, wit you well, your great travail nor your good love shall not be lost, for I consider your great labour and your hardiness, your bounty and your goodness as me ought to do. And, therefore, go on your way and look that you be of good comfort, for all shall be for your worship and for the best—and, parde, a twelve-month will soon be done. And trust me, fair knight, I shall be true to you and never betray you, but to my death I shall love you and none other.'

And therewithal she turned from the window and Sir Beaumains rode awayward from the castle making great dole. And so he rode now here, now there, he wist not whither, till it was dark night. And then it happened him to come to a poor man's house, and there he was harboured all that night. But Sir Beaumains had no rest, but wallowed and writhed for the love of the lady of that castle.

And so upon the morn he took his horse and rode until undern, and then he came to a broad water. And there he alighted to sleep and laid his head upon his shield and betook his horse to the dwarf and commanded the dwarf to watch all night.

Now turn we to the lady of the same castle that thought much upon Beaumains. And then she called unto her Sir Gringamore, her brother, and prayed him in all manner, as he loved her heartily, that he would ride after Sir Beaumains, 'And ever have you wait upon him till you may find him sleeping, for I am sure in his heaviness he will alight down in some place and lay him down to sleep. And, therefore, have you your wait upon him in privy manner and take his dwarf and come your way with him as fast as you may, for my sister Lyonet tells me that he can tell of what kindred he is come of. And, in the meanwhile, I and my sister will ride to your castle to wait when you bring with you the dwarf, and then will I have him in examination myself, for, till I know what is his right name and of what kindred he is come, shall I never be merry at my heart.'

'Sister,' said Sir Gringamore, 'all this shall be done after your intent.'

And so he rode all that other day and the night till he had lodged him. And when he saw Sir Beaumains fast asleep he came stilly stalking behind the dwarf and plucked him fast under his arm and so rode his way with him to his own castle. And this Sir Gringamore was all in black, his armour and his horse and all that to him longs. But ever as he rode with the dwarf toward the castle he cried to his lord and prayed him for help. And therewith awoke Sir Beaumains and up he leapt lightly and saw where the black knight rode his way with the dwarf, and so he rode out of his sight.

[VII.20] Then Sir Beaumains put on his helm and buckled on his shield and took his horse and rode after him all that ever he might, through moors and fells and great sloughs, that many times his horse and he plunged over their heads in deep mires, for he knew not the way but took the gaynest way in that woodness, that many times he was like to perish. And at the last him happened to come to a fair green way and there he met with a poor man of the country and asked him whether he met not with a knight upon a black horse and all black harness and a little dwarf sitting behind him with heavy cheer.

'Sir,' said the poor man, 'here by me came Sir Gringamore, the knight, with such a dwarf, and therefore I rede you not to follow him for he is one of the perilest knights of the world and his castle is here near-hand but two miles. Therefore we advise you, ride not after Sir Gringamore but if you owe him good will.'

So leave we Sir Beaumains riding toward the castle and speak we of Sir Gringamore and the dwarf. Anon as the dwarf was come to the castle, Dame Lyoness and Dame Lyonet, her sister, asked the dwarf where was his master born and of what lineage was he come. 'And but if thou tell me,' said Dame Lyoness, 'thou shalt never escape this castle but ever here to be prisoner.'

'As for that,' said the dwarf, 'I fear not greatly to tell his name and of what kin he is come of. Wit you well, he is a king's son and a queen's, and his father hight King Lot of Orkney, and his mother is sister to King Arthur, and he is brother to Sir Gawain, and his name is Sir Gareth of Orkney. And now I have told you his right name I pray you, fair lady, let me go to my lord again, for he will never out of this country till he have me again. And if he is angry he will do harm ere that he is stinted and work you wrake in this country.'

'As for that, be as be may.'

'Nay,' said Sir Gringamore, 'as for that threating, we will go to dinner!'

And so they washed and went to meat and made them

97

merry and well-at-ease. Because the Lady Lyoness of the
Castle Perilous was there, they made the greater joy.

'Truly, madam,' said Lyonet unto her sister, 'well may he
be a king's son, for he has many good tacches: for he is
courteous and mild, and the most suffering man that ever I
met withal. For I dare say there was never gentlewoman
reviled man in so foul a manner as I have rebuked him,
and at all times he gave me goodly and meek answers
again.'

And, as they sat thus talking, there came Sir Gareth in at
the gate with his sword drawn in his hand and cried aloud
that all the castle might hear, 'Thou traitor knight, Sir
Gringamore! Deliver me my dwarf again or, by the faith that
I owe to God and to the high Order of Knighthood, I shall
do thee all the harm that may lie in my power!'

Then Sir Gringamore looked out at a window and said,
'Sir Gareth of Orkney, leave thy boasting words, for thou
gettest not thy dwarf again!'

'Then, coward knight,' said Gareth, 'bring him with thee
and come and do battle with me and win him and take him.'

'So will I do,' said Sir Gringamore, 'and me list – but for all
thy great words thou gettest him not.'

'Ah! fair lady,' said Dame Lyonet, 'I would he had his
dwarf again, for I would he were not wroth, for, now he has
told me all my desire, I keep no more of the dwarf. And also,
brother, he has done much for me and delivered me from the
Red Knight of the Red Laundes. And, therefore, brother, I
owe him my service before all knights living, and wit you
well that I love him before all other knights living, and full
fain I would speak with him. But in no wise I would not
that he wist what I were, but as I were another strange
lady.'

'Well, sister,' said Sir Gringamore, 'sithen that I know
now your will, I will obey me now unto him.'

And so therewith he went down and said, 'Sir Gareth, I

cry you mercy, and all that I have misdone I will amend it at your will. And therefore I pray you that you would alight and take such cheer as I can make you in this castle.'

'Shall I have my dwarf?' said Sir Gareth.

'Yea! sir, and all the pleasure that I can make you, for as soon as your dwarf told me what you were and of what kind you are come and what noble deeds you have done in these marches, then I repented me of my deeds.'

Then Sir Gareth alighted and there came his dwarf and took his horse. 'Ah! my fellow,' said Sir Gareth, 'I have had much adventures for thy sake!'

And so Sir Gringamore took him by the hand and led him into the hall where his own wife was. [VII.21] And then came forth Dame Lyoness arrayed like a princess, and there she made him passing good cheer and he her again, and they had goodly language and lovely countenance. And Sir Gareth thought many times, 'Jesu! would that the lady of [the] Castle Perilous were so fair as she is.'

And there was all manner of games and plays, of dancing and singing, and evermore Sir Gareth beheld that lady. And the more he looked on her the more he burned in love that he passed himself far in his reason. And forth towards night they yode unto supper, and Sir Gareth might not eat for his love was so hot that he wist not where he was. And these looks espied Sir Gringamore, and then, after supper, he called his sister, Dame Lyoness, into a chamber and said:

'Fair sister, I have well espied your countenance betwixt you and this knight and I will, sister, that you wit he is a full noble knight and if you can make him to abide here I will do him all the pleasure that I can, for, and you were better than you are, you were well bewared upon him.'

'Fair brother,' said Dame Lyoness, 'I understand well that the knight is a good knight and come he is out of a noble house. Notwithstanding I will essay him better, howbeit I

am most beholden to him of any earthly man, for he has had
great labour for my love and passed many dangerous passages.'

Right so Sir Gringamore went unto Sir Gareth and said,
'Sir, make you good cheer, for you shall have none other
cause, for this lady, my sister, is yours at all times, her
worship saved, for wit you well she loves you as well as you
do her and better, if better may be.'

'And I wist that,' said Sir Gareth, 'there lived not a
gladder man than I would be!'

'Upon my worship,' said Sir Gringamore, 'trust unto my
promise! And, as long as it likes you, you shall sojourn with
me, and this lady shall be with us daily and nightly to make
you all the cheer that she can.'

'I will well,' said Sir Gareth, 'for I have promised to be
nigh this country this twelve-month, and well I am sure
King Arthur and other noble knights will find me where
that I am within this twelve-month, for I shall be sought and
found, if that I am alive.'

And then Sir Gareth went unto the lady, Dame Lyoness,
and kissed her many times and either made great joy of other
and there she promised him her love, certainly to love him
and none other days of her life. Then this lady, Dame
Lyoness, by the assent of her brother, told Sir Gareth all the
truth what she was and how she was the same lady that he
did battle for and how she was lady of the Castle Perilous.
And there she told him how she caused her brother to take
away his dwarf, [VII.22] 'for this cause, to know the certain,
what was your name and of what kin you were come'. And
then she let fetch before him her sister, Lyonet, that had
ridden with him many a wilsom way.

Then was Sir Gareth more gladder than he was before.
And then they troth-plight other to love and never to fail
while their life lasts. And so they burned both in hot love
that they were accorded to abate their lusts secretly. And

there Dame Lyoness counselled Sir Gareth to sleep in none other place but in the hall, and there she promised him to come to his bed a little before midnight.

This counsel was not so privily kept but it was understood, for they were but young, both, and tender of age, and had not used such crafts before. Wherefore the damsel Lyonet was a little displeased, and she thought her sister, Dame Lyoness, was a little overhasty that she might not abide her time of marriage. And, for saving of her worship, she thought to abate their hot lusts, and she let ordain by her subtle crafts that they had not their intents, neither with other, as in their delights, until they were married.

And so it passed on. At after-supper was made a clean avoidance, that every lord and lady should go unto his rest. But Sir Gareth said plainly he would go no further than the hall, for in such places, he said, was convenient for an errant knight to take his rest in. And so there was ordained great couches and thereon feather beds, and there he laid him down to sleep. And within a while came Dame Lyoness wrapped in a mantle furred with ermine, and laid her down by the side of Sir Gareth. And therewithal he began to clip her and to kiss her.

And therewithal he looked before him and saw an armed knight with many lights about him and this knight had a long gisarne in his hand and made a grim countenance to smite him. When Sir Gareth saw him come in that wise he leapt out of his bed and got in his hand a sword and leapt toward that knight. And when the knight saw Sir Gareth come so fiercely upon him he smote him with a foin through the thick of the thigh that the wound was a shaftemonde broad and had cut in two many veins and sinews. And therewithal Sir Gareth smote him upon the helm such a buffet that he fell grovelling, and then he leapt over him and unlaced his helm and smote off his head from the body. And then he bled so fast that he might not stand, but so he laid him down upon his bed and there he swooned and lay as he had been dead.

Then Dame Lyoness cried aloud that Sir Gringamore heard it and came down. And when he saw Sir Gareth so shamefully wounded he was sore displeased and said, 'I am shamed that this noble knight is thus dishonoured. Sir,' said Sir Gringamore, 'how may this be that this noble knight is thus wounded?'

'Brother,' she said, 'I cannot tell you, for it was not done by me nor by mine assent, for he is my lord and I am his, and he must be mine husband. Therefore, brother, I will that you wit I shame not to be with him nor to do him all the pleasure that I can.'

'Sister,' said Gringamore, 'and I will that you wit it and Gareth, both, that it was never done by me, nor by mine assent this unhappy deed was never done.'

And there they staunched his bleeding as well as they might and great sorrow made Sir Gringamore and Dame Lyoness. And forthwithal came Dame Lyonet and took up the head in the sight of them all and anointed it with an ointment thereas it was smitten off, and in the same wise she did to the other part thereas the head stuck. And then she set it together and it stuck as fast as ever it did. And the knight arose lightly up and the damsel Lyonet put him in her chamber.

All this saw Sir Gringamore and Dame Lyoness, and so did Sir Gareth, and well he espied that it was Dame Lyonet that rode with him through the perilous passages.

'Ah! well, damsel,' said Sir Gareth, 'I weened you would not have done as you have done.'

'My lord, Sir Gareth,' said Lyonet, 'all that I have done I will avow it, and all shall be for your worship and us all.' . . .

Going to bed with Dame Lyoness a second time, Sir Gareth suffers again in the same way. Queen Morgause arrives at court and, having been greeted by her other three sons, Gawain, Gaheris and Aggra-

vaine, rebukes her brother, Arthur, for having misused her youngest
son, Gareth. In a tournament before the Castle Perilous Gareth and
Launcelot avoid fighting each other. Later, Gareth and Gawain, in
ignorance, fight and almost kill each other but are healed by Dame
Lyonet.

[VII.34] . . . Then said King Arthur unto the damsel
Saveage, 'I marvel that your sister, Dame Lyoness, comes not
hither to me, and, in especial, that she comes not to visit her
knight, my nephew, Sir Gareth, that has had so much
travail for her love.'

'My lord,' said the damsel Lyonet, 'you must, of your
good grace, hold her excused, for she knows not that my
lord, Sir Gareth, is here.'

'Go you, then, for her,' said King Arthur, 'that we may be
appointed what is best to do according to the pleasure of
my nephew.'

'Sir,' said the damsel, 'it shall be done.'

And so she rode unto her sister, and as lightly as she might
make her ready she came on the morn with her brother, Sir
Gringamore, and with her forty knights. And so, when she
was come, she had all the cheer that might be done both of
the King and of many other knights and also queens.
[VII.35] And among all these ladies she was named the
fairest and peerless. Then, when Sir Gareth met with her,
there was many a goodly look and goodly words, that all men
of worship had joy to behold them.

Then came King Arthur and many other kings, and Dame
Guenevere and Queen Morgause, his mother. And there the
King asked his nephew, Sir Gareth, whether he would have
this lady as paramour or else to have her to his wife.

'My lord, wit you well that I love her above all ladies
living.'

'Now, fair lady,' said King Arthur, 'what say you?'

'My most noble King,' said Dame Lyoness, 'wit you well
that my lord, Sir Gareth, is to me more lever to have and

welde as my husband than any king or prince that is
christened. And if I may not have him, I promise you I will
never have none. For, my lord, Arthur,' said Dame Lyoness,
'wit you well he is my first love, and he shall be the last. And
if you will suffer him to have his will and free choice, I dare
say he will have me.'

'That is truth,' said Sir Gareth, 'and I have not you and
welde you as my wife, there shall never lady nor gentlewoman rejoice me.'

'What, nephew?' said the King. 'Is the wind in that door?
For, wit you well, I would not for the stint [of] my crown to
be causer to withdraw your hearts. And, wit you well, you
cannot love so well but I shall rather increase it than decrease
it. And also you shall have my love and my lordship in the
uttermost wise that may lie in my power.'

And in the same wise said Sir Gareth's mother. So anon
there was made a provision for the day of marriage, and, by
the King's advice, it was provided that it should be at
Michaelmas following, at Kinke Kenadonne by the seaside,
for there is a plenteous country. And so it was cried in all the
places through the realm.

And then Sir Gareth sent his summons to all those knights
and ladies that he had won in battle before, that they should
be at his day of marriage at Kinke Kenadonne by the seaside.

And then Dame Lyoness and the damsel, Lyonet, with
Sir Gringamore rode to their castle, and a goodly and a rich
ring she gave to Sir Gareth and he gave her another. And
King Arthur gave her a rich bye of gold, and so she departed.

And King Arthur and his fellowship rode toward Kinke
Kenadonne, and Sir Gareth brought his lady on the way and
so came to the King again and rode with him. Lord! the
great cheer that Sir Launcelot made of Sir Gareth and he of
him. For there was no knight that Sir Gareth loved so well as
he did Sir Launcelot, and ever, for the most part, he would
ever be in Sir Launcelot's company.

For ever, after Sir Gareth had espied Sir Gawain's conditions, he withdrew himself from his brother, Sir Gawain's, fellowship, for he was ever vengeable and where he hated he would be avenged with murder. And that hated Sir Gareth.

[VII.36] So it drew fast to Michaelmas that hither came the lady, Dame Lyoness, the Lady of the Castle Perilous, and her sister, the damsel Lyonet, with Sir Gringamore, her brother, with them, for he had the conduct of these ladies. And there they were lodged at the devise of King Arthur.

And upon Michaelmasday the Bishop of Canterbury made the wedding between Sir Gareth and Dame Lyoness with great solemnity. And King Arthur made Sir Gaheris to wed the damsel Saveage, Dame Lyonet. And Sir Aggravaine King Arthur made to wed Dame Lyoness' niece, a fair lady. Her name was Dame Laurell. . . .

Then those whom Gareth has conquered report to Arthur's court and ask to be made the officers of Gareth's household. There is a final joust. 'But when this joust was done, Sir Lamorak and Sir Tristram departed suddenly and would not be known, for the which King Arthur and all the court was sore displeased.'

Book Five

Principally of Sir Tristram

❧

The son of King Melyodas of Lyonesse and Queen Elizabeth, sister of King Mark of Cornwall, Tristram is so named ('the sorrowful-born child') because his mother dies in childbirth.

[VIII.3] . . . And so Tristram learned to be an harper passing all other, that there was none such called in no country. And so in harping and on instruments of music in his youth he applied him for to learn. And after, as he grew in might and strength, he laboured in hunting and in hawking—never gentleman more that ever we heard read of. And, as the book says, he began good measures of blowing of beasts of venery and beasts of chase and all manner of vermins, and all the terms we have yet of hawking and hunting. And therefore the book of [venery, of hawking and hunting is called the book of] Sir Tristram.

Wherefore, as me seems, all gentlemen that bear old arms ought of right to honour Sir Tristram for the goodly terms that gentlemen have and use and shall do unto the Day of Doom, that thereby in a manner all men of worship may discover a gentleman from a yeoman and a yeoman from a villain. For he that gentle is will draw him to gentle tacches and to follow the noble customs of gentlemen. . . .

Having fought successfully for King Mark against Marhalt, who was claiming for his brother-in-law, King Angwysh of Ireland, tribute from Cornwall, Tristram goes to Ireland in disguise, for only there can he be healed of a wound made by Marhalt's poisoned spear. There he falls in love with the King's daughter, La Beall Isode, and, defeating Palomydes, the Saracen, whose love La Beall Isode and her parents reject, such is his prowess that he is mistaken for Launcelot. While he is taking a bath, Isode's mother sees that his sword lacks such a piece as she recovered from Marhalt's mortal wound. She tries unsuccessfully to kill Tristram who killed her brother. He has to leave the country. King Mark and he both fall in love with the wife of Segwarides. Wounded by Mark, without recognizing him, Tristram stains this lady's bed with blood so that her husband knows her adultery. Out of prudence Segwarides does nothing, but 'as long as King Mark lived he loved never after Sir Tristram'. Thinking it will mean Tristram's death, King Mark asks him to return to Ireland with his servant Governayle to bring back La Beall Isode as his Queen. On the way, however, as King Angwysh's champion, he fights Blamour in return for the promise of a boon, but will not kill him, so that Blamour and Bleoberis, who are Launcelot's nephews, swear they will never fight Tristram again, 'and for that gentle battle all the blood of Sir Launcelot loved Sir Tristram for ever.' King Angwysh and Tristram arrive in Ireland.

[VIII.24] . . . Then upon a day King Angwysh asked Sir Tristram why he asked not his boon. Then said Sir Tristram, 'Now it is time, sir, this is all that I will desire, that you will give La Beall Isode, your daughter, not for myself but for mine uncle, King Mark, [that] shall have her to wife, for so have I promised him.'

'Alas!' said the King. 'I had lever than all the land that I have that you would have wedded her yourself.'

'Sir, and I did so, I were shamed for ever in this world and false to my promise. Therefore,' said Sir Tristram, 'I require you, hold your promise that you promised me. For this is my desire, that you will give me La Beall Isode to go with me into Cornwall for to be wedded unto King Mark, mine uncle.'

'As for that,' King Angwysh said, 'you shall have her with you to do with her what it please you: that is for to say, if that you list to wed her yourself, that is me levest, and if you will give her unto King Mark, your uncle, that is in your choice.'

So, to make short conclusion, La Beall Isode was made ready to go with Sir Tristram. And Dame Brangwain went with her for her chief gentlewoman with many others. (The Queen, Isode's mother, gave Dame Brangwain unto her to be her gentlewoman.) And also she and Governayle had a drink from the Queen, and she charged them that, where King Mark should wed, that same day they should give them that drink that King Mark should drink to La Beall Isode. 'And then,' said the Queen, 'either shall love other days of their life.'

So this drink was given unto Dame Brangwain and unto Governayle. So Sir Tristram took the sea, and La Beall Isode. [And when they] were in their cabin it happed so they were thirsty. And then they saw a little flaket of gold stand by them and it seemed by the colour and the taste that it was noble wine. So Sir Tristram took the flaket in his hand and said, 'Madame Isode, here is a draught of good wine that Dame Brangwain, your maiden, and Governayle, my servant, have kept for themselves.'

Then they laughed and made good cheer and either drank to other freely and they thought never drink that ever they drank so sweet neither so good to them. But, by that drink was in their bodies, they loved either other so well that never their love departed for well nor for woe. And thus it happed first, the love betwixt Sir Tristram and La Beall Isode, the which love never departed days of their life. . . .

Tristram hears much of Launcelot's prowess as he escorts La Beall Isode to King Mark and says, 'and I had not this message in hand with this fair lady, truly I would never stint ere I had found Sir Launcelot.' He fights Palomydes again on account of La Beall

Isode. Because Palomydes is unchristened, she has Tristram spare his life and send him to Queen Guenevere, with this message, 'There are, within this land, but four lovers, and that is Sir Launcelot and Dame Guenevere, and Sir Tristram and Queen Isode.'

[VIII.34] . . . By the way they ⟨Sir Lamorak and Sir Dryaunt⟩ met with a knight that was sent from Dame Morgan le Fay unto King Arthur. And this knight had a fair horn harnessed with gold and the horn had such a virtue that there might no lady nor gentlewoman drink of that horn but if she were true to her husband. And if she were false she should spill all the drink, and if she were true to her lord she might drink thereof peaceably. And because of the Queen Guenevere, and in the despite of Sir Launcelot, this horn was sent unto King Arthur. And so by force Sir Lamorak made that knight to tell all the cause why he bore the horn, and so he told him all whole.

'Now shalt thou bear this horn,' said Sir Lamorak, 'to King Mark, or choose to die. For in the despite of Sir Tristram thou shalt bear it him, that horn, and say that I sent it him for to assay his lady: and if she be true he shall prove her.'

So this knight went his way unto King Mark and brought him that rich horn and said that Sir Lamorak sent it him, and so he told him the virtue of that horn. Then the King made his Queen to drink thereof and an hundred ladies with her, and there were but four ladies of all those that drank clean.

'Alas!' said King Mark, 'this is a great despite,' and swore a great oath that she should be burnt, and the other ladies also.

Then the barons gathered them together and said plainly they would not have those ladies burnt for an horn made by sorcery that came 'from the false sorceress and witch most that is now living, for that horn did never good, but caused strife and bate!' And always, in her days, she was an enemy to all true lovers. So there were many knights made their avow that, and ever they met with Morgan le Fay, that they would show her short courtesy. Also Sir Tristram was passing wroth that Sir Lamorak sent that horn unto King Mark, for well he knew that it was done in the despite of him and therefore he thought to quite Sir Lamorak.

Then Sir Tristram used daily and nightly to go to Queen Isode ever when he might, and ever Sir Andret, his cousin, watched him night by night for to take him with La Beall Isode. And so upon a night Sir Andret espied his hour and the time when Sir Tristram went to his lady. Then Sir Andret got unto him twelve knights and at midnight he set upon Sir Tristram secretly and suddenly. And there Sir Tristram was taken naked in bed with La Beall Isode. And so was he bound hand and foot and kept till day.

And then, by the assent of King Mark and of Sir Andret and of some of the barons, Sir Tristram was led unto a chapel that stood upon the sea-rocks, there for to take his judgement. And so he was led bound with forty knights, and when Sir Tristram saw that there was none other boot but needs he must die, then said he, 'Fair lords! Remember what I have done for the country of Cornwall and what jeopardy I have been in for the weal of you all. For when I fought with Sir Marhalt, the good knight, I was promised to be better rewarded when you all refused to take the battle. Therefore, as you are good, gentle knights, see me not thus shamefully to die, for it is shame to all knighthood thus to see me die. For I dare say,' said Sir Tristram, 'that I met never with no knight but I was as good as he or better.'

'Fie upon thee!' said Sir Andret, 'false traitor thou art with thine advantage! For all thy boast thou shalt die this day!'

'Ah! Andret, Andret,' said Sir Tristram, 'thou shouldest be my kinsman and now art to me full unfriendly. But, and there were no more but thou and I, thou wouldest not put me to death.'

'No?' said Sir Andret, and therewith he drew his sword and would have slain him.

So when Sir Tristram saw him make that countenance he looked upon both his hands that were fast bound unto two knights and suddenly he pulled them both unto him and unwraiste his hands and leapt unto his cousin, Sir Andret, and wroth his sword out of his hands. And then he smote Sir Andret that he fell down to the earth. And so he fought that he killed ten knights. So then Sir Tristram got the chapel and kept it mightily. Then the cry was great and people drew fast unto Sir Andret, more than an hundred. So when Sir Tristram saw the people draw unto him he remembered he was naked, and sparde fast the chapel door and broke the bars of a window. And so he leapt out and fell upon the crags in the sea.

And so at that time Sir Andret nor none of his fellows might not get him. [VIII.35] But, when they were departed, Governayle and Sir Lambegus and Sir Sentrayle de Lushon, that were Sir Tristram's men, sought sore after their master when they heard he was escaped. And so on the rocks they found him and with towels pulled him up. And then Sir Tristram asked where was La Beall Isode.

'Sir,' said Governayle, 'she is put in a lazar-cote.'

'Alas!' said Sir Tristram, 'that is a full ungoodly place for such a fair lady. And, if I may, she shall not be long there!'

And so he took his men and went thereas was La Beall Isode and fetched her away and brought her into a fair forest to a fair manor. And so he abode there with her. So now this good knight bade his men depart, for at that time he might not help them. And so they departed, all save Governayle.

And so upon a day Sir Tristram yode into the forest for to disport him, and there he fell asleep. And so happened there came to Sir Tristram a man that he had slain his brother. And so when this man had found him he shot him through the shoulder and anon Sir Tristram started up and killed that man.

And in the meantime it was told unto King Mark how Sir Tristram and La Beall Isode were in that same manor, and thither he came with many knights to slay Sir Tristram. And when he came there he found him gone and anon he took La Beall Isode home with him and kept her strait that by no means she might never write nor send.

And when Sir Tristram came toward the manor he found the track of many horses and looked about in the place and knew that his lady was gone. And then Sir Tristram took great sorrow and endured with great sorrow and pain long time, for the arrow that he was hurt withal was envenomed.

So by the mean of ⟨Dame Brangwain⟩ she [told] a lady that was cousin unto ⟨La Beall Isode⟩, and she came unto Sir Tristram and told him that he might not be whole by no means, 'for thy lady, Isode, may not help thee. Therefore she bids you haste you into Bretayne unto King Howell and there shall you find his daughter that is called Isode le Blaunche Mains, and there shall you find that she shall help you.'

Then Sir Tristram and Governayle got them shipping and so sailed into Bretayne. And when King Howell knew that it was Sir Tristram he was full glad of him.

'Sir,' said Sir Tristram, 'I am come unto this country to have help of your daughter.' And so she healed him.

[VIII.36] There was an earl that hight Grype, and this earl made great war upon him and put the King to the worse and besieged him. And on a time Sir Keyhydyns that was son to the King Howell, as he issued out he was sore wounded nigh to the death. Then Governayle went to the King and said, 'Sir, I counsel you to desire my lord, Sir Tristram, as in your need to help you.'

'I will do by your counsel,' said the King. And so he yode unto Sir Tristram and prayed him as in his wars to help him, 'for my son, Sir Keyhydyns, may not go unto the field.'

'Sir,' said Sir Tristram, 'I will go to the field and do what I may.'

So Sir Tristram issued out of the town with such fellowship as he might make and did such deeds that all Bretayne spoke of him. And then, at the last, by great force he slew the earl Grype ⟨by⟩ his own hands, and more than an hundred knights he slew that day. And then Sir Tristram was received into the city worshipfully with procession. Then King Howell embraced him in his arms and said, 'Sir Tristram, all my kingdom I will resign to you!'

'God defend!' said Sir Tristram, 'for I am beholden thereto for your daughter's sake to do for you more than that.'

So by the great means of the King and his son there grew great love betwixt Isode and Sir Tristram, for that lady was both good and fair and a woman of noble blood and fame, and, for because that Sir Tristram had such cheer and riches and all other plesaunce, that he had almost forsaken La Beall Isode. And so upon a time Sir Tristram agreed to wed this Isode le Blaunche Mains. And so, at the last, they were wedded and solemnly held their marriage. And so when they were in bed, both, Sir Tristram remembered him of his old lady, La Beall Isode, and then he took such a thought suddenly that he was all dismayed, and other cheer made he none [but] with clipping and kissing. As for [other] fleshly lusts, Sir Tristram had never ado with her—such mention makes the French book. Also it makes mention that the lady weened there had been no pleasure but kissing and clipping.

And, in the meantime, there was a knight in Bretayne—his name was Sir Suppynabyles. And he came over the sea into England and so he came into the court of King Arthur. And there he met with Sir Launcelot du Lake and told him of the marriage of Sir Tristram. Then said Sir Launcelot, 'Fie upon

him! untrue knight to his lady! That so noble a knight as Sir
Tristram is should be found to his first lady and love untrue,
that is the Queen of Cornwall! But say you to him thus,' said
Sir Launcelot, 'that of all knights in the world I have loved
him, and all was for his noble deeds. And let him wit that the
love between him and me is done for ever, and that I give
him warning, from this day forth I will be his mortal enemy!'

[VIII.37] So departed Sir Suppynabyles unto Bretayne
again and there he found Sir Tristram and told him that he
had been in King Arthur's court. Then Sir Tristram said,
'Heard you anything of me?'

'So God me help,' said Sir Suppynabyles, 'there I heard
Sir Launcelot speak of you great shame, and that you are a
false knight to your lady. And he bade me to do you to wit
that he will be your mortal foe in every place where he may
meet you.'

'That me repents,' said Sir Tristram, 'for of all knights I
loved most to be in his fellowship.'

Then Sir Tristram was ashamed and made great moan
that ever any knights should defame him for the sake of his
lady. And so, in this meanwhile, La Beall Isode made a letter
unto Queen Guenevere complaining her of the untruth of
Sir Tristram, how he had wedded the King's daughter of
Bretayne. So Queen Guenevere sent her another letter and
bade her be of good comfort, for she should have joy after
sorrow. For Sir Tristram was so noble a knight called that by
crafts of sorcery ladies would make such noble [men] to wed
them. 'But the end,' Queen Guenevere said, 'should be thus,
that he shall hate her and love you better than ever he did.' . . .

After a fierce fight, Tristram and Lamorak, as knights of equal
prowess, yield to each other and swear not to compete again.

[IX.12] . . . And this meanwhile came Sir Palomydes, the
good knight, following the Questing Beast that had in shape
like a serpent's head and a body like a leopard, buttocked

like a lion and footed like an hart. And in his body there was
such a noise as it had been twenty couple of hounds questing,
and such noise that beast made wheresoever he went. And
this beast evermore Sir Palomydes followed, for it was called
his quest.

And right so, as he followed this beast, it came by Sir
Tristram and soon after came Sir Palomydes. And, to brief
this matter, he smote down Sir Tristram and Sir Lamorak
both with one spear and so he departed after the Beste
Glatyssaunte (that was called the Questing Beast). Wherefore these two knights were passing wroth that Sir Palomydes
would not fight with them on foot.

Here men may understand, that are men of worship, that
man was never formed that all times might attain, but sometime he was put to the worse by malfortune and at sometime
the weaker knight put the bigger knight to a rebuke. . . .

[IX.13] . . . And, as they stood thus fighting, by fortune
came Sir Launcelot and Sir Bleoberis, and then Sir Launcelot
rode betwixt them and asked them for what cause they fought
so together, 'and you are both of the court of King Arthur!'

[IX.14] 'Sir,' said Sir Mellyagaunce, 'I shall tell you for
what cause we do this battle. I praised my lady, Queen
Guenevere, and said she was the fairest lady of the world,
and Sir Lamorak said nay thereto, for he said Queen
Morgause of Orkney was fairer than she and more of
beauty.'

'Ah!' said Sir ⟨Launcelot, 'Sir⟩ Lamorak, why sayest
thou so? It is not thy part to dispraise thy princess that thou
art under obeisance, and we all.' And therewithal Sir Launcelot alighted on foot. 'And, therefore, make thee ready, for I
will prove upon thee that Queen Guenevere is the fairest lady
and most of bounty in the world.'

'Sir,' said Sir Lamorak, 'I am loath to have ado with you
in this quarrel, for every man thinks his own lady fairest, and,
though I praise the lady that I love most, you should not be

wroth. For, though my lady, Queen Guenevere, is fairest in your eye, wit you well Queen Morgause of Orkney is fairest in mine eye, and so every knight thinks his own lady fairest. And, wit you well, sir, you are the man in the world, except Sir Tristram, that I am most loathest to have ado withal. But, and you will needs have ado with me, I shall endure you as long as I may.'

Then spoke Sir Bleoberis and said, 'My lord, Sir Launcelot, I wist you never so misadvised as you be at this time, for Sir Lamorak says to you but reason and knightly. For I warn you, I have a lady and me thinks that she is the fairest lady of the world. Were this a great reason that you should be wroth with me for such language? And well you wot that Sir Lamorak is a noble knight as I know any living, and he has owed you and all us ever good will. Therefore I pray you, be friends!'

Then Sir Launcelot said, 'Sir, I pray you, forgive me mine offence and evil will, and, if I was misadvised, I will make amends.'

'Sir,' said Sir Lamorak, 'the amends is soon made betwixt you and me.'

And so Sir Launcelot and Sir Bleoberis departed, and Sir Lamorak and Sir Mellyagaunce took their horses and either departed from other. . . .

Tristram secretly returns to La Beall Isode in Cornwall with Keyhydyns, 'and to tell the joys that were betwixt La Beall Isode and Sir Tristram there is no maker can make it, neither no heart can think it, neither no pen can write it, neither no mouth can speak it'. Keyhydyns immediately falls in love with La Beall Isode who unwisely replies on one occasion to his letters. Discovering this, Tristram attacks Keyhydyns for his treachery. Escaping out of a bay-window beneath which King Mark is playing chess, Keyhydyns pretends that he was asleep in the window and fell out. Thus, though he 'dread him lest he were discovered to the King that he was there', Tristram is able to escape into the forest where he lives, a half-naked madman and fool, with herdsmen and shepherds. La Beall Isode banishes Keyhydyns and he and Palomydes 'complained to other of their hot love that they loved La Beall Isode'. They charge King Mark with responsibility for Tristram's state but he blames the letter Tristram discovered. Thinking Tristram is dead, La Beall Isode tries to kill herself by running on a sword, but King Mark saves her. Unrecognized as Tristram, a madman is taken into Tintagel Castle but La Beall Isode's little dog discovers him as he lies in the garden in the sun. 'And thereupon La Beall Isode fell down in a swoon.' Recovered from his madness, Tristram is banished by King Mark. Palomydes laments that 'I may never win worship where Sir Tristram is . . . and if he be away for the most part I have the gre unless that Sir Launcelot be there or else Sir Lamorak.' At a tournament before the Castle of Maidens 'the cry was cried through the field, "Sir Launcelot has won the field this day!" Sir Launcelot made another cry contrary, "Sir Tristram has won the field."' Later, Darras imprisons Tristram, Palomydes and Dinadan because Tristram slew his three sons.

[IX.37] . . . So Sir Tristram endured there great pain, for sickness had undertaken him, and that is the greatest pain a prisoner may have. For all the while a prisoner may have his health of body he may endure under the mercy of God and in hope of good deliverance, but when sickness touches a prisoner's body then may a prisoner say all wealth is him bereft, and then has he cause to wail and weep. Right so did Sir Tristram when sickness had undertaken him, for then he took such sorrow that he had almost slain himself. . . .

His sickness makes Darras relent and the prisoners are released. After a battle in ignorance, Launcelot and Tristram yield to each other as knights of equal prowess and, with Gawain and Gaheris, who have been seeking Tristram, go to Camelot where Tristram is made a knight of the Round Table in Marhalt's place. Concerned at Tristram's increased fame, King Mark sets out for England intending to kill him treacherously for 'he had great suspicion of Sir Tristram because of his Queen'. Learning that a knight who

challenges him is Launcelot, he yields without fighting and is taken
to King Arthur whom he promises, ' "right as your lordship will
require me, unto my power I will make a large amends"—for he
was a fair speaker and false thereunder'. He promises to cherish
Tristram (though Launcelot utterly distrusts him) and the two ride
back to Cornwall 'and all was for the intent to see La Beall Isode,
for without the sight of her Sir Tristram might not endure'.

Gawain and his brothers send for their mother, Morgause, for
they wish to kill Lamorak, and know that, since he is her lover, he
will come to her bed in a castle beside Camelot. Finding him there,
however, Gaheris beheads Morgause saying to Lamorak, ' "thy
father slew our father, and thou to lie by our mother is too much
shame for us to suffer. And as for thy father, King Pellinore, my
brother, Sir Gawain, and I slew him." "You did the more wrong,"
said Sir Lamorak, "for my father slew not your father—it was Balin
le Saveage. . . ." ' Launcelot deplores the departure of Lamorak,
foreseeing that Gawain and his brothers will kill him, and that
Tristram, out of love for him, will eschew Arthur's court, also.

Galahad, the Haute Prince (not Galahad of the Grail), lord of
Surluse, cries a joust to which Guenevere goes with Launcelot.

[X.47] . . . 'Well,' said the Haute Prince, 'this day must
noble knights joust and at after-dinner we shall see how you
can do.'

Then they blew to jousts. And in came Sir Dinadan and
met with Sir Geryne, a good knight, and he threw him down
over his horse's crupper. And Sir Dinadan overthrew four
knights more, and there he did great deeds of arms, for he
was a good knight. But he was a great scoffer and a japer, and
the merriest knight among fellowship that was that time
living. And he loved every good knight and every good
knight loved him.

So when the Haute Prince saw Sir Dinadan do so well he
sent unto Sir Launcelot and bade him strike him adown, 'and
so bring him before me and Queen Guenevere'. Then Sir
Launcelot did as he was required. Then came Sir Launcelot
and smote down many knights and raced off helms and drove

all the knights before him, and Sir Launcelot smote adown Sir Dinadan and made his men to unarm him, and so brought him to the Queen. And then the Haute Prince laughed at Sir Dinadan that they might not stand.

'Well,' said Sir Dinadan, 'yet have I no shame, for the old shrew, Sir Launcelot, smote me down.'

So they went to dinner, all the court, and had great disport at Sir Dinadan. . . .

First prize at the tournament goes to Launcelot, second to Lamorak, third to Palomydes and the fourth to King Bagdemagus.

Because of King Mark's treachery Tristram and Isode flee to England where Launcelot houses them in his own castle of Joyous Garde and King Arthur is very glad. Palomydes reports the death of Lamorak at the hands of Gawain and his brothers as he left a tournament.

[X.55] . . . Now turn we unto Sir Tristram that as he rode ahunting he met with Sir Dinadan that was come into the country to seek Sir Tristram. And anon Sir Dinadan told Sir Tristram his name but Sir Tristram would not tell his name. Wherefore Sir Dinadan was wroth, 'for such a foolish knight as you are,' said Sir Dinadan, 'I saw but late this day lying by a well, and he fared as he slept. And there he lay like a fool grinning and would not speak and his shield lay by him and his horse also stood by him. And well I wot he was a lover!'

'Ah! fair sir,' said Sir Tristram, 'are not you a lover?'

'Mary! fie on that craft!' said Sir Dinadan.

'Sir, that is evil said,' [said] Sir Tristram, 'for a knight may never be of prowess but if he be a lover.'

'You say well,' said Sir Dinadan. 'Now I pray you tell me your name, sith you be such a lover, or else I shall do battle with you.'

'As for that,' said Sir Tristram, 'it is no reason to fight with me, but if I tell you my name. And as for my name, you shall not wit as at this time for me.'

'Fie! for shame! Are you a knight and dare not tell your name to me? Therefore, sir, I will fight with you.'

'As for that,' said Sir Tristram, 'I will be advised, for I will not do battle, but if me list. And if I do battle with you,' said Sir Tristram, 'you are not able to withstand me.'

'Fie on thee, coward!' said Sir Dinadan.

And thus, as they [hoved] still, they saw a knight come riding against them.

'Lo!' said Sir Tristram, 'see where comes a knight riding which will joust with you.'

Anon as Sir Dinadan beheld him, he said, 'By my faith! That same is the doted knight that I saw lie by the well, neither sleeping nor waking.'

'Well!' said Sir Tristram. 'I know that knight well with the covered shield of azure, for he is the King's son of Northumberland. His name is Sir Epynogrys and he is as great a lover as I know and he loves the King's daughter of Wales, a full fair lady. And now I suppose,' said Sir Tristram, 'and you require him, he will joust with you, and then shall you prove whether a lover be better knight, or you that will not love no lady.'

'Well,' said Sir Dinadan, 'now shalt thou see what I shall do.'

And therewithal Sir Dinadan spoke on hight and said, 'Sir knight, make thee ready to joust with me, for joust you must needs, for it is the custom of knights errant for to make a knight to joust, will he or nill he.'

'Sir,' said Sir Epynogrys, 'is that the rule and custom of you?'

'As for that,' said Sir Dinadan, 'make ready, for here is for me!'

And therewithal they spurred their horses and met together so hard that Sir Epynogrys smote down Sir Dinadan. And anon Sir Tristram rode to Sir Dinadan and said, 'How now? Me seems the lover has well sped!'

'Fie on thee, coward!' said Sir Dinadan. 'And if thou be a good knight, revenge me!'

'Nay,' said Sir Tristram, 'I will not joust as at this time. But take your horse, and let us go hence.'

'God defend me,' said Sir Dinadan, 'from thy fellowship, for I never sped well since I met with thee.'

And so they departed. . . .

[X.58] '. . . And of the death of Sir Lamorak,' said Sir Tristram, 'it was over-great pity, for I dare say he was the cleanest-mighted man and the best-winded of his age that was alive. For I knew him that he was one of the best knights that ever I met withal, but if it were Sir Launcelot.'

'Alas!' said Sir Dinadan and Sir Tristram, 'that full woe is us for his death! And if they were not the cousins of my lord, King Arthur, that slew him, they should die for it, all that were consenting to his death.'

'And for such things,' said Sir Tristram, 'I fear to draw unto the court of King Arthur. Sir, I will that you wot it,' said Sir Tristram unto Sir Gareth.

'As for that, I blame you not,' said Sir Gareth, 'for well I understand the vengeance of my brethren, Sir Gawain, Sir Aggravaine, Sir Gaheris and Sir Mordred. But as for me,' said Sir Gareth, 'I meddle not of their matters, and therefore there is none that loves me of them. And for cause that I understand they are murderers of good knights, I left their company, and would God I had been beside Sir Gawain when that most noble knight, Sir Lamorak, was slain!'

'Now, as Jesu be my help,' said Sir Tristram, 'it is passingly well said of you, for I had lever,' said Sir Tristram, 'than all the gold betwixt this and Rome I had been there.'

'Iwis,' said Sir Palomydes, 'so would I, and yet had I never the gre at no jousts nor tournament and that noble knight Sir Lamorak had been there, but either on horseback or else on foot he put me ever to the worse. And that day that Sir Lamorak was slain he did the most deeds of arms that

ever I saw knight do in my life, and when he was given the
gre by my lord, King Arthur, Sir Gawain and his three
brethren, Sir Aggravaine, Sir Gaheris and Sir Mordred, set
upon Sir Lamorak in a privy place and there they slew his
horse. And so they fought with him on foot more than three
hours, both before him and behind him, and so Sir Mordred
gave him his death's wound behind him at his back and all
to-hew him, for one of his squires told me that saw it.'

'Now, fie upon treason!' said Sir Tristram, 'for it slays
mine heart to hear this tale.'

'And so it does mine,' said Sir Gareth, 'brethren as they
are mine.'

'Now speak we of other deeds,' said Sir Palomydes, 'and
let him be, for his life you may not get again.'

'That is the more pity!' said Sir Dinadan. 'For Sir Gawain
and his brethren—except you, Sir Gareth—hate all good
knights of the Round Table for the most part. For well I
wot, and they might, privily they hate my lord, Sir Launcelot,
and all his kin, and great privy despite they have at him. And
certainly that is my lord, Sir Launcelot, well aware of, and
that causes him the more to have the good knights of his kin
about him.'

[X.59] 'Now, sir,' said Sir Palomydes, 'let us leave off this
matter and let us see how we shall do at this tournament.
And, sir, by mine advice, let us four hold together against all
that will come.'

'Not by my counsel,' said Sir Tristram, 'for I see by their
pavilions there will be four hundred knights. And doubt you
not,' said Sir Tristram, 'but there will be many good knights,
and be a man never so valiant nor so big but he may be over-
matched. And so have I seen knights do many, and, when
they weened best to have won worship, they lost it, for manhood is not worth but if it be meddled with wisdom. And as
for me,' said Sir Tristram, 'it may happen I shall keep mine
own head as well as another.'

So thus they rode until they came to Humber bank where they heard a cry and a doleful noise. . . .

After a tournament at Lonazep Palomydes is rebuked by La Beall Isode for his treachery caused by envy of Tristram. He tells Sir Epynogrys, 'I well deserved that rebuke, for I did not knightly, and therefore I have lost the love of her and of Sir Tristram for ever.'

[X.86] . . . ever Sir Palomydes faded and mourned that all men had marvel wherefore he faded so away. So upon a day in the dawning Sir Palomydes went into the forest by himself alone and there he found a well and anon he looked into the well and in the water he saw his own visage, how he was discoloured and defaded, a nothing like as he was.

'Lord Jesu! what may this mean?' said Sir Palomydes. And thus he said to himself, 'Ah! Palomydes, Palomydes, why art thou thus defaded and ever was wont to be called one of the fairest knights of [the] world? Forsooth, I will no more live this life, for I love that I may never get nor recover.'

And therewithal he laid him down by the well, and so began to make a rhyme of La Beall Isode and of Sir Tristram. And so, in the meanwhile, Sir Tristram was ridden into the same forest to chase an hart of grece. But Sir Tristram would not ride ahunting nevermore unarmed because of Sir Brewnes Saunze Pité. And so Sir Tristram rode into the forest up and down, and, as he rode, he heard one sing marvellously loud, and that was Sir Palomydes which lay by the well.

And then Sir Tristram rode softly thither for he deemed that there was some knight errant which was at the well. And when Sir Tristram came nigh he descended down from his horse and tied his horse fast to a tree. And so he came near on foot and soon after he was aware where lay Sir Palomydes by the well and sang loud and merrily. And ever the complaints were of La Beall Isode which was marvellously well said and piteously and full dolefully. And all the whole song Sir Tristram heard word by word, and when he had heard all Sir Palomydes' complaint he was wroth out of measure and thought for to slay him thereas he lay. Then Sir Tristram remembered himself that Sir Palomydes was unarmed and of so noble a name that Sir Palomydes had, and also the noble name that himself had. Then he made a restraint of his anger and so he went unto Sir Palomydes a soft pace and said,

'Sir Palomydes, I have heard your complaint and of your treason that you have owed me long and, wit you well, therefore you shall die! And, if it were not for shame of knighthood, thou shouldest not escape my hands, for now I know well thou hast awaited me with treason. And, therefore,' said Sir Tristram, 'tell me how thou wilt acquit thee.'

'Sir, I shall acquit me thus: as for Queen La Beall Isode, thou shalt wit that I love her above all other ladies in this world, and well I wot it shall befall by me, as for her love, as befell on the noble knight Sir Keyhydyns, that died for the love of La Beall Isode. And now, Sir Tristram, I will that you wot that I have loved La Beall Isode many a long day and she has been the causer of my worship. And else I had been the most simplest knight in the world, for by her, and because of her, I have won the worship that I have. For when I remembered me of Queen Isode I won the worship wheresoever I came, for the most part. And yet I had never reward nor bounty of her, days of my life, and yet I have been her knight long guerdonless. And, therefore, Sir Tristram, as for any death I dread not, for I had as lief die as live. And if I were armed as you are I should lightly do battle with thee.'

'Sir, well have you uttered your treason,' said Sir Tristram.

'Sir, I have done to you no treason,' said Sir Palomydes, 'for love is free for all men and, though I have loved your lady, she is my lady as well as yours. Howbeit that I have wrong, if any wrong be, for you rejoice her and have your desire of her, and so had I never nor never [am] like to have, and yet shall I love her to the uttermost, days of my life, as well as you.'

[X.87] Then said Sir Tristram, 'I will fight with you to the utterest!'

'I grant,' said Sir Palomydes, 'for in a better quarrel keep I never to fight. For, and I die at your hands, at a better knight's hands might I never be slain. And sithen I understand that I shall never rejoice La Beall Isode, I have as good will to die as to live.'

'Then set you a day,' said Sir Tristram, 'that we shall do battle.'

'Sir, this day fifteen days,' said Sir Palomydes, 'I will meet with you hereby, in the meadow under Joyous Garde.'

'Now, fie for shame!' said Sir Tristram. 'Will you set so long a day? Let us fight tomorn.'

'Not so,' said Sir Palomydes, 'for I am meagre and have been long sick for the love of La Beall Isode. And, therefore, I will repose me till I have my strength again.'

So then Sir Tristram and Sir Palomydes promised faithfully to meet at the well that day fifteen days.

'But now I am remembered,' said Sir Tristram to Sir Palomydes, 'that you broke me once a promise when that I rescued you from Sir Brewnes Saunze Pité and nine knights. And then you promised to meet me at the perowne and the grave beside Camelot, whereas that time you failed of your promise.'

'Wit you well,' said Sir Palomydes unto Sir Tristram, 'I was at that day in prison that I might not hold my promise. But wit you well,' said Sir Palomydes, 'I shall you promise now and keep it.'

'So God me help,' said Sir Tristram, 'and you had held your promise, this work had not been here now at this time.'

Right so departed Sir Tristram and Sir Palomydes. And

so Sir Palomydes took his horse and his harness and so he rode unto King Arthur's court. And there he got him four knights and four sergeants-of-arms and so he returned again unto Joyous Garde.

And so, in the meanwhile, Sir Tristram chased and hunted at all manner of venery. And about three days before the battle that should be, as Sir Tristram chased an hart there was an archer shot at the hart and by misfortune he smote Sir Tristram in the thick of the thigh. And the same arrow slew Sir Tristram's horse under him. When Sir Tristram was so hurt he was passing heavy, and, wit you well, he bled passing sore. And then he took another horse and rode unto Joyous Garde with great heaviness, more for the promise that he had made unto Sir Palomydes to do battle with him within three days after [than for any hurt]. Wherefore there was neither man nor woman that could cheer him, for ever he deemed that Sir Palomydes had smitten him so because he should not be able to do battle with him at the day appointed. [X.88] But in no wise there was no knight about Sir Tristram that would believe that Sir Palomydes would hurt him, neither by his own hands nor by none other consenting.

And so, when the fifteenth day was come, Sir Palomydes came to the well with four knights with him of King Arthur's court and three sergeants-of-arms. And for this intent Sir Palomydes brought those knights with him and the sergeants-of-arms, for they should bear record of the battle betwixt Sir Tristram and him. And one sergeant brought in his helm and the other his spear and the third his sword. So Sir Palomydes came into the field and there he abode nigh two hours, and then he sent a squire unto Sir Tristram and desired him to come into the field to hold his promise.

When the squire was come unto Joyous Garde, anon as Sir Tristram heard of his coming, he commanded that the squire should come to his presence thereas he lay in his bed.

'My lord, Sir Tristram,' said Sir Palomydes' squire, 'wit you well, my lord, Sir Palomydes, abides you in the field and he would wit whether you would do battle or not.'

'Ah! my fair brother,' said Sir Tristram, 'wit you well that I am right heavy for these tidings. But tell your lord, Sir Palomydes, and I were well at ease, I would not lie here, neither he should have had no need to send for me, and I might either ride or go. And for thou shalt see that I am no liar'—Sir Tristram showed him his thigh and the deepness of the wound was six inches deep. 'And now thou hast seen my hurt, tell thy lord that this is no feigned matter and tell him that I had lever than all the gold that King Arthur has that I were whole. And let him wit that, as for me, as soon as I may ride I shall seek him endlong and overthwart this land. And that I promise you, as I am a true knight. And if ever I may meet him, tell your lord, Sir Palomydes, he shall have of me his fill of battle.'

And so the squire departed. And when Sir Palomydes knew that Sir Tristram was hurt then he said thus, 'Truly, I am glad of his hurt and for this cause, for now I am sure I shall have no shame. For I wot well, and we had meddled, I should have had hard handling of him, and by likelihood I must needs have had the worse. For he is the hardiest knight in battle that now is living except Sir Launcelot.'

And then departed Sir Palomydes whereas fortune led him. And within a month Sir Tristram was whole of his hurt, and then he took his horse and rode from country to country, and all strange adventures he achieved wheresoever he rode. And always he inquired for Sir Palomydes, but of all that quarter of summer Sir Tristram could never meet with Sir Palomydes.

But thus, as Sir Tristram sought and inquired after Sir Palomydes, Sir Tristram achieved many great battles, wherethrough all the noise and brewte fell to Sir Tristram and the name ceased of Sir Launcelot. And therefore Sir Launcelot's brethren and his kinsmen would have slain Sir Tristram because of his fame. But when Sir Launcelot wist how his kinsmen were set he said to them openly,

'Wit you well that, and any of you all be so hardy to wait my lord, Sir Tristram, with any hurt, shame or villainy, as I am true knight, I shall slay the best of you all ⟨with⟩ mine own hands. Alas! fie for shame! should you for his noble deeds await to slay him. Jesu defend,' said Sir Launcelot, 'that ever any noble knight, as Sir Tristram is, should be destroyed with treason!'

So of this noise and fame sprang into Cornwall and unto them of Lyonesse, whereof they were passing glad and made great joy. And then they of Lyonesse sent letters unto Sir Tristram of recommendation, and many great gifts to maintain Sir Tristram's estate. And ever, between, Sir Tristram resorted unto Joyous Garde whereas La Beall Isode was, that loved him ever.

Now leave we Sir Tristram de Lyonesse and speak we of Sir Launcelot du Lake and of Sir Galahad, Sir Launcelot's son, how he was begotten and in what manner. . . .

[XI.1] . . . And therewithal came King Pelles, the good and noble King, and salewed Sir Launcelot and he him again.

'Now, fair knight,' said the King, 'what is your name? I require you, of your knighthood, tell you me.'

[XI.2] 'Sir,' said Sir Launcelot, 'wit you well, my name is Sir Launcelot du Lake.'

'And my name is King Pelles, King of the foreign country and cousin nigh unto Joseph of Arimathea.'

And then either of them made much of other and so they went into the castle to take their repast. And anon there came in a dove at a window and in her mouth there seemed a little [censer] of gold and therewithal there was such a savour as all the spicery of the world had been there. And forthwithal there was upon the table all manner of meats and drinks that they could think upon. So there came in a damsel passing fair and young, and she bore a vessel of gold betwixt her hands. And thereto the King kneeled devoutly and said his prayers, and so did all that were there.

'Ah! Jesu,' said Sir Launcelot, 'what may this mean?'

'Sir,' said the King, 'this is the richest thing that any man has, living, and when this thing goes abroad the Round Table shall be broken for a season. And, wit you well,' said the King, 'this is the Holy Sankgreall that you have here seen.'

So the King and Sir Launcelot led their life the most part of that day together. And fain would King Pelles have found the means that Sir Launcelot should have lain by his daughter, fair Elayne, and for this intent: the King knew well that Sir Launcelot should get a pusil upon his daughter which should be called Sir Galahad, the good knight, by whom all the foreign country should be brought out of danger, and by him the Holy Grail should be achieved.

Then came forth a lady that hight Dame Brusen and she said unto the King, 'Sir, wit you well, Sir Launcelot loves no lady in the world but all only Queen Guenevere. And, therefore, work you by my counsel and I shall make him to lie with your daughter, and he shall not wit but that he lies by Queen Guenevere.'

'Ah! fair lady,' said the King, 'hope you that you may bring this matter about?'

'Sir,' said she, 'upon pain of my life, let me deal!' For this Dame Brusen was one of the greatest enchanters that was that time in the world. And so anon by Dame Brusen's wit she made one to come to Sir Launcelot that he knew well, and this man brought a ring from Queen Guenevere like as it had come from her. And when Sir Launcelot saw that token, wit you well, he was never so fain.

'Where is my lady?' said Sir Launcelot.

E

'In the Castle of Case,' said the messenger, 'but five miles hence.'

Then thought Sir Launcelot to be there the same night. And then this Dame Brusen, by the commandment of King Pelles, she let send Elayne to this castle with five and twenty knights unto the Castle of Case. Then Sir Launcelot, against night, rode unto the castle and there anon he was received worshipfully with such people, to his seeming, as were about Queen Guenevere secret. So, when Sir Launcelot was alighted, he asked where the Queen was. So Dame Brusen said she was in her bed.

And then people were avoided and Sir Launcelot was led into her chamber. And then Dame Brusen brought Sir Launcelot a cup of wine and anon as he had drunk that wine he was so assotted and mad that he might make no delay but without any let he went to bed. And so he weened that maiden Elayne had been Queen Guenevere. And wit you well that Sir Launcelot was glad, and so was that lady, Elayne, that she had got Sir Launcelot in her arms, for well she knew that that same night should be begotten Sir Galahad upon her, that should prove the best knight of the world.

And so they lay together until undern of the morn. And all the windows and holes of that chamber were stopped that no manner of day might be seen. And anon Sir Launcelot remembered him and arose up and went to the window [XI.3] and, anon as he had unshut the window, the enchantment was passed. Then he knew himself that he had done amiss. 'Alas!' he said, 'that I have [lived] so long, for now am I shamed.'

And anon he got his sword in his hand and said, 'Thou traitress! What art thou that I have lain by all this night? Thou shalt die right here of mine hands!'

Then this fair lady, Elayne, skipped out of her bed all naked and said, 'Fair, courteous knight, Sir Launcelot,' kneeling before him, 'you are come of King's blood and therefore I require you have mercy upon me! And, as thou art renowned the most noble knight of the world, slay me not, for I have in my womb begotten of thee that shall be the most noblest knight of the world.'

'Ah! false traitress! Why hast thou betrayed me? Tell me anon,' said Sir Launcelot, 'what thou art.'

'Sir,' she said, 'I am Elayne, the daughter of King Pelles.'

'Well,' said Sir Launcelot, 'I will forgive you.' And therewith he took her up in his arms and kissed her, for she was a fair lady and thereto lusty and young and wise as any was that time living. 'So God me help,' said Sir Launcelot, 'I may not wite you, but her that made this enchantment upon me and between you and me. And I may find her, that same lady, Dame Brusen, shall lose her head for her witchcrafts, for there was never knight deceived as I am this night.'

Then she said, 'My lord, Sir Launcelot, I beseech you, see me as soon as you may, for I have obeyed me unto the prophecy that my father told me. And by his commandment, to fulfil this prophecy, I have given thee the greatest riches and the fairest flower that ever I had, and that is my maidenhood that I shall never have again. And, therefore, gentle knight, owe me your good will.'

And so Sir Launcelot arrayed him and armed him and took his leave mildly of that young lady, Elayne. And so he departed and rode to the Castle of Corbyn where her father was.

And as fast as her time came she was delivered of a fair child, and they christened him, Galahad. And, wit you well, that child was well kept and well nourished, and he was so named, Galahad, because Sir Launcelot was so named at the fountain stone. (And after that the Lady of the Lake confirmed him Sir Launcelot du Lake.) . . .

[XI.7] . . . And when she came to Camelot King Arthur and Queen Guenevere said with all the knights that Dame

Elayne was the best besene lady that ever was seen in that court. And, anon as King Arthur wist that she was come, he met her and salewed her and so did the most part of all the knights of the Round Table, both Sir Tristram, Sir Bleoberis and Sir Gawain, and many more that I will not rehearse.

But when Sir Launcelot saw her he was so ashamed that, because he drew his sword to her on the morn after that he had lain by her, that he would not salewe her neither speak with her. And yet Sir Launcelot thought that she was the fairest woman that ever he saw in his life days. But when Dame Elayne saw Sir Launcelot would not speak unto her she was so heavy she weened her heart would have to-brast, for, wit you well, out of measure she loved him. And then Dame Elayne said unto her woman, Dame Brusen, 'The unkindness of Sir Launcelot slays mine heart near.'

'Ah! peace, madam,' said Dame Brusen, 'I shall undertake that this night he shall lie with you, and you will hold you still.'

'That were me lever,' said Dame Elayne, 'than all the gold that is above earth.'

'Let me deal!' said Dame Brusen.

So when Dame Elayne was brought unto the Queen either made other good cheer as by countenance, but nothing with their hearts. But all men and women spoke of the beauty of Dame Elayne. And then it was ordained that Dame Elayne should sleep in a chamber nigh by the Queen and all under one roof. And so it was done as the King commanded. Then the Queen sent for Sir Launcelot and bade him come to her chamber that night, 'or else,' said the Queen, 'I am sure that you will go to your lady's bed, Dame Elayne, by whom you got Galahad.'

'Ah! madam,' said Sir Launcelot, 'never say you so, for that I did was against my will.'

'Then,' said the Queen, 'look that you come to me when I send for you.'

'Madam,' said Sir Launcelot, 'I shall not fail you, but I shall be ready at your commandment.'

So this bargain was not so soon done and made between them but Dame Brusen knew it by her crafts and told it unto her lady, Dame Elayne.

'Alas!' said she, 'how shall I do?'

'Let me deal!' said Dame Brusen, 'for I shall bring him by the hand even to your bed and he shall ween that I am Queen Guenevere's messenger.'

'Then well were me!' said Dame Elayne, 'for all the world I love not so much as I do Sir Launcelot.'

[XI.8] So when time came that all folks were to bed, Dame Brusen came to Sir Launcelot's bed-side and said, 'Sir Launcelot du Lake, sleep you? My lady, Queen Guenevere, lies and awaits upon you.'

'Ah! my fair lady,' said Sir Launcelot, 'I am ready to go with you whither you will have me.'

So Launcelot threw upon him a long gown and so he took his sword in his hand. And then Dame Brusen took him by the finger and led him to her lady's bed, Dame Elayne, and then she departed and left them there in bed together. And, wit you well, this lady was glad, and so was Sir Launcelot, for he weened that he had had another in his arms.

Now leave we them kissing and clipping as was a kindly thing and now speak we of Queen Guenevere that sent one of her women that she most trusted unto Sir Launcelot's bed. And when she came there she found the bed cold and he was not therein. And so she came to the Queen and told her all.

'Alas!' said the Queen, 'where is that false knight become?' So the Queen was nigh out of her wits, and then she writhed and waltered as a mad woman and might not sleep a four or a five hours.

Then Sir Launcelot had a condition that he used of custom to clatter in his sleep and to speak often of his lady, Queen Guenevere. So Sir Launcelot had awaked as long as it had

pleased him and so, by course of kind, he slept and Dame
Elayne, both. And in his sleep he talked and clattered as a jay
of the love that had been betwixt Queen Guenevere and him,
and so, as he talked so loud, the Queen heard him thereas she
lay in her chamber. And when she heard him so clatter she
was wroth out of measure, and then she coughed so loud that
Sir Launcelot awaked. And anon he knew her hemming and
then he knew well that he lay by the Queen Elayne. And
therewith he leapt out of his bed as he had been a wood man,
in his shirt, and anon the Queen met him in the floor and
thus she said:

'Ah! thou false traitor knight! Look thou never abide in
my court and lightly that thou void my chamber! And not so
hardy, thou false traitor knight, that evermore thou come in
my sight!'

'Alas!' said Sir Launcelot. And therewith he took such an
heartly sorrow at her words that he fell down to the floor in a
swoon. And therewithal Queen Guenevere departed. And
when Sir Launcelot awoke out of his swoon he leapt out at a
bay-window into a garden and there with thorns he was all
to-crached of his visage and his body, and so he ran forth he
knew not whither and was as wild as ever was man. And so
he ran two years and never man had grace to know him.

[XI.9] Now turn we unto Queen Guenevere and to the
fair lady Elayne, that when Dame Elayne heard the Queen
so rebuke Sir Launcelot and how also he swooned and how
he leapt out of the bay-window, then she said unto Queen
Guenevere, 'Madam, you are greatly to blame for Sir
Launcelot, for now have you lost him. For I saw and heard
by his countenance that he is mad for ever. And, therefore,
alas! madam, you have done great sin and yourself great dishonour, for you have a lord royal of your own, and therefore
it were your part for to love him, for there is no queen in this
world that hath such another king as you have. And if you
were not, I might have got the love of my lord, Sir Launcelot,

and a great cause I have to love him for he had my maiden-hood, and by him I have borne a fair son whose [name] is Sir Galahad. And he shall be in his time the best knight of the world.'

'Well, Dame Elayne,' said the Queen, 'as soon as it is daylight I charge you to avoid my court. And, for the love you owe unto Sir Launcelot, discover not his counsel, for, and you do, it will be his death!'

'As for that,' said Dame Elayne, 'I dare undertake he is marred for ever, and that have you made. For neither you nor I are like to rejoice him, for he made the most piteous groans when he leapt out at yonder bay-window that ever I heard man make. Alas!' said fair Elayne.

And, 'Alas!' said the Queen, 'for now I wot well that we have lost him for ever.' . . .

Ector, Bors and Lionel, Launcelot's kinsmen, seek for him, supported by the Queen's treasury. So, also, do Gawain, Uwayne, Sagramour, Agglovale and Percival, but with no success.

[XI.10] . . . And so Sir Agglovale and Sir Percival rode together unto their mother which was a queen in those days. And, when she saw her two sons, for joy she wept tenderly, and then she said, 'Ah! my dear sons, when your father was slain he left me four sons of the which now be two slain. And for the death of my noble son, Sir Lamorak, shall mine heart never be glad!'

And then she kneeled down upon her knees before Sir Agglovale and Sir Percival and besought them to abide at home with her.

'Ah! my sweet mother,' said Sir Percival, 'we may not, for we are come of king's blood of both parties. And, therefore, mother, it is our kind to haunt arms and noble deeds.'

'Alas! my sweet sons,' then she said, 'for your sakes I shall first lose my liking and lust, and then wind and weather I may not endure, what for the [death] of King Pellinore, your

father, that was shamefully slain by the hands of Sir Gawain
and his brother, Sir Gaheris. And they slew him not manly
but by treason. And alas! my dear sons, this is a piteous
complaint for me of your father's death, considering also the
death of Sir Lamorak that of knighthood had but few fellows.
And now, my dear sons, have this in your mind.'

And so there was but weeping and sobbing in the court
when they should depart, and she fell in swooning in the
midst of the court. [XI.11] And, when she was awaked,
after them she sent a squire with spending enough. And so
when the squire had overtaken them they would not suffer
him to ride with them but sent him home again to comfort
their mother, praying her meekly of her blessing. . . .

> In their quest for Launcelot, Bors and Percival fight each other in
> ignorance and are healed by a vision of the Sankgreall. Launcelot
> suffers many adventures in his madness and is, latterly, wounded by
> a boar and tended by a hermit.

[XII.3] . . . And then upon a day Sir Launcelot ran his
way into the forest. And by the adventure he came to the
city of Corbyn where Dame Elayne was that bore Galahad,
Sir Launcelot's son. And so when he was entered into the
town he ran through the town to the castle, and then all the
young men of that city ran after Sir Launcelot, and there
they threw turves at him and gave him many sad strokes.
And ever as Sir Launcelot might reach any of them, he
threw them so that they would never come in his hands no
more, for of some he broke the legs and arms.

And so he fled into the castle and then came out knights
and squires and rescued Sir Launcelot. When they beheld
him and looked upon his person they thought they never saw
so goodly a man. And when they saw so many wounds upon
him they deemed that he had been a man of worship. And
then they ordained him clothes to his body and straw and
litter under the gate of the castle to lie in. And so every day

they would throw him meat and set him drink, but there was
but few that would bring him meat to his hands.

[XII.4] So it befell that King Pelles had a nephew whose
name was Castor. And so he desired of the King to be made
knight, and at his own request the King made him knight at
the feast of Candlemas. And when Sir Castor was made
knight, that same day he gave many gowns. And then Sir
Castor sent for the fool which was Sir Launcelot. And when
he was come before Sir Castor he gave Sir Launcelot a robe
of scarlet and all that longed unto him. And when Sir
Launcelot was so arrayed like a knight he was the seemliest
man in all the court and none so well made.

So when he saw his time he went into the garden and there
he laid him down by a well and slept. And so at afternoon
Dame Elayne and her maidens came into the garden to sport
them. And as they romed up and down one of Dame Elayne's
maidens espied where lay a goodly man by the well sleeping.

'Peace!' said Dame Elayne, 'and say no word, but show
me that man where he lies.'

So anon she brought Dame Elayne where he lay. And
when that she beheld him, anon she fell in remembrance of
him and knew him verily for Sir Launcelot. And therewithal
she fell aweeping so heartily that she sank even to the earth.
And when she had thus wept a great while then she arose
and called her maidens and said she was sick. And so she
yode out of the garden as straight to her father as she could,
and there she took him by herself apart. And then she said,
'Ah! my dear father, now I have need of your help, and, but
if that you help me now, farewell my good days for ever!'

'What is that, daughter?' said King Pelles.

'In your garden I was to sport me, and there, by the well,
I found Sir Launcelot du Lake sleeping.'

'I may not believe it!' said King Pelles.

'Truly, sir, he is there!' she said. 'And me seems he should
be yet distracted out of his wits.'

'Then hold you still,' said the King, 'and let me deal.'

Then the King called unto him such as he most trusted, a four persons and Dame Elayne, his daughter, and Dame Brusen, her servant. And when they came to the well and beheld Sir Launcelot, anon Dame Brusen said to the King, 'We must be wise how we deal with him, for this knight is out of his mind, and if we awake him rudely what he will do we all know not. And, therefore, abide you a while and I shall throw an enchantment upon him that he shall not awake of an hour.'

And so she did. And then the King commanded that all people should avoid, that none should be in that way thereas the King would come. And so, when this was done, these four men and these ladies laid hand on Sir Launcelot and so they bore him into a tower and so into a chamber where was the holy vessel of the Sankgreall. And before that holy vessel Sir Launcelot was laid. And there came an holy man and unhilled that vessel, and so, by miracle and by virtue of that holy vessel, Sir Launcelot was healed and recovered.

And as soon as he was awaked, he groaned and sighed and complained him sore of his woodness and strokes that he had had. [XII.5] And as soon as Sir Launcelot saw King Pelles and Dame Elayne, he waxed ashamed and said thus, 'Ah! Lord Jesu, how came I hither? For God's sake, my fair lord, let me wit how that I came hither!'

'Sir,' said Dame Elayne, 'into this country you came like a mazed man, clean out of your wit. And here have you been kept as a fool, and no creature here knew what you were, until by fortune a maiden of mine brought me unto you whereas you lay sleeping by a well. And anon, as I verily beheld you, [I knew you]. Then I told my father, and so were you brought before this holy vessel and, by the virtue of it, thus were you healed.'

'Ah! Jesu, mercy!' said Sir Launcelot. 'If this be sooth, how many are there that know of my woodness?'

'So God me help,' said Dame Elayne, 'no more but my father and I and Dame Brusen.'

'Now, for Christ's love,' said Sir Launcelot, 'keep it counsel and let no man know it in the world! For I am sore ashamed that I have been misfortuned, for I am banished the country of England.'

And so Sir Launcelot lay more than a fortnight ere ever that he might stir for soreness. And then upon a day he said unto Dame Elayne these words: 'Fair Lady Elayne, for your sake I have had much care and anguish, it needs not to rehearse it, you know how. Notwithstanding, I know well I have done foul to you when that I drew my sword to you to have slain you upon the morn after when that I had lain with you. And all was for the cause that you and Dame Brusen made me for to lie by you magre mine head. And, as you say, Sir Galahad, your son, was begotten.'

'That is truth,' said Dame Elayne.

'Then will you, for my sake,' said Sir Launcelot, 'go you unto your father and get me a place of him wherein I may dwell? For in the court of King Arthur may I never come.'

'Sir,' said Dame Elayne, 'I will live and die with you, only for your sake, and if my life might not avail you and my death might avail you, wit you well, I would die for your sake. And I will to my father, and I am right sure there is [no]thing that I can desire of him but I shall have it. And where you be, lord, Sir Launcelot, doubt you not but I will be with you with all the service that I may do.'

So forthwithal she went to her father and said, 'Sir, my lord, Sir Launcelot, desires to be here by you in some castle of yours.'

'Well, daughter,' said the King, 'sithen it is his desire to abide in these marches, he shall be in the Castle of Blyaunte and there shall you be with him and twenty of the fairest young ladies that are in this country, and they shall be all of the greatest blood in this country. And you shall have twenty

knights with you. For, daughter, I will that you wit we all be
honoured by the blood of Sir Launcelot.'

[XII.6] Then went Dame Elayne unto Sir Launcelot and
told him all how her father had devised. Then came a knight
which was called Sir Castor, that was nephew unto King
Pelles, and he came unto Sir Launcelot and asked him what
was his name.

'Sir,' said Sir Launcelot, 'my name is Le Shyvalere Ill
Mafeete, that is to say, "the knight that has trespassed".'

'Sir,' said Sir Castor, 'it may well be so, but ever me seems
your name should be Sir Launcelot du Lake for ere now I
have seen you.'

'Sir,' said Sir Launcelot, 'you are not gentle. For I put a
case that my name were Sir Launcelot and that it list me not
to discover my name, what should it grieve you here to keep
my counsel, and you not hurt thereby? But, wit you well, and
ever it lie in my power, I shall grieve you, and ever I meet
with you in my way!'

Then Sir Castor kneeled adown and besought Sir
Launcelot for mercy, 'for I shall never utter what you are,
while that you are in these parts'.

Then Sir Launcelot pardoned him. And so King Pelles
with twenty knights and Dame Elayne with her twenty
ladies rode unto the Castle of Blyaunte that stood in an
island beclosed environ with a fair water deep and large.
And, when they were there, Sir Launcelot let call it the
Joyous Isle, and there was he called none otherwise but Le
Shyvalere Mafeete, 'the knight that has trespassed'.

Then Sir Launcelot let make him a shield all of sable and
a queen crowned in the midst, of silver, and a knight, clean
armed, kneeling before her. And every day once, for any
mirths that all the ladies might make him, he would once
every day look towards the realm of Logres, where King
Arthur and Queen Guenevere was, and then would he fall
upon aweeping as his heart should to-brast. . . .

Percival and Ector Discover Launcelot at Joyous Isle

[XII.9] . . . So it befell on a day that Sir Ector and Sir Percival came unto Sir Launcelot and asked of him what he would do and whether he would go with them unto King Arthur.

'Nay!' said Sir Launcelot, 'that may I not do by no means, for I was vengeably defended the court, that I cast me never to come there more.'

'Sir,' said Sir Ector, 'I am your brother, and you are the man in the world that I love most. And, if I understood that it were your disworship, you may understand that I would never counsel you thereto. But King Arthur and all his knights, and, in especial, Queen Guenevere, make such dole and sorrow for you that it is marvel to hear and see. And you must remember the great worship and renown that you are of, how that you have been more spoken of than any other knight that is now living—for there is none that bears the name now but you and Sir Tristram. And, therefore, brother,' said Sir Ector, 'make you ready to [ride to] the court with us. And I dare say and make it good,' said Sir Ector, 'it has cost my lady, the Queen, twenty thousand pounds, the seeking of you.'

'Well, brother,' said Sir Launcelot, 'I will do after your counsel and ride with you.'

So then they took [their horses] and made ready, and anon they took their leave of King Pelles and of Dame Elayne. And when Sir Launcelot should depart, Dame Elayne made great sorrow. 'My lord, Sir Launcelot,' said Dame Elayne, 'this same feast of Pentecost shall your son and mine, Galahad, be made knight, for he is now fully fifteen winters old.'

'Madam, do as you list,' said Sir Launcelot, 'and God give him grace to prove a good knight.'

'As for that,' said Dame Elayne, 'I doubt not he shall prove the best man of his kin except one.'

'Then shall he be a good man enough,' said Sir Launcelot.

[XII.10] So anon they departed and within fifteen days' journey they came unto Camelot, that is in English called Winchester. And when Sir Launcelot was come among them the King and all the knights made great joy of his home-coming. And there Sir Percival and Sir Ector de Maris began and told the whole adventures, how Sir Launcelot had been out of his mind in the time of his absence and how he called himself Le Shyvalere Mafeete, 'the knight that had tres-passed', and in three days within Joyous Isle Sir Launcelot smote down five hundred knights. And ever as Sir Ector and Sir Percival told these tales of Sir Launcelot, Queen Guene-vere wept as she should have died. Then the Queen made him great cheer.

'Ah! Jesu,' said King Arthur, 'I marvel for what cause you, Sir Launcelot, went out of your mind. For I and many others deem it was for the love of fair Elayne, the daughter of King Pelles, by whom you are noised that you have got a child, and his name is Galahad. And men say that he shall do many marvellous things.'

'My lord,' said Sir Launcelot, 'if I did any folly, I have that I sought.'

And therewithal the King spoke no more. But all Sir Launcelot's kinsmen knew for whom he went out of his mind. And then there was made great feasts, and great joy was there among them. And all lords and ladies made great joy when they heard how Sir Launcelot was come again unto the court.

Now will we leave of this matter and speak we of Sir [Tristram] and of Sir Palomydes, that was the Saracen unchristened.

[XII.11] When Sir Tristram was come home unto Joyous Garde from his adventures—and all this while that Sir Launcelot was thus missed, two years and more, Sir

Tristram bore the brewte and renown through all the realm of Logres, and many strong adventures befell him and full well and worshipfully he brought them to an end—so when he was come home, La Beall Isode told of the great feast that should be at Pentecost next following. And there she told him how Sir Launcelot had been missed two years and all that while he had been out of his mind, and how he was helped by the holy vessel of the Sankgreall.

'Alas!' said Sir Tristram, 'that caused some debate betwixt him and Queen Guenevere.'

'Sir,' said Dame Isode, 'I know it all, for Queen Guenevere sent me a letter, all how it was done, for because I should require you to seek him. And now, blessed be God,' said La Beall Isode, 'he is whole and sound and come again to the court.'

'Ah! Jesu, thereof am I fain,' said Sir Tristram. 'And now shall you and I make us ready, for both you and I will be at that feast.'

'Sir,' said Dame Isode, 'and it please you, I will not be there, for through me you are marked by many good knights and that causes you for to have much more labour for my sake than needs you to have.'

'Then will I not be there,' said Sir Tristram, 'but if you be there.'

'God defend!' said La Beall Isode, 'for then shall I be spoken of shame among all queens and ladies of estate. For you that are called one of the noblest knights of the world and a knight of the Round Table, how may you be missed at the feast? For what shall be said of you among all knights?—"Ah! see how Sir Tristram hunts and hawks and cowers within a castle with his lady and forsakes us! Alas!" shall some say, "it is pity that ever he was knight or ever he should have the love of a lady." Also, what shall queens and ladies say of me?—"It is pity that I have my life that I would hold so noble a knight as you are from his worship." '

'So God me help,' said Sir Tristram unto La Beall Isode,
'it is passingly well said of you and nobly counselled. And
now I well understand that you love me. And, like as you
have counselled me, I will do a part thereafter, but there
shall no man nor child ride with me but myself alone. And so
I will ride on Tuesday next coming and no more harness of
war but my spear and my sword.' . . .

On his way, Tristram fights Palomydes who ultimately yields to
him, for 'mine offence is to you not so great but that we may be
friends, for all that I have offended is and was for the love of La
Beall Isode'. Palomydes is then baptized and they ride to Camelot.

Book Six

'*The noble tale of the Sankgreall*'

This same Pentecost, when Palomydes, newly baptized, comes to Arthur's court, there also comes a good old man who brings with him Galahad whom he seats in the 'Sege Perilous' at the Round Table where it is written, 'Four hundred winters and four and fifty accomplished after the Passion of our Lord Jesu Christ ought this sege to be fulfilled.' It is reported that a great stone is floating on the river and in it sticks a sword.

[XIII.4] . . . Then the King took him by the hand and went down from the palace to show Galahad the adventures of the stone. [XIII.5] Then the Queen heard thereof and came after with many ladies and showed her the stone where it hoved on the water.

'Sir,' said the King unto Sir Galahad, 'here is a great marvel as ever I saw and right good knights have essayed and failed.'

'Sir,' said Sir Galahad, 'it is no marvel, for this adventure is not theirs but mine. And for the surety of this sword I brought none with me, but here by my side hangs the scabbard.'

And anon he laid his hand on the sword and lightly drew it out of the stone and put it in the sheath and said unto the King, 'Now it goes [better than it did beforehand].'

'Sir,' said the King, 'a shield God may send you.'

'Now have I the sword that sometime was the good knight's, Balin le Saveage, and he was a passing good knight of his hands. And with this sword he slew his brother Balan, and that was great pity for he was a good knight. And either slew other through a dolorous stroke that Balin gave unto King Peiles, the which is not yet whole, nor naught shall be till that I heal him.'

So therewith the King had espied come riding down the river a lady on a white palfrey a great pace toward them. Then she salewed the King and the Queen and asked if that Sir Launcelot were there. And then he answered himself and said, 'I am here, my fair lady!'

Then she said all with weeping there, 'Ah! Sir Launcelot, how your great doing is changed sithen this day in the morn!'

'Damsel, why say you so?'

'Sir, I say you sooth,' said the damsel, 'for you were this day in the morn the best knight of the world. But who should say so now, he should be a liar, for there is now one better than you are, and well it is proved by the adventure of the sword whereto you durst not set to your hand. And that is the change of your name and living. Wherefore I make unto you a remembrance that you shall not ween from henceforth that you are the best knight of the world.'

'As touching unto that,' said Sir Launcelot, 'I know well I was never none of the best.'

'Yes,' said the damsel, 'that were you and are yet, of any sinful man of the world. And, sir King, Nacien the hermit sends thee word that thee shall befall the greatest worship that ever befell king in Bretayne, and I say you wherefore, for this day the Sankgreall appeared in thy house and fed thee and all thy fellowship of the Round Table.'

So she departed and went the same way that she came.

[XIII.6] 'Now,' said the King, 'I am sure at this quest of the Sankgreall shall all you of the Round Table depart and never shall I see you again whole together. Therefore once shall I see you together in the meadow all whole together. Therefore I will see you all whole together in the meadow of Camelot to joust and to tourney, that, after your death, men may speak of it that such good knights were here, such a day, whole together.'

As unto that counsel and at the King's request they accorded all and took on the harness that longed unto jousting. But all this moving of the King was for this intent for to see Galahad proved. For the King deemed he should not lightly come again unto the court after this departing. So were they assembled in the meadow, both more and less. Then Sir Galahad, by the prayer of the King and the Queen, did on a noble gesseraunt upon him and also he did on his helm, but shield would he take none for no prayer of the King. So then Sir Gawain and other knights prayed him to take a spear. Right so he did. So the Queen was in a tower with all her ladies for to behold that tournament.

Then Sir Galahad dressed him in midst of the meadow and began to break spears marvellously that all men had wonder of him, for he there surmounted all other knights. For within a while he had defouled many good knights of the Table Round save all only twain, that was Sir Launcelot and Sir Percival. [XIII.7] Then the King, at the Queen's desire, made him to alight and to unlace his helm that the Queen might see him in the visage. When she advised him she said, 'I dare well say soothly that Sir Launcelot begot him, for never two men resembled more in likeness. Therefore it is no marvel though he is of great prowess.'

So a lady that stood by the Queen said, 'Madam, for God's sake, ought he of right to be so good a knight?'

'Yea! forsooth,' said the Queen, 'for he is of all parties come of the best knights of the world and of the highest lineage. For Sir Launcelot is come but of the eighth degree from our Lord Jesu Christ, and Sir Galahad is the ninth degree from our Lord Jesu Christ. Therefore I dare say they are the greatest gentlemen of the world.'

And then the King and all the estates went home unto Camelot and so went unto evensong to the great monastery. And so after upon that to supper, and every knight set in his own place as they were beforehand. Then anon they heard cracking and crying of thunder that them thought the palace should all to-drive. So in the midst of the blast entered a sunbeam more clearer by seven times than ever they saw day, and all they were alighted of the grace of the Holy Ghost. Then began every knight to behold other, and either saw other, by their seeming, fairer than ever they were before. Notforthan there was no knight that might speak one word a great while, and so they looked every man on other as they had been dumb.

Then entered into the hall the Holy Grail covered with white samite, but there was none that might see it nor whom that bore it. And there was all the hall fulfilled with good odours and every knight had such meats and drinks as he best loved in this world. And when the Holy Grail had been borne through the hall, then the holy vessel departed suddenly, that they wist not where it became. Then had they all breath to speak, and then the King yielded thankings to God of his good grace that he had sent them.

'Certes,' said the King, 'we ought to thank our Lord Jesu Christ, greatly that he has showed us this day at the reverence of this high feast of Pentecost.'

'Now,' said Sir Gawain, 'we have been served this day with what meats and drinks we thought on. But one thing beguiled us, that we might not see the Holy Grail, it was so preciously covered. Wherefore I will make here a vow that tomorn, without longer abiding, I shall labour in the quest of the Sankgreall, and that I shall hold me out a twelve-month and a day or more if need be, and never shall I return unto the court again till I have seen it more openly than it has been shown here. And, if I may not speed, I shall return again as he that may not be against the will of God.'

So when they of the Table Round heard Sir Gawain say so, they arose up, the most part, and made such avows as Sir Gawain has made. Anon as King Arthur heard this he was greatly displeased, for he wist well he might not againsay their avows. 'Alas!' said King Arthur unto Sir Gawain, 'you have nigh slain me for the avow that you have made, for, through you, you have bereft me the fairest and the truest of knighthood that ever was seen together in any realm of the world. For when they depart from hence I am sure they all shall never meet more together in this world, for they shall die many in the quest. And so it forthinks not me a little, for I have loved them as well as my life. Wherefore it shall grieve me right sore the departition of this fellowship, for I have had an old custom to have them in my fellowship.' [XIII.8] And therewith the tears fell in his eyes and then he said, 'Sir Gawain! you have set me in great sorrow, for I have great doubt that my true fellowship shall never meet here more again.'

'Ah! sir,' said Sir Launcelot, 'comfort yourself! For it shall be unto us a great honour, and much more than we died in other places, for of death we are siker.'

'Ah! Launcelot,' said the King, 'the great love that I have had unto you all the days of my life makes me to say such doleful words! For there was never Christian king that ever had so many worthy men at his table as I have had this day at the Table Round. And that is my great sorrow.'

When the Queen, ladies and gentlewomen knew of this tiding they had such sorrow and heaviness that there might no tongue tell, for those knights had held them in honour and charity. But, above all others, Queen Guenevere made great sorrow. 'I marvel,' said she, 'that my lord will suffer them to depart from him.'

Thus was all the court troubled for the love of the departing

of these knights, and many of those ladies that loved
knights would have gone with their loves. And so had they
done, had not an old knight come among them in religious
clothing and spoken all on hight and said, 'Fair lords, which
have sworn in the quest of the Sankgreall, thus sends you
Nacien, the hermit, word that none in this quest lead lady nor
gentlewoman with him, for it is not to do in so high a service
as they labour in. For I warn you, plain, he that is not clean
of his sins, he shall not see the mysteries of our Lord Jesu
Christ.'

And for this cause they left these ladies and gentlewomen. . . .

Among other adventures Galahad undertakes to 'do away the
wicked customs' of the Castle of Maidens which has been seized by
seven knights who, when it is prophesied that a knight will soon
overthrow them, vow 'there shall never lady nor knight pass this
Castle but they shall abide . . . or die therefore till that knight be
come. . . . And, therefore, it is called the Maidens' Castle for they
have devoured many maidens.' Routed, when they ride out against
Galahad, they flee back into the castle.

[XIII.16] . . . So they ⟨Sir Gawain, Sir Gareth and Sir
Uwaine⟩ departed and rode by fortune till that they came by
the Castle of Maidens. And there the seven brethren espied
the three knights and said, 'Sithen we are flemed by one
knight from this castle we shall destroy all the knights of
King Arthur's that we may overcome, for the love of Sir
Galahad.'

And therewith the seven knights set upon them three
knights. And by fortune Sir Gawain slew one [of] the
brethren and each one of his fellows overthrew another and
so slew all the remnant. And then they took the way under
the castle and there they lost the way that Sir Galahad rode.
And there every⟨one⟩ of them departed from other.

And Sir Gawain rode till he came to an hermitage and
there he found the good man saying his evensong of our

Lady. And there Sir [Gawain] asked harbour for charity and the good man granted him gladly. Then the good man asked him what he was.

'Sir,' he said, 'I am a knight of King Arthur's that am in the quest of the Sankgreall, and my name is Sir Gawain.'

'Sir,' said the good man, 'I would wit how it stands betwixt God and you.'

'Sir,' said Sir Gawain, 'I will with a good will show you my life, if it please you.' There he told the hermit how a monk of an abbey 'called me wicked knight'.

'He might well say it,' said the hermit, 'for, when you were made first knight, you should have taken you to knightly deeds and virtuous living. And you have done the contrary, for you have lived mischievously many winters. And Sir Galahad is a maid and sinned never, and that is the cause he shall achieve where he goes that you, nor none such, shall never attain, neither none in your fellowship, for you have used the most untruest life that ever I heard knight live. For, certes, had you not been so wicked as you are, never had the seven brethren been slain by you and your two fellows. For Sir Galahad himself alone beat them all seven the day before, but his living is such that he shall slay no man lightly.

'Also, I may say you that the Castle of Maidens betokens the good souls that were in prison before the Incarnation of our Lord Jesu Christ. And the seven knights betoken the seven deadly sins that reigned that time in the world. And I may liken the good knight, Galahad, unto the Son of the High Father that light within a maiden and bought all the souls out of thrall: so did Sir Galahad deliver all the maidens out of the woeful castle. Now, Sir Gawain,' said the good man, 'thou must do penance for thy sin.'

'Sir, what penance shall I do?'

'Such as I will give thee,' said the good man.

'Nay,' said Sir Gawain, 'I may do no penance, for we

knights adventurous many times suffer great woe and pain.'

'Well,' said the good man. And then he held his peace.

And on the morn then Sir Gawain departed from the hermit and betaught him unto God. And by adventure he met with Sir Agglovale and Sir Gryfflet, two knights of the Round Table, and so they three rode four days without finding of any adventure. And at the fifth day they departed and every⟨one⟩ held as fell them by adventure.

Here leaves the tale of Sir Gawain and his fellows and speaks of Sir Galahad.

[XIII.17] So when Sir Galahad was departed from the Castle of Maidens he rode till he came to a waste forest and there he met with Sir Launcelot and Sir Percival. But they knew him not, for he was new disguised. Right so his father, Sir Launcelot, dressed his spear and broke it upon Sir Galahad, and Sir Galahad smote him so again that he bore down horse and man. And then he drew his sword and dressed him unto Sir Percival and smote him so on the helm that it rove to the coif of steel, and, had not the sword swerved, Sir Percival had been slain. And with the stroke he fell out of his saddle.

So these jousts was done before the hermitage where a recluse dwelt. And when she saw Sir Galahad ride she said, 'God be with thee, best knight of the world! Ah! certes,' said she all aloud, that Sir Launcelot and Percival might hear, 'and yonder two knights had known thee as well as I do, they would not have encountered with thee.'

When Sir Galahad heard her say so he was adread to be known, and therewith he smote his horse with his spurs and rode a great pace fromward them. Then perceived they both that he was Sir Galahad and up they got on their horses and rode fast after him. But within a while he was out of their sight and then they turned again with heavy cheer and said,

'Let us spirre some tidings,' said Percival, 'at yonder recluse.'

'Do as you list,' said Sir Launcelot.

So when Sir Percival came to the recluse she knew him well enough and Sir Launcelot, both. But Sir Launcelot rode overthwart and endlong a wild forest and held no path but as wild adventure led him. And at the last he came to a stony cross which departed two ways in waste land, and by the cross was a stone that was a marble, but it was so dark that Sir Launcelot might not wit what it was. Then Sir Launcelot looked beside him and saw an old chapel and there he weened to have found people.

And anon Sir Launcelot fastened his horse to a tree and there he did off his shield and hung it upon a tree and then he went to the chapel door and found it waste and broken. And within he found a fair altar full richly arrayed with cloth of clean silk, and there stood a clean fair candlestick which bore six great candles therein, and the candlestick was of silver. And when Sir Launcelot saw this light he had great will for to enter into the chapel, but he could find no place where he might enter. Then was he passing heavy and dismayed, and returned again and came to his horse and did off his saddle and bridle and let him pasture him, and unlaced his helm and ungirt his sword and laid him down to sleep upon his shield before the cross.

[XIII.18] And so he fell asleep, and, half-waking and half-sleeping, he saw coming by him two palfreys, all fair and white, which bore a litter, and therein lying a sick knight. And when he was nigh the cross he there abode still. All this Sir Launcelot saw and beheld it, for he slept not verily, and he heard him say, 'Ah! sweet Lord! When shall this sorrow leave me, and when shall the holy vessel come by me where-through I shall be healed? For I have endured thus long for little trespass, a full great while!'

Thus complained the knight and always Sir Launcelot heard it. So with that Sir Launcelot saw the candlestick with the [six] tapers came before the cross and he saw nobody that brought it. Also there came a table of silver and the holy vessel of the Sankgreall which Sir Launcelot had seen beforetime in King [Pescheor's] house. And therewith the sick knight sat him up and held up both his hands and said, 'Fair, sweet Lord, which is here within the holy vessel, take heed unto me that I may be whole of this malady!'

And therewith on his hands and knees he went so nigh that he touched the holy vessel and kissed it, and anon he was whole. And then he said, 'Lord God! I thank thee, for I am healed of this sickness.'

So when the holy vessel had been there a great while it went unto the chapel with the chandelier and the light so that Sir Launcelot wist not where it was become, for he was overtaken with sin that he had no power to rise again the holy vessel. Wherefore after that many men said him shame, but he took repentance after that.

Then the sick knight dressed him up and kissed the cross. Anon his squire brought him his arms and asked his lord how he did. 'Certes,' said he, 'I thank God, right well! Through the holy vessel I am healed. But I have marvel of this sleeping knight that he had no power to awake when this holy vessel was brought hither.'

'I dare well say,' said the squire, 'that he dwells in some deadly sin whereof he was never confessed.'

'By my faith,' said the knight, 'whatsoever he is, he is unhappy. For, as I deem, he is of the fellowship of the Round Table, which is entered in the quest of the Sankgreall.'

'Sir,' said the squire, 'here I have brought you all your arms save your helm and your sword, and, therefore, by mine assent, now may you take this knight's helm and his sword.'

And so he did. And when he was clean armed he took there Sir Launcelot's horse, for he was better than his, and so departed they from the cross. [XIII.19] Then anon Sir

Launcelot waked and sat him up and bethought him what he had seen there and whether it were dreams or not. Right so heard he a voice that said, 'Sir Launcelot, more harder than is the stone, and more bitter than is the wood, and more naked and barer than is the leaf of the fig-tree! Therefore go thou from hence and withdraw thee from these holy places!'

And when Sir Launcelot heard this he was passing heavy and wist not what to do, and so departed sore weeping and cursed the time that he was born, for then he deemed never to have worship more. For those words went to his heart till that he knew wherefore he was called so. Then Sir Launcelot went to the cross and found his helm, his sword and his [horse] away. And then he called himself a very wretch and most unhappy of all knights and there he said, 'My sin and my wickedness have brought me unto great dishonour! For when I sought worldly adventures for worldly desires I ever achieved them and had the better in every place, and never was I discomforted in no quarrel, were it right, were it wrong. And now I take upon me the adventures to seek of holy things, now I see and understand that mine old sin hinders me and shames me, that I had no power to stir nor speak when the holy blood appeared before me.'

So thus he sorrowed till it was day and heard the fowls sing. Then somewhat he was comforted. But when Sir Launcelot missed his horse and his harness then he wist well God was displeased with him. And so he departed from the cross on foot into a fair forest and so by prime he came to an high hill and found an hermitage and an hermit therein which was going unto mass. And then Sir Launcelot kneeled down and cried on our Lord mercy for his wicked works. So, when mass was done, Sir Launcelot called him and prayed him for saint charity for to hear his life.

'With a good will,' said the good man, and asked him whether he was of King Arthur's and of the fellowship of the Table Round.

'Yea! forsooth, sir, and my name is Sir Launcelot du Lake, that has been right well said of. And now my good fortune is changed, for I am the most wretch of the world.'

The hermit beheld him and had marvel why he was so abashed. 'Sir,' said the hermit, 'you ought to thank God more than any knight living, for he has caused you to have more worldly worship than any knight that is now living. And for your presumption to take upon you in deadly sin for to be in his presence where his flesh and his blood was—which caused you you might not see it with your worldly eyes, for he will not appear where such sinners are but if it be unto their great hurt or unto their shame. And there is no knight now living that ought to yield God so great thanks as you, for he has given you beauty, bounty, seemliness and great strength over all other knights. And therefore you are the more beholden unto God than any other man to love him and dread him, for your strength and your manhood will little avail you, and God be against you.'

[XIII.20] Then Sir Launcelot wept with heavy heart and said, 'Now I know well you say me sooth.'

'Sir,' said the good man, 'hide none old sin from me.'

'Truly,' said Sir Launcelot, 'that were me full loath to discover, for this fourteen year I never discovered one thing that I have used, and ⟨on⟩ that may I now wite my shame and my misadventures.'

And then he told there the good man all his life and how he had loved a queen unmeasurably and out of measure long. 'And all my great deeds of arms that I have done for the most part was for the Queen's sake, and for her sake would I do battle, were it right or wrong. And never did I battle all only [for] God's sake, but for to win worship and to cause me the better to be beloved, and little or nought I thanked never God of it.' Then Sir Launcelot said, 'Sir, I pray you counsel me.'

'Sir, I will counsel you,' said the hermit. 'You shall assure me, by your knighthood, you shall no more come in that queen's fellowship as much as you may forbear.'

And then Sir Launcelot promised him that he nolde, by the faith of his body.

'Sir, look that your heart and your mouth accord,' said the good man, 'and I shall assure you you shall have the more worship than ever you had.'

'Holy father,' said Sir Launcelot, 'I marvel of the voice that said to me marvellous words as you have heard beforehand.'

'Have you no marvel,' said the good man, 'thereof, for it seems well God loves you. For men may understand a stone is hard of kind and, namely, one more than another, and that is to understand by thee, Sir Launcelot, for thou wilt not leave thy sin for no goodness that God has sent thee. Therefore thou art more harder than any stone and wouldest never be made neish, neither by water nor by fire, and that is the heat of the Holy Ghost may not enter in thee.

'Now, take heed, in all the world men shall not find one knight to whom our Lord has given so much of grace as he has lent thee, for he has given thee fairness with seemliness; also he has given thee wit and discretion to know good from ill; he has also given prowess and hardiness and given thee to work so largely that thou hast had the better all thy days of thy life wheresoever thou came. And now our Lord would suffer thee no longer but that thou shalt know him, whether thou wilt or nilt. And why the voice called thee bitterer than the wood, for wheresoever much sin dwells there may be but little sweetness, wherefore thou art likened to an old rotten tree.

'Now have I showed thee why thou art harder than the stone and bitterer than the tree, now shall I show thee why thou art more naked and barer than the fig-tree. It befell that our Lord on Palm Sunday preached in Jerusalem, and there he found in the people that all hardness was harboured in them, and there he found in all the town not one that would

harbour him. And then he went out of the town and found in
midst the way a fig-tree which was right fair and well garnished of leaves, but fruit had it none. Then our Lord
cursed the tree that bore no fruit, that betokens, the fig-tree,
unto Jerusalem that had leaves and no fruit. So thou, Sir
Launcelot, when the Holy Grail was brought before thee, he
found in thee no fruit, neither good thought nor good will,
and defouled with lechery.'

'Certes,' said Sir Launcelot, 'all that you have said is true,
and from henceforward I cast me, by the grace of God, never
to be so wicked as I have been but as to sew knighthood and
to do feats of arms.'

Then this good man enjoined Sir Launcelot such penance
as he might do and to sew knighthood, and so absolved him
and prayed him to abide with him all that day.

'I will well,' said Sir Launcelot, 'for I have neither helm,
horse nor sword.'

'As for that,' said the good man, 'I shall help you ere
tomorn, at even, of an horse and all that longs unto you.'

And then Sir Launcelot repented him greatly of his
misdeeds.

Here leaves the tale of Sir Launcelot and begins of Sir
Percival de Galys. . . .

Gawain and Ector meet and regret that, in the quest of the Sankgreall, they can find no adventures. Gawain fights a knight who
challenges them, only to discover, as he dies, that he is Uwaine.
' "And now forgive thee, God, for it shall be ever rehearsed that the
one sworn brother has slain the other." "Alas!" said Sir Gawain,
"that ever this misadventure befell me!" ' Gawain and Ector ride to
Nacien's hermitage. He explains the allegorical meaning of their
experiences.

[XVI.5] . . . 'Certes,' said Sir Gawain, 'full soothly have
you said, that I see it openly. Now I pray you tell me why

we met not with so many adventures as we were wont to do?'

'I shall tell you gladly,' said the good man. 'The adventure of the Sankgreall, which is in showing now, for it appears not to no sinners, wherefore marvel you not, [though] you fail thereof and many others, for you are an untrue knight and a great murderer, and to good men signifies other things than murder. For I dare say, as sinful as ever Sir Launcelot has been, sith that he went into the quest of the Sankgreall he slew never man nor nought shall, till that he come to Camelot again, for he has taken [upon] him to forsake sin. And nere were that he is not stable, but by his thought he is likely to turn again, he should be next to achieve it save Sir Galahad, his son. But God knows his thought and his unstableness. And yet shall he die right an holy man and no doubt he has no fellow of none earthly sinful man living.'

'Sir,' said Sir Gawain, 'it seems ⟨to⟩ me by your words that for our sins it will not avail us to travail in this quest.'

'Truly,' said the good man, 'there are an hundred such as you are shall never prevail but to have shame.'

And when they had heard these words they commended him unto God. Then the good man called Sir Gawain and said, 'It is long time passed sith that you were made knight and never since served thou thy Maker. And now thou art so old a tree that in thee is neither leaf, nor grass, nor fruit. Wherefore bethink thee that thou yield to our Lord the bare rind, sith the fiend hath the leaves and the fruit.'

'Sir,' said Sir Gawain, 'and I had leisure I would speak with you, but my fellow, Sir Ector, is gone and abides me yonder beneath the hill.'

'Well,' said the good man, 'thou were better to be counselled.'

Then departed Sir Gawain and came to Sir Ector, and so took their horses and rode till that they came to a forester's house which harboured them right well. And on the morn departed from their host and rode long ere they could find any adventure.

Now turns this tale unto Sir Bors de Ganys. . . .

When Bors makes his confession the religious finds him 'in so marvellous a life and so stable that he felt he was never greatly corrupt in fleshly lusts but in one time that he begot Elayne le Blanke.' After many adventures Launcelot comes to the end of his quest.

[XVII.15] . . . Then Sir Launcelot kneeled adown before the chamber door, for well wist he that there was the Sankgreall within that chamber. Then said he, 'Fair sweet Father, Jesu Christ! If ever I did thing that pleased thee, Lord, for thy pity ne have [me] not in despite for my sins done before time, and that thou show me something of that I seek.'

And with that he saw the chamber door open and there came out a great clearness that the house was as bright as all the torches of the world had been there. So came he to the chamber door and would have entered. And anon a voice said unto him, 'Sir Launcelot, flee and enter not, for thou ought not to do it! For, and if thou enter, thou shalt forthink it.'

Then he withdrew him aback right heavy. Then looked he up into the midst of the chamber and saw a table of silver and the holy vessel covered with red samite and many angels about it, whereof one held a candle of wax burning, and the other held a cross and the ornaments of an altar. And before the holy vessel he saw a good man clothed as a priest and it seemed that he was at the sakering of the mass. And it seemed to Sir Launcelot that above the priest's hands were three men, whereof the two put the youngest by likeness between the priest's hands, and so he lifted [him] up right high, and it seemed to show so to the people. And then Sir Launcelot marvelled not a little, for him thought the priest was so greatly charged of the figure that him seemed that he should fall to the earth. And when he saw none about him that would help him, then came he to the door a great pace and said, 'Fair Father, Jesu Christ, ne take it for no sin if I help the good man which hath great need of help.'

Right so entered he into the chamber and came towards the table of silver, and when he came nigh it he felt a breath that him thought it was entromedled with fire which smote him so sore in the visage that him thought it burnt his visage. And therewith he fell to the earth and had no power to arise, as he that had lost the power of his body and his hearing and sight. Then felt he many hands which took him up and bore him out of the chamber door and left him there seeming dead to all people.

So upon the morrow, when it was fair day, they within were risen and found Sir Launcelot lying before the chamber door. All they marvelled how that he came in. And so they looked upon him and felt his pulse to wit whether were any life in him. And so they found life in him but he might not stand nor stir no member that he had. And so they took him by every part of the body and bore him into a chamber and laid him in a rich bed far from folk. And so he lay four days. Then one said he was alive and another said nay, he was dead.

'In the name of God,' said an old man, 'I do you verily to wit he is not dead but he is as full of life as the strongest of us all. Therefore I rede you all that he be well kept till God send life in him again.'

[XVII.16] So in such manner they kept Sir Launcelot four-and-twenty days and also many nights, that ever he lay still as a dead man. And at the twenty-fifth day befell him after midday that he opened his eyes. And when he saw folk he made great sorrow and said, 'Why have you awaked me? for I was more at ease than I am now. Ah! Jesu Christ! Who might be so blessed that might see openly thy great marvels of sweetness there where no sinner may be!'

'[What] have you seen?' [said they about him.

'I have seen],' said he, 'great marvels that no tongue may

F

tell and more than any heart can think. And had not my sin been beforetime, else I had seen much more.'

Then they told him how he had lain there four-and-twenty days and nights. Then him thought it was punishment for the four[-and-twenty] years that he had been [a] sinner, wherefore our Lord put him in penance the four[-and-twenty] days and nights. Then looked Launcelot before him and saw the hair⟨shirt⟩ which he had borne nigh a year: for that he forthought him right much that he had broken his promise unto the hermit which he had avowed to do.

Then they asked how [it] stood with him.

'Forsooth,' said he, 'I am whole of body, thanked be our Lord! Therefore, for God's love, tell me where I am.' Then said they all that he was in the Castle of Carbonek. Therewith came a gentlewoman and brought him a shirt of small linen cloth. But he changed not there but took the hair⟨shirt⟩ to him again.

'Sir,' said they, 'the quest of the Sankgreall is achieved now right in you, and never shall you see of Sankgreall more than you have seen.'

'Now I thank God,' said Sir Launcelot, 'for his great mercy, for that I have seen, for it suffices me. For, as I suppose, no man in this world have lived better than I have done to achieve that I have done.'

And therewith he took the hair⟨shirt⟩ and clothed him in it, and above that he put a linen [shirt] and after that a robe of scarlet, fresh and new. And when he was so arrayed they marvelled all, for they knew him well that he was Sir Launcelot, the good knight. And then they said all, 'Ah! my lord, Sir Launcelot!—you are he?'

And he said, 'Yea! truly, I am he.'

Then came word to the King Pelles that the knight that had lain so long dead was the noble knight, Sir Launcelot. Then was the King right glad and went to see him. And when Sir Launcelot saw him come he dressed him against him, and then made the King great joy of him. And there the King told him tidings how his fair daughter was dead. Then Sir Launcelot was right heavy and said, 'Me forthinks of the death of your daughter, for she was a full fair lady, fresh and young. And well I wot she bore the best knight that is now on earth or that ever was since God was born.'

So the King held him there four days and on the morrow he took his leave of King Pelles and of all the fellowship and thanked them of the great labour. . . .

Having got as near the Grail as he can, Launcelot returns to Camelot. Galahad arrives at the Castle of Carbonek.

[XVII.20] . . . therewithal beseemed them that there came an old man and four angels from Heaven, clothed in likeness of a bishop and had a cross in his hand. And these four angels bore him up in a chair and set him down before the table of silver whereupon the Sankgreall was. And it seemed that he had in midst of his forehead letters which said, 'See you here, Joseph, the first Bishop of Christendom, the same which our Lord succoured in the City of Sarras in the spiritual [palace].' Then the knights marvelled for that Bishop was dead more than three hundred years before. 'Ah! knights,' said he, 'marvel not, for I was sometime an earthly man.'

So with that they heard the chamber door open and there they saw angels. And two bore candles of wax and the third bore a towel and the fourth a spear which bled marvellously, that the drops fell within a box which he held with his other hand. And anon they set the candles upon the table and the third the towel upon the vessel and the fourth the holy spear even upright upon the vessel.

And then the Bishop made semblance as though he would have gone to the sakering of a mass, and then he took an obley which was made in likeness of bread. And, at the lifting up, there came a figure in likeness of a child, and the visage

was as red and as bright as any fire, and smote himself into
the bread that all they saw it that the bread was formed of a
fleshly man. And then he put it into the holy vessel again and
then he did that longed to a priest to do mass. And then he
went to Sir Galahad and kissed him and bade him go and kiss
his fellows. And so he did anon.

'Now,' said he, 'the servants of Jesu Christ, you shall be
fed before this table with sweet meats that never knights
yet tasted.'

And when he had said he vanished away. And they set
them at the table in great dread and made their prayers.
Then looked they and saw a man come out of the holy vessel
that had all the signs of the Passion of Jesu Christ bleeding
all openly and said, 'My knights and my servants and my
true children, which are come out of deadly life into the
spiritual life, I will no longer cover me from you, but you
shall see now a part of my secrets and of my hidden things.
Now hold and receive the High Order and meet which you
have so much desired.'

Then took he himself the holy vessel and came to Sir
Galahad. And he kneeled adown and received his Saviour.
And after him so received all his fellows. And they thought
it so sweet that it was marvellous to tell. Then said he to Sir
Galahad, 'Son, wotest thou what I hold betwixt my hands?'

'Nay!' said he, 'but if you tell me.'

'This is,' said he, 'the holy dish wherein I ate the lamb on
Easter Day and now hast thou seen that thou most desired to
see. But yet hast thou not seen it so openly as thou shalt see it
in the City of Sarras, in the spiritual palace. Therefore thou
must go hence and bear with thee this holy vessel, for this
night it shall depart from the realm of Logres and it shall
nevermore be seen here. And knowest thou wherefore? For
he is not served nor worshipped to his right by them of this
land, for they be turned to evil living, and therefore I shall
disherit them of the honour which I have done them. And

164

therefore go you three unto the sea where you shall find your ship ready, and with you take the sword with the strong girdles, and no more with you but Sir Percival and Sir Bors. Also I will that you take with you of this blood of this spear for to anoint the Maimed King, both his legs and his body, and he shall have his health.'

'Sir,' said Galahad, 'why shall not these other fellows go with us?'

'For this cause, for right as I depart my apostles, one here and another there, so I will that you depart. And two of you shall die in my service, and one of you shall come again and tell tidings.'

Then gave he them his blessing and vanished away. [XVII.21] And Sir Galahad went anon to the spear which lay upon the table, and touched the blood with his fingers and came after to the Maimed Knight and anointed his legs and his body. And therewith he clothed him anon and started upon his feet out of his bed as an whole man and thanked God that he had healed him. And anon he left the world and yielded himself to a place of religion of white monks, and was a fully holy man. . . .

Galahad, Percival and Bors ride and sail to the City of Sarras where, after a period in prison, Galahad becomes king and, after a short while, dies, bidding Bors greet 'Sir Launcelot, my father, and, as soon as you see him, bid him remember of this world unstable.' His soul ascends to Heaven and with him the Sankgreall and the spear. Percival dies a year or so later in a hermitage and Bors then returns to Camelot and gives Galahad's message to Launcelot.

Book Seven

Sir Launcelot and Queen Guenevere

[XVIII.1] So after the quest of the Sankgreall was fulfilled and all knights that were left alive were come home again unto the Table Round, as the Book of the Sankgreall makes mention, then was there great joy in the court, and, in especial, King Arthur and Queen Guenevere made great joy of the remnant that were come home. And passing glad was the King and the Queen of Sir Launcelot and of Sir Bors, for they had been passing long away in the quest of the Sankgreall.

Then, as the book says, Sir Launcelot began to resort unto Queen Guenevere again, and forgot the promise and the perfection that he made in the quest. For, as the book says, had not Sir Launcelot been in his privy thoughts and in his mind so set inwardly to the Queen as he was in seeming outward to God, there had no knight passed him in the quest of the Sankgreall. But ever his thoughts privily were on the Queen, and so they loved together more hotter than they did beforehand and had many such privy draughts together that many in the court spoke of it and, in especial, Sir Aggravaine, Sir Gawain's brother, for he was ever open-mouthed.

So it befell that Sir Launcelot had many resorts of ladies and damsels which daily resorted unto him to be their champion. In all such matters of right Sir Launcelot applied him daily to do for the pleasure of our Lord Jesu Christ, and ever, as much as he might, he withdrew him from the company of Queen Guenevere for to eschew the slander and noise. Wherefore the Queen waxed wroth with Sir Launcelot. So on a day she called him to her chamber and said thus: 'Sir Launcelot, I see and feel daily that your love begins to slake, for you have no joy to be in my presence, but ever you are out of this court, and quarrels and matters you have nowadays for ladies, maidens and gentlewomen [more] than ever you were wont to have beforehand.'

'Ah! madam,' said Sir Launcelot, 'in this you must hold me excused for divers causes: one is, I was but late in the quest of the Sankgreall, and I thank God of his great mercy, and never of my deserving, that I saw in that my quest as much as ever saw any sinful man living, and so was it told me. And if that I had not had my privy thoughts to return to [your] love again, as I do, I had seen as great mysteries as ever saw my son, Sir Galahad, Percival or Sir Bors. And, therefore, madam, I was but late in that quest, and, wit you well, madam, it may not be yet lightly forgotten, the high service in whom I did my diligent labour.

'Also, madam, wit you well that there be many men speak of our love in this court and have you and me greatly in await, as these Sir Aggravaine and Sir Mordred. And, madam, wit you well, I dread them more for your sake than for any fear of them I have of them myself, for I may happen to escape and ride myself in a great need where, madam, you must abide all that will be said unto you. And then, if that you fall in any distress throughout wilful folly, then is there none other help but by me and my blood.

'And, wit you well, madam, the boldness of you and me will bring us to shame and slander, and that were me loath to see you dishonoured. And that is the cause I take upon me more for to do for damsels and maidens than ever I did before, that men should understand my joy and delight is my pleasure to have ado for damsels and maidens.'

[XVIII.2] All this while the Queen stood still and let Sir Launcelot say what he would. And when he had all said she brast out weeping and so she sobbed and wept a great while. And when she might speak she said, 'Sir Launcelot, now I well understand that thou art a false, recrayed knight and a common lecherer, and lovest and holdest other ladies, and of me thou hast disdain and scorn. For, wit thou well, now I understand thy falsehood, I shall never love thee more, and look thou be never so hardy to come in my sight. And right here I discharge thee this court that thou never come within it, and I forfend thee my fellowship and upon pain of thy head that thou see me nevermore!'

Right so Sir Launcelot departed with great heaviness that unneth he might sustain himself for great dole-making. Then he called Sir Bors, Ector de Maris and Sir Lionel and told them how the Queen had forfend him the court and so he was in will to depart into his own country.

'Fair sir,' said Bors de Ganys, 'you shall [not] depart out of this land, by mine advice, for you must remember you what you are and renowned the most noblest knight of the world, and many great matters you have in hand. And women in their hastiness will do oftentimes that, after, them sore repents. And, therefore, by mine advice, you shall take your horse and ride to the good hermitage here beside Windsor, that sometime was a good knight. His name is Sir Brastias. And there shall you abide till that I send you word of better tidings.'

'Brother,' said Sir Launcelot, 'wit you well, I am full loath to depart out of this realm, but the Queen has defended me so highly that me seems she will never be my good lady as she has been.'

'Say you never so!' said Sir Bors, 'for many times ere this she has been wroth with you, and, after that, she was the first [that] repented it.'

'You say well,' said Sir Launcelot, 'for now will I do by

your counsel and take mine horse and mine harness and ride to the hermit, Sir Brastias, and there will I repose me till I hear some manner of tidings from you. But, fair brother, in that you can, get me the love of my lady, Queen Guenevere.'

'Sir,' said Sir Bors, 'you need not to move me of such matters, for, well you wot, I will do what I may to please you.'

And then Sir Launcelot departed suddenly and no creature wist where he was become but Sir Bors. So, when Sir Launcelot was departed, the Queen outward made no manner of sorrow in showing to none of his blood nor to none other. But, wit you well, inwardly, as the book says, she took great thought. But she bore it out with a proud countenance as though she felt no thought nor danger. . . .

To show that all knights are as pleasing to her as Launcelot, Queen Guenevere gives a large dinner at which she provides fruit, Gawain's delight. Pyonell poisons it intending to kill Gawain who slew Lamorak, his cousin. By mistake Patryse is poisoned and Guenevere is accused. King Arthur wishes Launcelot were present to defend her. Bors promises to be her champion but, warned by Bors, Launcelot appears on the day and wins, explaining that he owes a debt to Arthur for knighting him, and to Guenevere, for returning to him his lost sword that day. ' "And, therefore, . . . I promised her at that day ever to be her knight in right or in wrong." . . . And evermore the Queen . . . wept . . . that he had done to her so great kindness where she showed him great unkindness.'

Elayne of Astolat falls in love with Launcelot and nurses him when wounded in a tournament at which he was disguised and wore her favour. Guenevere is jealous. Bors wishes Launcelot could find it in him to love Elayne.

[XVIII.18] . . . And so, upon the morn, when Sir Launcelot should depart, fair Elayne brought her father with her, and Sir Lavayn and Sir Tirry, and then thus she said, [XVIII.19] 'My lord, Sir Launcelot, now I see you will depart from me. Now, fair knight and courteous knight,' said she, 'have mercy upon me, and suffer me not to die for your love.'

'Why, what would you that I did?' said Sir Launcelot.

'Sir, I would have you to my husband,' said Elayne.

'Fair damsel, I thank you heartily,' said Sir Launcelot, 'but truly,' said he, 'I cast me never to be wedded man.'

'Then, fair knight,' said she, 'will you be my paramour?'

'Jesu defend me!' said Sir Launcelot, 'for then I rewarded your father and your brother full evil for their great goodness.'

'Alas! then,' said she, 'I must die for your love.'

'You shall not do so,' said Sir Launcelot, 'for, wit you well, fair maiden, I might have been married, and I had willed, but I never applied me yet to be married. But because, fair damsel, that you love me as you say you do, I will, for your good will and kindness, show to you some goodness. That is this, that wheresoever you will beset your heart upon some good knight that will wed you, I shall give you together a thousand pound yearly, to you and to your heirs. This much will I give you, fair maiden, for your kindness, and always while I live to be your own knight.'

'Sir, of all this,' said the maiden, 'I will none, for, but if you will wed me, or to be my paramour at the least, wit you well, Sir Launcelot, my good days are done.'

'Fair damsel,' said Sir Launcelot, 'of these two things you must pardon me.'

Then she shrieked shrilly and fell down in a swoon. And then women bore her into her chamber and there she made overmuch sorrow. And then Sir Launcelot would depart, and there he asked Sir Lavayn what he would do.

'Sir, what should I do,' said Sir Lavayn, 'but follow you, but if you drive me from you or command me to go from you?'

Then came Sir Barnarde to Sir Launcelot and said to him, 'I cannot see but that my daughter will die for your sake.'

'Sir, I may not do withal,' said Sir Launcelot, 'for that me sore repents, for I report me to yourself that my proffer is fair. And me repents,' said Sir Launcelot, 'that she loves me as she does, for I was never the causer of it. For I report me unto your son I never, early nor late, proffered her bounty nor fair behests. And as for me,' said Sir Launcelot, 'I dare do that a knight should do and say that she is a clean maiden for me, both for deed and will. For I am right heavy of her distress. For she is a full fair maiden, good and gentle, and well taught.'

'Father,' said Sir Lavayn, 'I dare make good she is a clean maiden as for my lord, Sir Launcelot. But she does as I do, for sithen I saw first my lord, Sir Launcelot, I could never depart from him, neither nought I will, and I may follow him.'

Then Sir Launcelot took his leave and so they departed and came to Winchester. And, when King Arthur wist that Sir Launcelot was come whole and sound, the King made great joy of him, and so did Sir Gawain and all the knights of the Round Table except Sir Aggravaine and Sir Mordred. Also Queen Guenevere was wood wroth with Sir Launcelot and would by no means speak with him, but estranged herself from him. And Sir Launcelot made all the means that he might for to speak with the Queen, but it would not be.

Now speak we of the Fair Maiden of Astolat that made such sorrow day and night that she never slept, ate, nor drank, and ever she made her complaint unto Sir Launcelot. So when she had thus endured a ten days that she feebled so that she must needs pass out of this world, then she shrove her clean and received her Creator. And ever she complained still upon Sir Launcelot. Then her ghostly father bade her leave such thoughts. Then she said,

'Why should I leave such thoughts? Am I not an earthly woman? And all the while the breath is in my body I may complain me, for my belief is that I do none offence – though

I love an earthly man—unto God, for he formed me thereto
and all manner of good love comes of God. And other than
good love loved I never Sir Launcelot du Lake. And I take
God to record, I loved never none but him, nor never shall, of
earthly creature. And a clean maiden I am for him and for all
others. And sithen it is the sufferance of God that I shall die
for so noble a knight, I beseech thee, high Father of Heaven,
have mercy upon me and my soul, and upon mine innumer-
able pains that I suffer may be aligeaunce of part of my sins.
For, sweet Lord Jesu,' said the fair maiden, 'I take God to
record I was never to thee great offender nor against thy
laws, but that I loved this noble knight, Sir Launcelot, out of
measure. And of myself, good Lord, I had no might to withstand the fervent love wherefore I have my death.'

And then she called her father, Sir Barnarde, and her
brother, Sir Tirry, and heartily she prayed her father that her
brother might write a letter like as she did endite, and so her
father granted her. And when the letter was written, word by
word like as she devised it, then she prayed her father that
she might be watched until she were [dead].

'And while my body is hot let this letter be put in my
right hand and my hand bound fast to the letter until that I
be cold. And let me be put in a fair bed with all the richest
clothes that I have about me, and so let my bed and all my
richest clothes be led with me in a chariot unto the next place
where the Thames is, and there let me be put within a barget
and but one man with me, such as you trust, to stir me
thither, and that my barget be covered with black samite
over and over. And thus, father, I beseech you, let it be
done.'

So her father granted her faithfully all things should be
done like as she had devised. Then her father and her brother
made great dole for her. And when this was done, anon she
died. And when she was dead the corpse and the bed all was
led the next way unto the Thames and there a man and the

corpse and all things as she had devised was put in the Thames. And so the man stirred the barget unto West-minster, and there it rubbed and rolled to and fro a great while ere any man espied it.

[XVIII.20] So by fortune King Arthur and Queen Guenevere were talking together at a window and so, as they looked into the Thames, they espied that black barget and had marvel what it meant. Then the King called Sir Kay and showed it him.

'Sir,' said Sir Kay, 'wit you well, there is some new tidings.'

'Therefore go you thither,' said the King to Sir Kay, 'and take with you Sir Braundiles and Sir Aggravaine and bring me ready word what is there.'

Then these three knights departed and came to the barget and went in. And there they found the fairest corpse lying in a rich bed that ever they saw, and a poor man sitting in the barget's end and no word would [he] speak. So these three knights returned unto the King again and told him what they found.

'That fair corpse will I see,' said the King.

And so the King took the Queen by the hand and went thither. Then the King made the barget to be held fast, and then the King and the Queen went in with certain knights with them, and there he saw the fairest woman lie in a rich bed, covered unto her middle with many rich cloths and all was of cloth of gold. And she lay as she had smiled.

Then the Queen espied the letter in her right hand and told the King. Then the King took it and said, 'Now am I sure this letter will tell us what she was and why she is come hither.'

So then the King and the Queen went out of the barget and so commanded a certain ⟨number⟩ to wait upon the barget. And so when the King was come to his chamber he called many knights about him and said that he would wit openly what was written within that letter. Then the King broke it and made a clerk to read it, and this was the intent of the letter:

'Most noble knight, my lord, Sir Launcelot, now has death made us two at debate for your love. And I was your lover, that men called the Fair Maiden of Astolat. Therefore unto all ladies I make my moan, yet for my soul you pray and bury me at the least, and offer you my mass-penny. This is my last request. And a clean maiden I died, I take God to witness. And pray for my soul, Sir Launcelot, as thou art peerless.'

This was all the substance in the letter. And when it was read the King, the Queen and all the knights wept for pity of the doleful complaints. Then was Sir Launcelot sent for and, when he was come, King Arthur made the letter to be read to him. And when Sir Launcelot heard it, word by word, he said,

'My lord, Arthur, wit you well, I am right heavy of the death of this fair lady. And God knows I was never causer of her death by my willing, and that will I report me unto her own brother that here is, Sir Lavayn. I will not say nay,' said Sir Launcelot, 'but that she was both fair and good, and much I was beholden unto her. But she loved me out of measure.'

'Sir,' said the Queen, 'you might have showed her some bounty and gentleness which might have preserved her life!'

'Madam,' said Sir Launcelot, 'she would none other ways be answered but that she would be my wife or else my paramour, and of these two I would not grant her. But I proffered her, for her good love that she showed me, a thousand pounds yearly to her and to her heirs, and to wed any manner of knight that she could find best to love in her heart. For, madam,' said Sir Launcelot, 'I love not to be constrained to love, for love must only arise of the heart's self and not by none constraint.'

'That is truth, sir,' said the King, 'and with many knights love is free in himself, and never will be bound, for where he is bound he looses himself.'

Then said the King unto Sir Launcelot, 'Sir, it will be your worship that you oversee that she be interred worshipfully.'

'Sir,' said Sir Launcelot, 'that shall be done as I can best devise.'

And so many knights yode thither to behold that fair dead maiden. And so upon the morn she was interred richly. And Sir Launcelot offered her mass-penny. And all those knights of the Table Round that were there at that time offered with Sir Launcelot. And then the poor [man] went again with the barget. Then the Queen sent for Sir Launcelot and prayed him of mercy, for why that she had been wroth with him causeless.

'This is not the first time,' said Sir Launcelot, 'that you have been displeased with me causeless. But, madam, ever I must suffer you, but what sorrow that I endure, you take no force.'

So this passed on all that winter with all manner of hunting and hawking, and jousts and tourneys were many betwixt many great lords. And ever in all places Sir Lavayn got great worship, that he was nobly defamed among many knights of the Table Round.

[XVIII.21] Thus it passed on till Christmas, and then every day there was jousts made for a diamond—who that jousted best should have a diamond. But Sir Launcelot would not joust but if it were a great jousts cried. But Sir Lavayn jousted there all the Christmas passingly well and was best praised, for there were but few that did so well. Wherefore all manner of knights deemed that Sir Lavayn should be made knight of the Table Round at the next feast of Pentecost. . . .

At a great joust on Candlemasday Launcelot, in disguise, but wearing Guenevere's favour, with Lavayn fights King Arthur and is joined by Gareth who sees his need and fights well. He is also disguised: 'Sir Launcelot knew not Sir Gareth, for, and Sir Tristram de Lyonesse or Sir Lamorak de Galys had been alive, Sir Launcelot would have deemed he had been one of them twain.' King Arthur also praises Gareth for helping Launcelot:

[XVIII.24] 'For ever it is,' said King Arthur, 'a worshipful knight's deed to help and succour another worshipful knight when he sees him in danger. For ever a worshipful man will be loath to see a worshipful man shamed, and he that is of no worship and meddles with cowardice, never shall he show gentleness nor no manner of goodness where he sees a man in danger, for then will a coward never show mercy. And always a good man will do ever to another man as he would be done to himself.'

So then there were made great feasts unto kings and dukes, and revel, game and play, and all manner of nobless was used. And he that was courteous, true and faithful to his friend was that time cherished.

[XVIII.25] And thus it passed on from Candlemas until Easter, that the month of May was come when every lusty heart begins to blossom and to burgeon. For, like as trees and herbs burgeon and flourish in May, in like wise every lusty heart that is any manner of lover springs, burgeons, buds and flourishes in lusty deeds. For it gives unto all lovers courage, that lusty month of May, in something to constrain him to some manner of thing more than in any other month, for diverse causes. For then all herbs and trees renew a man and woman, and in like wise lovers call to their mind old gentleness and old service and many kind deeds that was forgotten by negligence.

For, like as winter rasure does always arace and deface green summer, so fares it by unstable love in man and woman, for in many persons there is no stability. For [we] may see all day for a little blast of winter's rasure anon we shall deface and lay apart true love for little or nought that cost much thing. This is no wisdom neither no stability but it is feebleness of nature and great disworship, whosoever uses this.

Therefore, like as May month flowers and flourishes in every man's garden, so in like wise let every man of worship flourish his heart in this world, first unto God and next unto the joy of them that he promised his faith unto. For there was never worshipful man nor worshipful woman but they loved one better than another, and worship in arms may never be foyled. But first reserve the honour to God, and secondly thy quarrel must come of thy lady. And such love I call virtuous love.

But nowadays men cannot love seven-nights but they must have all their desires. That love may not endure by reason, for where they are soon accorded and hasty, heat soon cools. And right so fares the love nowadays, soon hot, soon cold. This is no stability. But the old love was not so, for men and women could love together seven years and no licorous lusts was betwixt them, and then was love, truth and faithfulness. And so in like wise was used such love in King Arthur's days.

Wherefore I liken love nowadays unto summer and winter, for, like as the one is cold and the other is hot, so fares love nowadays. And, therefore, all you that are lovers, call unto your remembrance the month of May, like as did Queen Guenevere, for whom I make here a little mention, that while she lived she was a true lover and therefore she had a good end.

[XIX.1] So it befell in the month of May, Queen Guenevere called unto her ten knights of the Table Round and she gave them warning that early upon the morn she would ride amaying into woods and fields beside Westminster, 'and I warn you that there be none of you but he is well horsed and that you all are clothed all in green or in silk or in cloth. And I shall bring with me ten ladies, and every knight shall have a lady by him. And every knight shall have a squire and two yeomen, and I will that all be well horsed.'

So they made them ready in the freshest manner, and these were the names of the knights: Sir Kay le Seneschal, Sir Aggravaine, Sir Braundiles, Sir Sagramour le Desyrus, Sir Dodynas le Saveage, Sir Ozanna le Cure Hardy, Sir Ladynas of the Forest Savayge, Sir Persaunte of Inde, Sir Ironsyde, that was called the knight of the Red Laundes, and Sir Pelleas the Lover. And these ten knights made them ready in the freshest manner to ride with the Queen.

And so upon the morn, ere it were day, in a May morning, they took their horses with the Queen and rode amaying in woods and meadows as it pleased them, in great joy and delights. For the Queen had cast to have been again with King Arthur at the furthest by ten of the clock, and so was that time her purpose.

Then there was a knight which hight Sir Mellyagaunce, and he was son unto King Bagdemagus, and this knight had that time a castle of the gift of King Arthur within seven miles of Westminster. And this knight, Sir Mellyagaunce, loved passingly well Queen Guenevere, and so had he done long and many years. And the book says he had lain in await for to steal away the Queen, but evermore he forbore for because of Sir Launcelot. For in no wise he would meddle with the Queen and Sir Launcelot were in her company or else and he were nearhand.

And that time was such a custom that the Queen rode never without a great fellowship of men of arms about her. And they were many good knights and the most part were young men that would have worship and they were called the Queen's Knights. And never in no battle, tournament nor jousts they bore none of them no manner of acknowledging of their own arms but plain white shields, and thereby they were called the Queen's Knights. And when it happed any of them to be of great worship by his noble deeds, then, at the next feast of Pentecost, if there were any slain or dead (as there was no year that there failed but there were some dead), then was there chosen in his stead that was dead the most man of worship that were called the Queen's Knights. And thus they came up first, ere they were renowned men of worship, both Sir Launcelot and all the remnant of them.

But this knight Sir Mellyagaunce had espied the Queen well and her purpose, and how Sir Launcelot was not with her, and how she had no men of arms with her but the ten noble knights all arrayed in green for maying. Then he purveyed him a twenty men of arms and an hundred archers for to distress the Queen and her knights, for he thought that time was best season to take the Queen.

[XIX.2] So as [the Queen] was out amaying with all her knights which were bedaished with herbs, mosses and flowers in the freshest manner, right so there came out of a wood Sir Mellyagaunce with an eight-score men, all harnessed as they should fight in a battle of arrest, and bade the Queen and her knights abide, for magre their heads they should abide.

'Traitor knight!' said Queen Guenevere, 'what cast thou to do? Wilt thou shame thyself? Bethink thee how thou art a king's son and a knight of the Table Round, and thou thus to be about to dishonour the noble king that made thee knight! Thou shamest all knighthood and thyself and me! And I let thee wit thou shalt never shame me, for I had lever cut mine own throat in twain rather than thou should dishonour me!'

'As for all this language,' said Sir Mellyagaunce, 'be as it be may! For, wit you well, madam, I have loved you many a year, and never ere now could I get you at such avail. And, therefore, I will take you as I find you.'

Then spoke all the ten noble knights at once and said, 'Sir

179

Mellyagaunce, wit thou well thou art about to jeopardy thy worship to dishonour, and also you cast to jeopardy your persons. Howbeit we be unarmed and you have us at a great advantage, for it seems by you that you have laid watch upon us. But rather than you should put the Queen to a shame and us all, we had as lief to depart from our lives, for, and we otherways did, we were shamed for ever.'

Then said Sir Mellyagaunce, 'Dress you as well as you can, and keep the Queen!'

Then the ten knights of the Round Table drew their swords, and these others let run at them with their spears, and the ten knights manly abode them and smote away their spears that no spear did them no harm. Then they lashed together with swords, and anon Sir Kay, Sir Sagramour, Sir Aggravaine, Sir Dodynas, Sir Ladynas and Sir Ozanna were smitten to the earth with grimly wounds. Then Sir Braundiles and Sir Persaunte, Sir Ironsyde and Sir Pelleas fought long, and they were sore wounded, for these ten knights, ere ever they were laid to the ground, slew forty men of the boldest and the best of them.

So when the Queen saw her knights thus dolefully wounded and needs must be slain at the last, then for very pity and sorrow she cried and said, 'Sir Mellyagaunce, slay not my noble knights! And I will go with thee upon this covenant, that thou save them and suffer them no more to be hurt, with this that they are led with me wheresoever thou leadest me. For I will rather slay myself than I will go with thee, unless that these noble knights may be in my presence.'

'Madam,' said Sir Mellyagaunce, 'for your sake they shall be led with you into mine own castle, with that you will be ruled and ride with me.'

Then the Queen prayed the four knights to leave their fighting and she and they would not depart.

'Madam,' said Sir Pelleas, 'we will do as you do, for, as for me, I take no force of my life nor death.' For, as the French

book says, Sir Pelleas gave such buffets there that none
armour might hold him.

[XIX.3] Then by the Queen's commandment they left
battle and dressed the wounded knights on horseback, some
sitting and some overthwart their horses, that it was pity to
behold. And then Sir Mellyagaunce charged the Queen and
all her knights that none of her fellowship should depart
from her, for full sore he dread Sir Launcelot du Lake, lest
he should have any knowledging. And all this espied the
Queen, and privily she called unto her a child of her chamber
which was swiftly horsed of a great advantage.

'Now go thou,' said she, 'when thou seest thy time, and
bear this ring unto Sir Launcelot du Lake and pray him, as
he loves me, that he will see me and rescue me, if ever he will
have joy of me. And spare not thy horse,' said the Queen,
'neither for water nor for land.'

So this child espied his time, and lightly he took his horse
with spurs and departed as fast as he might. And when Sir
Mellyagaunce saw him so flee, he understood that it was by
the Queen's commandment for to warn Sir Launcelot. Then
they that were best horsed chased him and shot at him, but
from them all the child went deliverly.

And then Sir Mellyagaunce said unto the Queen, 'Madam,
you are about to betray me, but I shall ordain for Sir
Launcelot that he shall not come lightly at you.'

And then he rode with her and all the fellowship in all the
haste that they might. And so by the way Sir Mellyagaunce
laid in buishment of the best archers that he had, of a thirty,
to await upon Sir Launcelot, charging them that, if they saw
such a manner of knight come by the way upon a white horse,
'that in any wise you slay his horse, but in no manner have
you ado with him bodily, for he is overhardy to be overcome'.
So this was done and they were come to his castle. But in no
wise the Queen would never let none of the ten knights and
her ladies out of her sight, but always they were in her

presence. For the book says Sir Mellyagaunce durst make
no maystries for dread of Sir Launcelot, insomuch he deemed
that he had warning.

So when the child was departed from the fellowship of Sir
Mellyagaunce, within a while ⟨he⟩ came to Westminster,
and anon he found Sir Launcelot. And when he had told his
message and delivered him the Queen's ring, 'Alas!' said Sir
Launcelot, 'now am I shamed for ever unless that I may
rescue that noble lady from dishonour!'

Then eagerly he asked his arms. And ever the child told
Sir Launcelot how the ten knights fought marvellously and
how Sir Pelleas, Sir Ironsyde, Sir Braundiles and Sir Persaunte of Inde fought strongly, but, namely, Sir Pelleas —
there might none harness hold him. And how they all fought
till they were laid to the [earth], and how the Queen made
appointment for to save their lives and to go with Sir
Mellyagaunce.

'Alas!' said Sir Launcelot, 'that most noble lady, that she
should be so destroyed! I had lever,' said Sir Launcelot, 'than
all France that I had been there, well armed.'

So when Sir Launcelot was armed and upon his horse he
prayed the child of the Queen's chamber to warn Sir Lavayn
how suddenly he was departed and for what cause. 'And pray
him, as he loves me, that he will hie him after me, and that he
stint not until he come to the castle where Sir Mellyagaunce
abides, for there,' said Sir Launcelot, 'he shall hear of me,
and I be a man living!'

[XIX.4] Then Sir Launcelot rode as fast as he might, and
the book says he took the water at Westminster Bridge and
made his horse swim over the Thames unto Lambeth. And
so within a while he came to the same place thereas the ten
noble knights fought with Sir Mellyagaunce. And then Sir
Launcelot followed the track until that he came to a wood,
and there was a strait way, and there the thirty archers bade
Sir Launcelot turn again and follow no longer that track.

'What commandment have you,' said Sir Launcelot, 'to cause me, that am a knight of the Round Table, to leave my right way?'

'These ways shalt thou leave or else thou shalt go it on thy foot, for, wit thou well, thy horse shall be slain.'

'That is little maystry,' said Sir Launcelot, 'to slay mine horse! But, as for myself, when my horse is slain I give right nought of you, not and you were five hundred more!'

So then they shot Sir Launcelot's horse and smote him with many arrows. And then Sir Launcelot avoided his horse and went on foot, but there were so many ditches and hedges betwixt them and him that he might not meddle with none of them.

'Alas! for shame!' said Sir Launcelot, 'that ever one knight should betray another knight! But it is an old-said saw, "A good man is never in danger but when he is in the danger of a coward." '

Then Sir Launcelot walked on a while and was sore encumbered with his armour, his shield and his spear. Wit you well he was full sore annoyed! And full loath he was for to leave anything that longed unto him, for he dread sore the treason of Sir Mellyagaunce. Then by fortune there came a chariot that came thither to fetch wood.

'Say me, carter,' said Sir Launcelot, 'what shall I give thee to suffer me to leap into thy chariot, and that thou wilt bring me unto a castle within these two miles?'

'Thou shalt not enter into this chariot,' said the carter, 'for I am sent for to fetch wood.'

'Unto whom?' said Sir Launcelot.

'Unto my lord, Sir Mellyagaunce,' said the carter.

'And with him would I speak,' said Sir Launcelot.

'Thou shalt not go with me!' said the carter.

When Sir Launcelot leapt to him and gave him backward with his gauntlet a reremain, that he fell to the earth stark dead, then the other carter, his fellow, was afraid, and

weened to have gone the same way. And then he said, 'Fair
lord! save my life and I shall bring you where you will.'

'Then I charge thee,' said Sir Launcelot, 'that thou drive
me and this chariot unto Sir Mellyagaunce's gate.'

'Then leap you up into the chariot,' said the carter, 'and
you shall be there anon.'

So the carter drove on a great wallop and Sir Launcelot's
horse followed the chariot with more than forty arrows in
him. And more than an hour and an half Queen Guenevere
was awaiting in a bay-window. Then one of her ladies espied
an armed knight standing in a chariot.

'Ah! see, madam,' said the lady, 'where rides in a chariot
a goodly armed knight, and we suppose he rides unto hanging.'

'Where?' said the Queen.

Then she espied by his shield that it was Sir Launcelot,
and then was she aware where came his horse after the chariot
and ever he trod his guts and his paunch under his feet.

'Alas!' said the Queen, 'now I may prove and see that well
is that creature that has a trusty friend. A! ha!' said Queen
Guenevere, 'I see well that you were hard bested when you
ride in a chariot!'

And then she rebuked that lady that likened Sir Launcelot
to ride in a chariot to hanging. 'Forsooth it was foul-
mouthed,' said the Queen, 'and evil likened, so for to liken
the most noble knight of the world unto such a shameful
death. Ah! Jesu defend him and keep him,' said the Queen,
'from all mischievous end!'

So by this was Sir Launcelot come to the gates of that
castle, and there he descended down and cried, that all the
castle might ring, 'Where art thou, thou false traitor, Sir
Mellyagaunce, and knight of the Table Round? Come forth,
thou traitor knight! thou and all thy fellowship with thee,
for here I am, Sir Launcelot du Lake, that shall fight with
you all!'

And therewithal he bore the gate wide open upon the porter and smote him under the ear with his gauntlet that his neck brast in two pieces. [XIX.5] When Sir Mellyagaunce heard that Sir Launcelot was come he ran unto the Queen and fell upon his knee and said, 'Mercy! madam, for now I put me wholly in your good grace.'

'What ails you now?' said Queen Guenevere. 'Parde, I might well wit that some good knight would revenge me, though my lord, King Arthur, knew not of this your work.'

'Ah! madam,' said Sir Mellyagaunce, 'all this that is amiss on my part shall be amended right as yourself will devise, and wholly I put me in your grace.'

'What would you that I did?' said the Queen.

'Madam, I would no more,' said Sir Mellyagaunce, 'but that you would take all in your own hands and that you will rule my lord, Sir Launcelot. And such cheer as may be made him in this poor castle you and he shall have until tomorn, and then may you and all they return again unto Westminster. And my body and all that I have I shall put in your rule.'

'You say well,' said the Queen, 'and better is peace than evermore war, and the less noise the more is my worship.'

Then the Queen and her ladies went down unto Sir Launcelot that stood wood wroth out of measure to abide battle, and ever he said, 'Thou traitor knight, come forth!' Then the Queen came unto him and said, 'Sir Launcelot, why be you so amoved?'

'Ah! madam,' said Sir Launcelot, 'why ask you me that question? For me seems you ought to be more wrother than I am, for you have the hurt and the dishonour. For, wit you well, madam, my hurt is but little in regard for the slaying of a mare's son, but the despite grieves me much more than all my hurt.'

'Truly,' said the Queen, 'you say truth, but heartily I

thank you,' said the Queen. 'But you must come in with me peaceably, for all thing is put in mine hand, and all that is amiss shall be amended, for the knight full sore repents him of this misadventure that is befallen him.'

'Madam,' said Sir Launcelot, 'sith it is so that you are accorded with him, as for me I may not againsay it, howbeit Sir Mellyagaunce has done full shamefully to me and cowardly. And, madam,' said Sir Launcelot, 'and I had wist that you would have been so lightly accorded with him I would not have made such haste unto you.'

'Why say you so?' said the Queen. 'Do you forthink yourself of your good deeds? Wit you well,' said the Queen. 'I accorded never with him for no favour nor love that I had unto him, but of every shameful noise, in wisdom, to lay adown.'

'Madam,' said Sir Launcelot, 'you understand full well I was never willing nor glad of shameful slander nor noise. And there is neither king, queen nor knight that bears the life, except my lord, King Arthur, and you, madam, that should let me, but I should make Sir Mellyagaunce's heart full cold ere ever I departed from hence!'

'That wot I well,' said the Queen, 'but what will you more? You shall have all thing ruled as you list to have it.'

'Madam!' said Sir Launcelot, 'so you be pleased, as for my part you shall soon please me.'

Right so the Queen took Sir Launcelot by the bare hand, for he had put off his gauntlet. And so she went with him to her chamber, and then she commanded him to be unarmed. And then Sir Launcelot asked the Queen where were her ten knights that were wounded with her. Then she showed them unto him and there they made great joy of the coming of Sir Launcelot, and he made great sorrow of their hurts. And there Sir Launcelot told them how cowardly and traitorly he set archers to slay his horse, and he was fain to put himself in a chariot. And thus they complained every ⟨one⟩ to other, and full fain they would have been revenged, but they kept the peace because of the Queen.

(Then, as the French book says, Sir Launcelot was called many days after Le Chevalier de la Charrette, and so he did many deeds and great adventures. And so we leave off here of 'Le Chevalier de la Charrette' and turn we to this tale.)

So Sir Launcelot had great cheer with the Queen. And then he made a promise with the Queen that the same night he should come to a window outward toward a garden, and that window was barred with iron. And there Sir Launcelot promised to meet her when all folks were asleep.

So then came Sir Lavayn driving to the gates saying, 'Where is my lord, Sir Launcelot?' And anon he was sent for. And when Sir Lavayn saw Sir Launcelot he said, 'Ah! my lord, I found how you were hard bested, for I have found your horse that is slain with arrows.'

'As for that,' said Sir Launcelot, 'I pray you, Sir Lavayn, speak you of other matters and let this pass, and right it another time, and we may.'

[XIX.6] Then the knights that were hurt were searched, and soft salves were laid to their wounds. And so it passed on till supper time. And all the cheer that might be made them there was done unto the Queen and all her knights. And when season was they went unto their chambers, but in no wise the Queen would not suffer her wounded knights to be from her, but that they were laid within draughts by her chamber, upon beds and pallets, that she might herself see unto them that they wanted nothing.

So when Sir Launcelot was in his chamber which was assigned unto him he called unto him Sir Lavayn and told him that night he must speak with his lady, Queen Guenevere.

'Sir,' said Sir Lavayn, 'let me go with you, and it please you, for I dread me sore of [the] treason of Sir Mellyagaunce.'

'Nay!' said Sir Launcelot, 'I thank you, but I will have nobody with me.'

Then Sir Launcelot took his sword in his hand and privily went to the place where he had espied a ladder beforehand, and that he took under his arm and bore it through the garden and set it up to the window. And anon the Queen was there ready to meet him. And then they made their complaints to other of many diverse things and then Sir Launcelot wished that he might have come in to her.

'Wit you well,' said the Queen, 'I would as fain as you that you might come in to me.'

'Would you so, madam,' said Sir Launcelot, 'with your heart, that I were with you?'

'Yea! truly,' said the Queen.

'Then shall I prove my might,' said Sir Launcelot, 'for your love.'

And then he set his hands upon the bars of iron and pulled at them with such a might that he brast them clean out of the stone walls. And therewithal one of the bars of iron cut the brawn of his hands throughout to the bone. And then he leapt into the chamber to the Queen.

'Make you no noise,' said the Queen, 'for my wounded knights lie here fast by me.'

So, to pass upon this tale, Sir Launcelot went to bed with the Queen and took no force of his hurt hand, but took his pleasaunce and his liking until it was the dawning of the day. For, wit you well, he slept not but watched. And, when he saw his time that he might tarry no longer, he took his leave and departed at the window and put it together as well as he might again, and so departed to his own chamber. And there he told Sir Lavayn how that he was hurt. Then Sir Lavayn dressed his hand [and staunched] it and put upon it a glove that it should not be espied. And so they lay long abed in the morning till it was nine of the clock.

Then Sir Mellyagaunce went to the Queen's chamber and found her ladies there ready clothed. 'Ah! Jesu, mercy,' said Sir Mellyagaunce, 'what ails you, madam, that you sleep this long?'

And therewithal he opened the curtain for to behold her. And then was he aware where she lay and all the head-sheet, pillow and over-sheet was all be-bled of the blood of Sir Launcelot and of his hurt hand. When Sir Mellyagaunce espied that blood, then he deemed in her that she was false to the King, and that some of the wounded knights had lain by her all that night.

'A! ha! madam,' said Sir Mellyagaunce, 'now I have found you a false traitress unto my lord, Arthur, for now I prove well it was not for nought that you laid these wounded knights within the bounds of your chamber. Therefore I call you of treason before my lord, King Arthur. And now I have proved you, madam, with a shameful deed. And that they be all false, or some of them, I will make it good, for a wounded knight this night has lain by you.'

'That is false!' said the Queen, 'that I will report me unto them.'

When the ten knights heard Sir Mellyagaunce's words they spoke all at once and said, 'Sir Mellyagaunce, thou falsely beliest my lady, the Queen, and that we will make good upon thee, any of us. Now choose which thou list of us, when we are whole of the wounds thou gavest us.'

'You shall not! Away with your proud language! For here you may all see that a wounded knight this night has lain by the Queen.'

Then they all looked and were sore ashamed when they saw that blood. And, wit you well, Sir Mellyagaunce was passing glad that he had the Queen at such advantage, for he deemed by that to hide his own treason. And so in this rumour came in Sir Launcelot and found them at a great affray.

[XIX.7] 'What array is this?' said Sir Launcelot.

Then Sir Mellyagaunce told them what he had found and so he showed him the Queen's bed.

'Now truly,' said Sir Launcelot, 'you did not your part nor knightly to touch a Queen's bed while it was drawn and she lying therein. And I dare say,' said Sir Launcelot, 'my lord, King Arthur, himself would not have displayed her curtains, and she being within her bed, unless that it had pleased him to have lain him down by her. And, therefore, Sir Mellyagaunce, you have done unworshipfully and shamefully to yourself.'

'Sir, I wot not what you mean,' said Sir Mellyagaunce, 'but well I am sure there has one of her hurt knights lain with her this night. And that will I prove with mine hands, that she is a traitress unto my lord, King Arthur.'

'Beware what you do,' said Sir Launcelot, 'for, an you say so and will prove it, it will be taken at your hands.'

'My lord, Sir Launcelot,' said Sir Mellyagaunce, 'I rede you beware what you do! For, though you are never so good a knight—as I wot well you are renowned the best knight of the world—yet should you be advised to do battle in a wrong quarrel, for God will have a stroke in every battle.'

'As for that,' said Sir Launcelot, 'God is to be dread! But, as to that, I say nay plainly—that this night there lay none of these ten knights wounded with my lady, Queen Guenevere! And that will I prove with mine hands, that you say untruly in that. Now, what say you?' said Sir Launcelot.

'Thus I say!' said Sir Mellyagaunce, 'Here is my glove that she is a traitress unto my lord, King Arthur, and that this night one of the wounded knights lay with her.'

'Well, sir, and I receive your glove!' said Sir Launcelot. And anon they were sealed with their signets and delivered unto the ten knights.

'At what day shall we do battle together?' said Sir Launcelot.

'This day eight days,' said Sir Mellyagaunce, 'in the field beside Westminster.'

'I am agreed,' said Sir Launcelot.

'But now,' said Sir Mellyagaunce, 'sithen it is so that we must needs fight together, I pray you as you are a noble knight, await me with no treason neither no villainy the meanwhile, neither none for you.'

'So God me help,' said Sir Launcelot, 'you shall right well wit that I was never of no such conditions. For I report me to all knights that ever have known me, I fared never with no treason, neither I loved never the fellowship of him that fared with treason.'

'Then let us go unto dinner,' said Sir Mellyagaunce, 'and after dinner the Queen and you may ride all unto Westminster.'

'I will well,' said Sir Launcelot.

Then Sir Mellyagaunce said unto Sir Launcelot, 'Sir, pleases you to see estures of this castle?'

'With a good will,' said Sir Launcelot.

And then they went together from chamber to chamber, for Sir Launcelot dreaded no perils, for ever a man of worship and of prowess dreads but little of perils, for they ween that every man is as they are. But ever he that fares with treason puts often a true man in great danger. And so it befell upon Sir Launcelot that no peril dreaded: as he went with Sir Mellyagaunce he trod on a trap and the board rolled and there Sir Launcelot fell down more than ten fathom into a cave full of straw. And then Sir Mellyagaunce departed and made no fare, no more than he that wist not where he was.

And when Sir Launcelot was thus missed they marvelled where he was become. And then the Queen and many of them deemed that he was departed, as he was wont to do, suddenly, for Sir Mellyagaunce made suddenly to put aside Sir Lavayn's horse that they might all understand that Sir Launcelot were departed suddenly.

So [then] it passed on till after-dinner, and then Sir Lavayn would not stint until he had horse-litters for the wounded knights that they might be carried in them. And so with the Queen both ladies and gentlewomen, and so they rode unto Westminster, and there the knights told how Sir Mellyagaunce had appealed the Queen of high treason and how Sir Launcelot received the glove of him, 'and this day, eight days, they shall do battle before you'.

'By my head,' said King Arthur, 'I am afraid Sir Mellyagaunce has charged himself with a great charge. But where is Sir Launcelot?' said the King.

'Sir, we wot not where he is, but we deem he is ridden to some adventure, as he is oftentimes wont to do, for he had Sir Lavayn's horse.'

'Let him be,' said the King, 'for he will be found, but if he is trapped with some treason.'

[XIX.8] Thus leave we Sir Launcelot lying within that cave in great pain. And every day there came a lady and brought his meat and his drink and wooed him every day to have lain by her, and ever Sir Launcelot said her nay. Then said she, 'Sir, you are not wise, for you may never out of this prison but if you have my help. And also your lady, Queen Guenevere, shall be burnt in your default, unless that you be there at the day of battle.'

'God defend,' said Sir Launcelot, 'that she should be burnt in my default! And if it be so,' said Sir Launcelot, 'that I may not be there, it shall be well understood, both by the King and the Queen and by all men of worship, that I am dead, sick, or in prison. For all men that know me will say for me that I am in some evil case and I am not that day there. And thus well I understand that there is some good knight, either of my blood, or some other that loves me, that will take my quarrel in hand. And, therefore,' said Sir Launcelot, 'wit you well, you shall not fear me, and if there were no more women in all this land but you, yet shall not I have ado with you.'

'Then are you shamed,' said the lady, 'and destroyed for ever.'

'As for world's shame, now Jesu defend me! And as for my distress, it is welcome, whatsoever it be that God sends me.'

So she came to him again the same day that the battle should be and said, 'Sir Launcelot, bethink you, for you are too hard-hearted. And, therefore, and you would but once kiss me, I should deliver you and your armour and the best horse that was within Sir Mellyagaunce's stable.'

'As for to kiss you,' said Sir Launcelot, 'I may do that and lose no worship. And, wit you well, and I understood there were any disworship for to kiss you, I would not do it.'

And then he kissed her. And anon she got him up unto his armour, and, when he was armed, she brought him to a stable where stood twelve good coursers and bade him to choose of the best. Then Sir Launcelot looked upon a white courser and that liked him best, and anon he commanded him to be saddled with the best saddle of war, and so it was done. Then he got his own spear in his hand and his sword by his side, and then he commended the lady unto God and said, 'Lady, for this day's deed I shall do you service, if ever it lie in my power.'

[XIX.9] Now leave we here Sir Launcelot, all that ever he might wallop, and speak we of Queen Guenevere that was brought to a fire to be burnt. For Sir Mellyagaunce was sure, him thought, that Sir Launcelot should not be at that battle, and therefore he ever cried upon Sir Arthur to do him justice or else bring forth Sir Launcelot.

Then was the King and all the court full sore abashed and shamed that the Queen should have been burnt in the default

of Sir Launcelot. 'My lord, King Arthur,' said Sir Lavayn,
'you may understand that it is not well with my lord, Sir
Launcelot, for, and he were alive, so he be not sick or in
prison, wit you well he would have been here. For never
heard you that ever he failed yet his part for whom he should
do battle for. And therefore,' said Sir Lavayn, 'my lord,
King Arthur, I beseech you that you will give me licence to
do battle here this day for my lord and master and for to
save my lady, the Queen.'

'Grauntmercy! gentle Sir Lavayn,' said King Arthur, 'for
I dare say all that Sir Mellyagaunce puts upon my lady, the
Queen, is wrong. For I have spoken with ail the ten wounded
knights and there is not one of them, and he were whole and
able to do battle, but he would prove upon Sir Mellyagaunce's body [that it is false that he puts upon my Queen].'

'And so shall I,' said Sir Lavayn, 'in the defence of my
lord, Sir Launcelot, and you will give me leave.'

'And I give you leave,' said King Arthur, 'and do your
best, for I dare well say there is some treason done to Sir
Launcelot.'

Then was Sir Lavayn armed and horsed and deliverly at
the lists' end to perform his battle. And right as the heralds
should cry, 'Lechés les alere!' right so came Sir Launcelot
driving with all the might of his horse. And then King
Arthur cried, 'Whoo!' and 'Abide!'

And then was Sir Launcelot called before King Arthur
and there he told openly before the King all how that Sir
Mellyagaunce had served him first and last. And when the
King and Queen and all the lords knew of the treason of Sir
Mellyagaunce they were all ashamed on his behalf. Then
was the Queen sent for and set by the King in the great trust
of her champion.

And then Sir Launcelot and Sir Mellyagaunce dressed
them together with spears as thunder, and there Sir Launcelot bore him quite over his horse's crupper. And then Sir

Launcelot alighted and dressed his shield on his shoulder and took his sword in his hand, and so they dressed to each other and smote many great strokes together. And at the last Sir Launcelot smote him such a buffet upon the helmet that he fell on the one side to the earth. And then he cried upon him loud and said, 'Most noble knight, Sir Launcelot, save my life! For I yield me unto you and I require you, as you are a knight and fellow of the Table Round, slay me not, for I yield me as overcome, and, whether I shall live or die, I put me in the King's hand and yours.'

Then Sir Launcelot wist not what to do, for he had lever than all the good in the world that he might be revenged upon him. So Sir Launcelot looked upon the Queen, if he might espy by any sign or countenance what she would have done. And anon the Queen wagged her head upon Sir Launcelot as who says, 'Slay him!' And full well knew Sir Launcelot by her signs that she would have him dead. Then Sir Launcelot bade him, 'Arise, for shame, and perform this battle with me to the utterance!'

'Nay!' said Sir Mellyagaunce, 'I will never arise until that you take me as yielded and recreant.'

'Well, I shall proffer you a large proffer!' said Sir Launcelot. 'That is for to say, I shall unarm my head and my left quarter of my body, all that may be unarmed as for that quarter, and I will let bind my left hand behind me there it shall not help me, and right so I shall do battle with you.'

Then Sir Mellyagaunce started up and said on hight, 'Take heed, my lord, Arthur, of this proffer, for I will take it. And let him be disarmed and bound according to his proffer.'

'What say you?' said King Arthur unto Sir Launcelot. 'Will you abide by your proffer?'

'Yea! my lord,' said Sir Launcelot, 'for I will never go from that I have once said.'

Then the King's porters of the field disarmed Sir Launcelot, first his head and then his left arm and his left side, and they bound his left arm to his left side fast behind his back without shield or anything. And anon they yode together. Wit you well there was many a lady and many a knight marvelled [that] Sir Launcelot would jeopardy himself in such wise.

Then Sir Mellyagaunce came with sword all on hight and Sir Launcelot showed him openly his bare head and the bare left side. And when he weened to have smitten him upon the bare hand then lightly he devoided the left leg and the left side and put his head and his sword to that stroke, and so put it aside with great slight. And then with great force Sir Launcelot smote him on the helmet such a buffet that the stroke carved the head in two parts.

Then there was no more to do but he was drawn out of the field and, at the great instance of the knights of the Table Round, the King suffered him to be interred and the mention made upon him who slew him and for what cause he was slain. And then the King and the Queen made more of Sir Launcelot, and more was he cherished than ever he was beforehand.

[XIX.10] Then, as the French book makes mention, there was a good knight in the land of Hungary whose name was Sir Urry. And he was an adventurous knight and in all places where he might hear any adventurous deeds and of worship there would he be.

So it happened in Spain there was an earl and his son's name was called Sir Alpheus. And at a great tournament in Spain this Sir Urry, knight of Hungary, and Sir Alpheus of Spain, encountered together for very envy, and so either undertook other to the utterance. And by fortune this Sir Urry slew Sir Alpheus, the earl's son of Spain. But this knight that was slain had given Sir Urry, ere ever he were slain, seven great wounds, three on the head and three on his body and one upon his left hand. And this Sir Alpheus had a mother [which] was a great sorceress, and she, for the despite of her son's death, wrought by her subtle crafts that Sir Urry should never be whole, but ever his wounds should one time fester and another time bleed, so that he should never be whole until the best knight of the world had searched his wounds. And thus she made her avaunt, wherethrough it was known that this Sir Urry should never be whole.

Then his mother let make an horse-litter and put him therein with two palfreys carrying him. And then she took with him his sister, a full fair damsel, whose name was Fyleloly, and a page with them to keep their horses. And so they led Sir Urry through many countries, for, as the French book says, she led him so seven years through all lands christened and never could find no knight that might ease her son.

So she came unto Scotland and into the bounds of England. And by fortune she came at the feast of Pentecost to King Arthur's court that at that time was held at Carlisle. And when she came there she made it to be openly known how that she was come into that land for to heal her son. Then King Arthur let call that lady and ask her the cause why she brought that hurt knight into that land.

'My most noble King,' said that lady, 'wit you well, I brought him hither to be healed of his wounds, that of all this seven years might never be whole.'

And thus she told the King, and where he was wounded and with whom, and how his mother discovered it in her pride how she had wrought by enchantment that he should never be whole until the best knight of the world had searched his wounds. 'And so I have passed all the lands christened through to have him healed except this land, and if I fail here in this land I will never take more pain upon me. And that is great pity, for he was a good knight and of great nobless.'

'What is his name?' said King Arthur.

'My good and gracious lord,' she said, 'his name is Sir Urry of the Mount.'

'In good time,' said the King, 'and, sithen you are come into this land, you are right welcome. And wit you well, here shall your son be healed and ever any Christian man heal him. And for to give all other men of worship a courage, I myself will essay to handle your son and so shall all the kings, dukes and earls that are here present at this time, not presuming upon me that I am so worthy to heal your son by my deeds, but I will courage other men of worship to do as I will do.'

And then the King commanded all the kings, dukes and earls, and all noble knights of the Round Table that were there that time present, to come into the meadow of Carlisle. And so at that time there were but an hundred and ten of the Round Table, for forty knights were that time away. And so here we must begin at King Arthur, as was kindly to begin at him that was that time the most man of worship christened.

[XIX.11] Then King Arthur looked upon Sir Urry and he thought he was a full likely man when he was whole. And then the King made to take him down from the litter and laid him upon the earth, and anon there was laid a cushion of gold that he should kneel upon. And then King Arthur said, 'Fair knight, me rews of thy hurt, and for to courage all other knights I will pray thee softly to suffer me to handle thy wounds.'

'My most noble christened King, do you as you list,' said Sir Urry, 'for I am at the mercy of God and at your commandment.'

So then King Arthur softly handled him. And then some of his wounds renewed upon bleeding.

Then King Claryaunce of Northumberland searched, and it would not be. And then Sir Barraunte le Apres, that was called the King with the Hundred Knights, he essayed and failed. So did King Uriens of the land of Gore. So did King

Angwysh of Ireland and so did King Nentres of Garlot. So did King Carados of Scotland. So did the duke, Sir Galahad the Haute Prince. So did Sir Constantyne that was King Cador's son of Cornwall. So did Duke Chalence of Claraunce. So did the Earl of Ulbawys. So did the Earl Lambayle. So did the Earl of Arystanse.

Then came in Sir Gawain with his three sons, Sir Gyngalyn, Sir Florence and Sir Lovell (these two were begotten upon Sir Braundiles' sister), and all they failed. Then came in Sir Aggravaine, Sir Gaheris and Sir Mordred, and the good knight Sir Gareth, that was of very knighthood worth all the brethren.

So came in the knights of Sir Launcelot's kin but Sir Launcelot was not [that] time in the court for he was that time upon his adventures. Then Sir Lionel, Sir Ector de Maris, Sir Bors de Ganys, Sir Blamour de Ganys, Sir Bleoberis de Ganys, Sir Gahalantine, Sir Galyhodyn, Sir Menaduke, Sir Vyllars the Valiaunt, Sir Hebes le Renowne –all these were of Sir Launcelot's kin and all they failed.

Then came in Sir Sagramour le Desyrus, Sir Dodynas le Saveage, Sir Dinadan, Sir Brunor le Noire that Sir Kay named La Cote Male Tayle, and Sir le Seneschal, Sir Kay d'Estraunges, Sir Mellyot de Logres, Sir Petipace of Wynchilsee, Sir Galleron of Galway, Sir Melyon of the Mountain, Sir Cardoke, Sir Uwaine les Avoutres, and Sir Ozanna le Cure Hardy. Then came in Sir Ascamore and Sir Grummor and Grummorson, Sir Crosseleme, Sir Severause le Brewse that was called a passing strong knight.

(For, as the book says, the chief lady of the Lady of the Lake feasted Sir Launcelot and Sir Severause le Brewse, and, when she had feasted them both at sundry times, she prayed them to give her a done, and anon they granted her. And then she prayed Sir Severause that he would promise her never to do battle against Sir Launcelot, and in the same

wise she prayed Sir Launcelot never to do battle against Sir
Severause, and so either promised her. For the French book
says that Sir Severause had never courage nor great lust to do
battle against no man but if it were against giants and
against dragons and wild beasts.)

So leave we this matter and speak we of them that at the
King's request [were there] at the high feast as knights of
the Round Table for to search Sir Urry. And to this intent
the King did it to wit which was the most noblest knight
among them all. Then came in Sir Agglovale, Sir Durnor
and Sir Torre that was begotten upon the cowherd's wife,
but he was begotten before Aries wedded her. (And King
Pellinore begot them all: first, Sir Torre, Sir Agglovale, Sir
Durnor, Sir Lamorak, the most noblest knight, one of them
that ever was, in King Arthur's days, as for a worldly knight;
and Sir Percival that was peerless, except Sir Galahad, in
holy deeds. But they died in the quest of the Sankgreall.)

Then came in Sir Gryfflet le Fyse de Du, Sir Lucan de
Butler, Sir Bedyvere, his brother, Sir Braundiles, Sir Constantyne, Sir Cador's son of Cornwall that was king after
Arthur's days, and Sir Clegis, Sir Sadok, Sir Dynas le
Seneschal de Cornwall, Sir Fergus, Sir Dryaunt, Sir Lambegus, Sir Clarrus of Cleremount, Sir Cloddrus, Sir Hecty-
mere, Sir Edward of Caernarvon, Sir Priamus, which was
christened by the means of Sir Tristram, the noble knight,
and these three were brethren; Sir Elayne le Blanke, that
was son unto Sir Bors, for he begot him upon King Brande-
gore's daughter, and Sir Bryan de Lystenoyse; Sir Gauter,
Sir Raynold, Sir Gyllymere, were three brethren which Sir
Launcelot won upon a bridge in Sir Kay's arms; Sir Gwyarte
le Petite, Sir Bellyngere le Bewse, that was son to the good
knight Sir Alysaunder le Orphelyne, that was slain by the
treason of King Mark.

(Also that traitor King slew the noble knight, Sir Tristram, as he sat harping before his lady, La Beall Isode, with

a trenchant glaive. For whose death was the most wailing of any knight that ever was in King Arthur's days, for there was never none so bewailed as was Sir Tristram and Sir Lamorak, for they were with treason slain, Sir Tristram by King Mark and Sir Lamorak by Sir Gawain and his brethren.

And this Sir Bellyngere revenged the death of his father, Sir Alysaunder, and Sir Tristram, for he slew King Mark. And La Beall Isode died swooning upon the cross of Sir Tristram, whereof was great pity. And all that were with King Mark, which were of assent of the death of Sir Tristram, were slain, as Sir Ardret and many others.)

Then came Sir Hebes, Sir Morganoure, Sir Sentrayle, Sir Suppynabyles, Sir Bellyaunce le Orgulus, that the good knight Sir Lamorak won in plain battle, Sir Neroveus and Sir Plenoryus, two good knights that Sir Launcelot won, Sir Darras, Sir Harry de Fyze Lake, Sir Hermynde, brother to King Hermaunce, for whom Sir Palomydes fought at the Red City with two brethren; and Sir Selyses of the Dolorous Tower, Sir Edward of Orkney, Sir Ironsyde, that was called the noble knight of the Red Laundes, that Sir Gareth won for the love of Dame Lyoness; Sir Arrok, Sir Degrevaunt, Sir Degrave Saunze Vylony, that fought with the giant of the Black Lowe; Sir Epynogrys, that was the King's son of Northumberland, Sir Pelleas, that loved the Lady Ettarde (and he had died for her sake had not been one of the Ladies of the Lake, whose name was Dame Nineve, and she wedded Sir Pelleas, and she saved him ever after that he was never slain by her days, and he was a full noble knight); and Sir Lamyell of Cardiff, that was a great lover, Sir Playne de Fors, Sir Melyaus de Lyle, Sir Boarte le Cure Hardy, that was King Arthur's son, Sir Madore de la Porte, Sir Collgrevaunce, Sir Hervyse de la Forest Saveage, Sir Marrok the good knight that was betrayed by his wife, for she made him seven years a werewolf, Sir Persaunte, Sir Pertolope, his brother, that was called the Green Knight, and Sir Perimones, brother unto them both, which was called the Red Knight, that Sir Gareth won when he was called Beaumains.

All these hundred knights and ten searched Sir Urry's wounds by the commandment of King Arthur.

[XIX.12] 'Mercy, Jesu!' said King Arthur, 'where is Sir Launcelot du Lake, that he is not here at this time?' And thus, as they stood and spoke of many things, there one espied Sir Launcelot that came riding toward them, and anon they told the King.

'Peace!' said the King. 'Let no man say nothing until he be come to us.'

So when Sir Launcelot had espied King Arthur he descended down from his horse and came to the King and salewed him and them all. And, anon as the damsel, Sir Urry's sister, saw Sir Launcelot, she romed to her brother thereas he lay in his litter and said, 'Brother, here is come a knight that my heart gives greatly unto.'

'Fair sister,' said Sir Urry, 'so does my heart light greatly against him and my heart gives me more unto him than to all these that have searched me.'

Then said King Arthur unto Sir Launcelot, 'Sir, you must do as we have done,' and told him what they had done and showed him them all that had searched him.

'Jesu defend me,' said Sir Launcelot, 'while so many noble kings and knights have failed, that I should presume upon me to achieve that all you, my lords, might not achieve.'

'You shall not choose,' said King Arthur, 'for I command you to do as we all have done.'

'My most renowned lord,' said Sir Launcelot, 'I know well I dare not, nor may not, disobey you. But, and I might or durst, wit you well, I would not take upon me to touch that wounded knight in that intent that I should pass all other knights. Jesu defend me from that shame!'

'Sir, you take it wrong,' said King Arthur, 'for you shall not do it for no presumption, but for to bear us fellowship,

insomuch as you are a fellow of the Round Table. And, wit
you well,' said King Arthur, 'and you prevail not and heal
him, I dare say there is no knight in this land that may heal
him. And therefore I pray you do as we have done.'

And then all the kings and knights for the most part
prayed Sir Launcelot to search him. And then the wounded
knight, Sir Urry, sat him up weakly and said unto Sir
Launcelot, 'Now, courteous knight, I require thee, for God's
sake, heal my wounds! For methinks ever sithen you came
here my wounds grieve me not so much as they did.'

'Ah! my fair lord,' said Sir Launcelot, 'Jesu would that I
might help you! For I shame sore with myself that I should
be thus required, for never was I able in worthiness to do so
high a thing.'

Then Sir Launcelot kneeled down by the wounded knight
saying, 'My lord, Arthur, I must do your commandment,
which is sore against my heart.'

And then he held up his hands and looked unto the east,
saying secretly unto himself, 'Now blessed Father, and Son
and Holy Ghost, I beseech thee of thy mercy that my simple
worship and honesty be saved, and thou, blessed Trinity,
thou mayst give me power to heal this sick knight by the
great virtue and grace of thee, but, good Lord, never of
myself.'

And then Sir Launcelot prayed Sir Urry to let him see his
head. And then, devoutly kneeling, he ransacked the three
wounds that they bled a little. And forthwithal the wounds
fair healed and seemed as they had been whole a seven year.
And in like wise he searched his body of other three wounds
and they healed in like wise. And then the last of all he
searched his hand, and anon it fair healed.

Then King Arthur and all the kings and knights kneeled
down and gave thankings and loving unto God and unto his
blessed Mother. And ever Sir Launcelot wept as he had
been a child that had been beaten.

Then King Arthur let ravish priests and clerks in the most devoutest wise to bring in Sir Urry into Carlisle with singing and loving to God. And when this was done, the King let clothe him in rich manner, and then was there but few better-made knights in all the court, for he was passingly well made and bigly. Then King Arthur asked Sir Urry how he felt himself.

'Ah! my good and gracious lord, I felt myself never so lusty.'

'Then will you joust and do any arms?' said King Arthur.

'Sir, and I had all that longed unto jousts, I would be soon ready.'

[XIX.13] Then King Arthur made a party [of] a hundred knights to be against an hundred, and so, upon the morn, they jousted for a diamond, but there jousted none of the dangerous knights. And so, for to shorten this tale, Sir Urry and Sir Lavayn jousted best that day, for there was none of them but he overthrew and pulled down a thirty knights. And then by assent of all the kings and lords Sir Urry and Sir Lavayn were made knights of the Table Round. And then Sir Lavayn cast his love unto Dame Fyleloly, Sir Urry's sister, and then they were wedded with great joy. And so King Arthur gave to every ⟨one⟩ of them a barony of lands.

And this Sir Urry would never go from Sir Launcelot, but he and Sir Lavayn awaited evermore upon him. And they were in all the court accounted for good knights and full desirous in arms. And many noble deeds they did for they would have no rest but ever sought upon their deeds. Thus they lived in all that court with great nobless and joy long times. But every night and day Sir Aggravaine, Sir Gawain's brother, awaited Queen Guenevere and Sir Launcelot to put them both to a rebuke and a shame.

And so I leave here of this tale and overleap great books of Sir Launcelot, what great adventures he did when he was called Le Chevalier de la Charrette. For, as the French book says, because of despite that knights and ladies called him, 'the knight that rode in the Chariot', like as he were judged to the gibbet, therefore, in the despite of all them that named him so, he was carried in a chariot a twelvemonth, for, but little after that he had slain Sir Mellyagaunce in the Queen's quarrel, he never of a twelvemonth came on horseback. And, as the French book says, he did that twelvemonth more than forty battles.

And because I have lost the very matter of 'Le Chevalier de la Charrette' I depart from the tale of Sir Launcelot, and here I go unto the 'Morte Arthur'—and that caused Sir Aggravaine.

Book Eight

'The most piteous tale of the death of Arthur'

[XX.1] In May, when every heart flourishes and burgeons (for, as the season is lusty to behold and comfortable, so man and woman rejoice and glad of summer coming with his fresh flowers, for winter with his rough winds and blasts causes lusty men and women to cower and to sit by fires), so this season it befell in the month of May a great anger and unhappy that stinted not till the flower of chivalry of the world was destroyed and slain.

And all was long upon two unhappy knights which were named Sir Aggravaine and Sir Mordred, that were brethren unto Sir Gawain. For this Sir Aggravaine and Sir Mordred had ever a privy hate unto the Queen, Dame Guenevere, and to Sir Launcelot. And daily and nightly they ever watched upon Sir Launcelot.

So it misfortuned Sir Gawain and all his brethren were in King Arthur's chamber, and then Sir Aggravaine said thus openly, and not in no council, that many knights might hear, 'I marvel that we all be not ashamed both to see and to know how Sir Launcelot lies daily and nightly by the Queen. And all we know well that it is so, and it is shamefully suffered of us all that we should suffer so noble a king as King Arthur is to be shamed.'

Then spoke Sir Gawain and said, 'Brother, Sir Aggravaine, I pray you and charge you, move no such matters no more before me, for, wit you well, I will not be of your counsel.'

'So God me help,' said Sir Gaheris and Sir Gareth, 'we will not be known of your deeds!'

'Then will I!' said Sir Mordred.

'I believe you well,' said Sir Gawain, 'for ever unto all unhappiness, sir, you will grant. And I would that you left and make you not so busy, for I know,' said Sir Gawain, 'what will fall of it.'

'Fall whatsoever fall may,' said Sir Aggravaine, 'I will disclose it to the King!'

'Not by my counsel,' said Sir Gawain, 'for, and there arise war and wrake between Sir Launcelot [and us], wit you well, brother, there will many kings and great lords hold with Sir Launcelot. Also, brother Sir Aggravaine,' said Sir Gawain, 'you must remember how oftentimes Sir Launcelot has rescued the King and the Queen. And the best of us all had been full cold at the heart-root had not Sir Launcelot been better than we, and that has he proved himself full oft. And, as for my part,' said Sir Gawain, 'I will never be against Sir Launcelot for one day's deed, that was when he rescued me from King Carados of the Dolorous Tower and slew him and saved my life. Also, brother, Sir Aggravaine and Sir Mordred, in like wise Sir Launcelot rescued you both and three score and two from Sir Tarquin. And, therefore, brother, me thinks such noble deeds and kindness should be remembered.'

'Do you as you list,' said Sir [Aggravaine], 'for I will laine it no longer.'

So with these words came in Sir Arthur.

'Now, brother,' said Sir Gawain, 'stint your strife!'

'That will I not,' said Sir Aggravaine and Sir Mordred.

'Well! will you so?' said Sir Gawain. 'Then God speed you, for I will not hear of your tales nor be of your counsel.'

'No more will I,' said Sir Gaheris.

'Nor I,' said Sir Gareth, 'for I shall never say evil by that man that made me knight.'

And therewithal they three departed making great dole.

'Alas!' said Sir Gawain and Sir Gareth, 'now is this realm wholly destroyed and mischieved, and the noble fellowship of the Round Table shall be disparbeled.'

[XX.2] So they departed and then King Arthur asked them what noise they made.

'My lord!' said Sir Aggravaine, 'I shall tell you, for I may keep it no longer. Here is I and my brother, Sir Mordred, broke unto my brother, Sir Gawain, Sir Gaheris and to Sir Gareth—for this is all, to make it short—we know all that Sir Launcelot holds your Queen and has done long. And we are your sister's sons—we may suffer it no longer. And all we wot that you should be above Sir Launcelot, and you are the King that made him knight, and therefore we will prove it that he is a traitor to your person.'

'If it be so,' said the King, 'wit you well, he is none other. But I would be loath to begin such a thing but I might have proofs of it, for Sir Launcelot is an hardy knight and all you know that he is the best knight among us all, and, but if he be taken with the deed, he will fight with him that brings up the noise, and I know no knight that is able to match him. Therefore, and it is sooth as you say, I would that he were taken with the deed.'

For, as the French book says, the King was full loath that such a noise should be upon Sir Launcelot and his Queen. For the King had a deeming of it, but he would not hear thereof, for Sir Launcelot had done so much for him and for the Queen so many times that, wit you well, the King loved him passingly well.

'My lord,' said Sir Aggravaine, 'you shall ride tomorn ahunting, and, doubt you not, Sir Launcelot will not go with you. And so, when it draws toward night, you may send the

Queen word that you will lie out all that night, and so may you send for your cooks. And then, upon pain of death, that night we shall take him with the Queen, and we shall bring him unto you, quick or dead.'

'I will well,' said the King. 'Then I counsel you to take with you sure fellowship.'

'Sir,' said Sir Aggravaine, 'my brother, Sir Mordred, and I will take with us twelve knights of the Round Table.'

'Beware,' said King Arthur, 'for I warn you, you shall find him wight.'

'Let us deal!' said Sir Aggravaine and Sir Mordred.

So, on the morn, King Arthur rode ahunting and sent word to the Queen that he would be out all that night. Then Sir Aggravaine and Sir Mordred got to them twelve knights and hid themselves in a chamber in the Castle of Carlisle. And these were their names: Sir Collgrevaunce, Sir Madore de la Porte, Sir Gyngalyn, Sir Mellyot de Logres, Sir Petipace of Wynchilsee, Sir Galleron of Galway, Sir Mellyon of the Mountain, Sir Ascamore, Sir Gromoresom Erioure, Sir Cursesalayne, Sir Florence and Sir Lovell. So these twelve knights were with Sir Mordred and Sir Aggravaine, and all they were of Scotland, or else of Sir Gawain's kin or [well-]willers to his brother.

So when the night came Sir Launcelot told Sir Bors how he would go that night and speak with the Queen.

'Sir,' said Sir Bors, 'you shall not go this night, by my counsel.'

'Why?' said Sir Launcelot.

'Sir, for I dread me ever of Sir Aggravaine that waits upon you daily to do you shame and us all. And never gave my heart against no going that ever you went to the Queen so much as now, for I mistrust that the King is out this night from the Queen [because, peradventure, he has lain some watch for you and the Queen]. Therefore I dread me sore of some treason.'

'Have you no dread,' said Sir Launcelot, 'for I shall go and come again and make no tarrying.'

'Sir,' said Sir Bors, 'that me repents, for I dread me sore that your going this night shall wrath us all.'

'Fair nephew,' said Sir Launcelot, 'I marvel me much why you say thus, sithen the Queen has sent for me. And, wit you well, I will not be so much a coward but she shall understand I will see her good grace.'

'God speed you well,' said Sir Bors, 'and send you sound and safe again!'

[XX.3] So Sir Launcelot departed and took his sword under his arm, and so he walked in his mantle, that noble knight, and put himself in great jeopardy. And so he passed on till he came to the Queen's chamber: and so lightly he was had into the chamber. For, as the French book says, the Queen and Sir Launcelot were together, and whether they were abed or at other manner of disports me list not thereof make no mention, for love that time was not as love is nowadays.

But thus, as they were together, there came Sir Aggravaine and Sir Mordred with twelve knights with them of the Round Table, and they said with great crying and scaring voice, 'Thou traitor, Sir Launcelot! now art thou taken!'

And thus they cried with a loud voice that all the court might hear it. And these fourteen knights all were armed at all points as they should fight in a battle.

'Alas!' said Queen Guenevere, 'now are we mischieved both.'

'Madam!' said Sir Launcelot, 'is there here any armour within you that might cover my body withal? And if there is any, give it me and I shall soon stint their malice, by the grace of God!'

'Now, truly,' said the Queen, 'I have none armour, neither helm, shield, sword, nor spear, wherefore I dread me sore our long love is come to a mischievous end. For I hear by their noise there be many noble knights, and well I wot they be surely armed and against them you may make no resistance. Wherefore you are likely to be slain, and then shall I be burnt! For, and you might escape them,' said the Queen, 'I would not doubt but that you would rescue me in what danger that I ever stood in.'

'Alas!' said Sir Launcelot, 'in all my life thus was I never bested that I should be thus shamefully slain for lack of mine armour.'

But ever Sir Aggravaine and Sir Mordred cried, 'Traitor knight, come out of the Queen's chamber! For, wit thou well, thou art beset so that thou shalt not escape!'

'Ah! Jesu, mercy!' said Sir Launcelot. 'This shameful cry and noise I may not suffer, for better were death at once than thus to endure this pain!'

Then he took the Queen in his arms and kissed her and said, 'Most noblest Christian Queen, I beseech you, as you have been ever my special good lady and I at all times your poor knight and true unto my power, and as I never failed you in right nor in wrong sithen the first day King Arthur made me knight, that you will pray for my soul if that I am slain. For well I am assured that Sir Bors, my nephew, and all the remnant of my kin, with Sir Lavayn and Sir Urry, that they will not fail you to rescue you from the fire. And therefore, mine own lady, recomfort yourself, whatsoever come of me, that you go with Sir Bors, my nephew, and they all will do you all the pleasure that they may, and you shall live like a queen upon my lands.'

'Nay! Sir Launcelot, nay!' said the Queen. 'Wit thou well that I will [never live] after thy days. But, and you be slain, I will take my death as meekly as ever did martyr take his death for Jesu Christ's sake.'

'Well, madam,' said Sir Launcelot, 'sith it is so that the day is come that our love must depart, wit you well, I shall sell my life as dear as I may. And a thousandfold,' said Sir

Launcelot, 'I am more heavier for you than for myself. And now I had lever than to be lord of all Christendom that I had sure armour upon me, that men might speak of my deeds ere ever I were slain.'

'Truly,' said the Queen, 'and it might please God, I would that they would take me and slay me and suffer you to escape.'

'That shall never be,' said Sir Launcelot. 'God defend me from such a shame! But, Jesu Christ, be thou my shield and mine armour!'

[XX.4] And therewith Sir Launcelot wrapped his mantle about his arm well and surely. And by then they had got a great form out of the hall and therewith they all rushed at the door.

'Now, fair lords,' said Sir Launcelot, 'leave your noise and your rushing and I shall set open this door and then may you do with me what it likes you.'

'Come off, then,' said they all, 'and do it, for it avails thee not to strive against us all. And therefore let us into this chamber, and we shall save thy life until thou come to King Arthur.'

Then Sir Launcelot unbarred the door and with his left hand he held it open a little that but one man might come in at once. And so there came striding a good knight, a much man and a large, and his name was called Sir Collgrevaunce of Gore. And he, with a sword, struck at Sir Launcelot mightily. And so he put aside the stroke and gave him such a buffet upon the helmet that he fell grovelling [dead] within the chamber door.

Then Sir Launcelot with great might drew the knight within the chamber door, and then Sir Launcelot, with help of the Queen and her ladies, he was lightly armed in Collgrevaunce's armour. And ever stood Sir Aggravaine and Sir Mordred, crying, 'Traitor knight! Come forth out of the Queen's chamber!'

'Sirs, leave your noise!' said Sir Launcelot. 'For, wit you well, Sir Aggravaine, you shall not prison me this night! And, therefore, and you do by my counsel, go you all from this chamber door and make you no such crying and such manner of slander as you do. For I promise you by my knighthood, and you will depart and make no more noise, I shall as tomorn appear before you all and before the King, and then let it be seen which of you all, or else you all, that will depreve me of treason. And there shall I answer you, as a knight should, that hither I came to the Queen for no manner of mal engine, and that will I prove and make it good upon you with my hands.'

'Fie upon thee, traitor!' said Sir Aggravaine and Sir Mordred, 'for we will have thee magre thine head and slay thee, and we list! For we let thee wit we have the choice of King Arthur to save thee or slay thee.'

'Ah! sirs,' said Sir Launcelot, 'is there none other grace with you? Then keep yourselves!'

And then Sir Launcelot set all open the chamber door and mightily and knightly he strode in among them. And anon, at the first stroke, he slew Sir Aggravaine and anon, after, twelve of his fellows. Within a while he had laid them down cold to the earth, for there was none of the twelve knights might stand Sir Launcelot one buffet. And also he wounded Sir Mordred and therewithal he fled with all his might. And then Sir Launcelot returned again unto the Queen and said, 'Madam, now wit you well, all our true love is brought to an end. For now will King Arthur ever be my foe. And, therefore, madam, and it like you that I may have you with me, I shall save you from all manner adventurous dangers.'

'Sir, that is not best,' said the Queen, 'me seems, for now you have done so much harm it will be best that you hold you still with this. And if you see that as tomorn they will put me unto death, then may you rescue me as you think best.'

'I will well,' said Sir Launcelot, 'for, have you no doubt, while I am a man living I shall rescue you.'

And then he kissed her and either of them gave other a ring, and so the Queen he left there and went to his lodging. [XX.5] When Sir Bors saw Sir Launcelot he was never so glad of his home-coming. 'Jesu, mercy!' said Sir Launcelot, 'why be you all armed? What means this?'

'Sir,' said Sir Bors, 'after you were departed from us we all, that are of your blood and your well-willers, were so [adretched] that some of us leapt out of our beds naked and some in their dreams caught naked swords in their hands. And therefore,' said Sir Bors, 'we deemed there was some great strife on hand and so we deemed that we were be-trapped with some treason. And therefore we made us thus ready, what need that ever we were in.'

'My fair nephew,' said Sir Launcelot unto Sir Bors, 'now shall you wit, all, that this night I was more hard bested than ever I was, days of my life. And thanked be God, I am myself escaped their danger.' And so he told them all how and in what manner, as you have heard beforehand. 'And, therefore, my fellows,' said Sir Launcelot, 'I pray you all that you will be of heart good, and help me in what need that ever I stand, for now is war come to us all.'

'Sir,' said Sir Bors, 'all is welcome that God sends us, and as we have taken much weal with you and much worship, we will take the woe with you as we have taken the weal.' And therefore they said, all the good knights, 'Look you take no discomfort! For there is no bands of knights under heaven but we shall be able to grieve them as much as they us, and therefore discomfort not yourself by no manner. And we shall gather together all that we love and that love us, and what that you will have done shall be done. And, therefore, let us take the woe and the joy together!'

'Grauntmercy,' said Sir Launcelot, 'of your good comfort, for, in my great distress, fair nephew, you comfort me greatly. But this, my fair nephew, I would that you did, in all haste that you may, [ere] it is far days past—that you will look in their lodging, that are lodged nigh here about the King, which will hold with me and which will not. For now I would know which were my friends from my foes.'

'Sir,' said Sir Bors, 'I shall do my pain, and, ere it be seven of the clock, I shall wit of such as you have [doubt] for, who that will hold with you.'

Then Sir Bors called unto him Sir Lionel, Sir Ector de Maris, Sir Blamour de Ganys, Sir Gahalantine, Sir Galy-hodyn, Sir Galihud, Sir Menaduke, Sir Vyllars the Valiaunte, Sir Hebes le Renowne, Sir Lavayn, Sir Urry of Hungary, Sir Neroveus, Sir Plenoryus (for these two were knights that Sir Launcelot won upon a bridge and therefore they would never be against him), and Sir Harry de Fyze Lake, and Sir Selyses of the Dolorous Tower, Sir Melyaus de Lyle, and Sir Bellyngere le Bewse that was Sir Alysaunder['s son] le Orphelyne—because his mother was kin unto Sir Launcelot he held with him. So came Sir Palomydes and Sir Saphir, his brother, Sir Clegis, Sir Sadok, Sir Dynas, and Sir Clarrus of Cleremount.

So these two-and-twenty knights drew them together and, by than they were armed and on horseback, they promised Sir Launcelot to do what he would. Then there fell to them, what of North Wales and of Cornwall, for Sir Lamorak's sake and for Sir Tristram's sake, to the number of a seven-score knights. Then spoke Sir Launcelot:

'Wit you well, I have been, ever since I came to this court, well-willed unto my lord, Arthur, and unto my lady, Queen Guenevere, unto my power. And this night, because my lady, the Queen, sent for me to speak with her, I suppose it was made by treason. Howbeit I dare largely excuse her person, notwithstanding I was there by near-hand slain, but as Jesu provided for me.'

And then that noble knight, Sir Launcelot, told them how

he was hard bested in the Queen's chamber, and how and in what manner he escaped from them. 'And, therefore, wit you well, my fair lords, I am sure there nis but war unto me and to mine. And for cause I have slain this night Sir Aggravaine, Sir Gawain's brother, and at the least twelve of his fellows, and for this cause now am I sure of mortal war. For these knights were sent by King Arthur to betray me, and therefore the King will in this heat and malice judge the Queen unto burning, and that may not I suffer that she should be burnt for my sake. For, and I may be heard and suffered and so taken, I will fight for the Queen, that she is a true lady unto her lord. But the King in his heat, I dread, will not take me as I ought to be taken.'

[XX.6] 'My lord, Sir Launcelot,' said Sir Bors, 'by mine advice you shall take the woe with the weal. And sithen it is fallen as it is, I counsel you to keep yourself, for, and you will yourself, there is no fellowship of knights christened that shall do you wrong. And also I will counsel you, my lord, that my lady, Queen Guenevere, and she be in any distress, insomuch as she is in pain for your sake, that you knightly rescue her, for, and you did any otherwise, all the world would speak you shame to the world's end. Insomuch as you were taken with her, whether you did right or wrong, it is now your part to hold with the Queen, that she be not slain and put to a mischievous death. For, and she so die, the shame shall be evermore yours.'

'Now Jesu defend me from shame,' said Sir Launcelot, 'and keep and save my lady, the Queen, from villainy and shameful death, and that she never be destroyed in my default! Wherefore, my fair lords, my kin and my friends,' said Sir Launcelot, 'what will you do?'

And anon they said all with one voice, 'We will do as you will do.'

'Then I put this case unto you,' said Sir Launcelot, 'that my lord, King Arthur, by evil counsel will tomorn in his heat put my lady, the Queen, unto the fire and there to be burnt. Then, I pray you, counsel me what is best for me to do.'

Then they said all at once with one voice, 'Sir, us thinks best that you knightly rescue the Queen. Insomuch as she shall be burnt, it is for your sake, and it is to suppose, and you might be handled, you should have the same death, or else a more shamefuller death. And, sir, we say, all, that you have rescued her from her death many times for other men's quarrels. Therefore us seems it is more your worship that you rescue the Queen from this quarrel, insomuch that she has it for your sake.'

Then Sir Launcelot stood still and said, 'My fair lords, wit you well, I would be loath to do that thing that should dishonour you or my blood. And, wit you well, I would be full loath that my lady, the Queen, should die such a shameful death. But, and it is so that you will counsel me to rescue her, I must do much harm ere I rescue her, and peradventure I shall there destroy some of my best friends. And if so be that I may win the Queen away, where shall I keep her?'

'Sir, that shall be the least care of us all,' said Sir Bors, 'for how did the most noble knight, Sir Tristram? By your good will, kept not he with him La Beall Isode, near three years in Joyous Garde, the which was done by your althers advice? And that same place is your own, and in likewise may you do, and you list, and take the Queen knightly away with you, if so be that the King will judge her to be burnt. And in Joyous Garde may you keep her long enough until the heat be past of the King, and then it may fortune you to bring the Queen again to the King with great worship, and peradventure you shall have then thanks for your bringing home, whether other may happen to have magre.'

'That is hard for to do,' said Sir Launcelot, 'for by Sir Tristram I may have a warning. For when by means of tretise Sir Tristram brought again La Beall Isode unto King

Mark from Joyous Garde, look you now what fell on the end, how shamefully that false traitor, King Mark, slew him as he sat harping before his lady, La Beall Isode. With a ground glaive he thrust him in behind to the heart, which grieves sore me,' said Sir Launcelot, 'to speak of his death, for all the world may not find such another knight.'

'All this is truth,' said Sir Bors, 'but there is one thing shall courage you and us all: you know well that King Arthur and King Mark were never like of conditions, for there was never yet man that ever could prove King Arthur untrue of his promise.'

But so, to make short tale, they were all condiscended that, for better or for worse, if so were that the Queen were brought on that morn to the fire, shortly they all would rescue her. And so by the advice of Sir Launcelot they put them all in a wood as nigh Carlisle as they might, and there they abode still to wit what the King would do.

[XX.7] Now turn we again, that when Sir Mordred was escaped from Sir Launcelot he got his horse and came to King Arthur sore wounded and all forbled, and there he told the King all how it was and how they were all slain save himself alone.

'Ah! Jesu, mercy! How may this be?' said the King. 'Took you him in the Queen's chamber?'

'Yea! so God me help!' said Sir Mordred. 'There we found him unarmed, and anon he slew Sir Collgrevaunce and armed him in his armour.' And so he told the King from the beginning to the ending.

'Jesu, mercy!' said the King. 'He is a marvellous knight of prowess. And, alas!' said the King, 'me sore repents that ever Sir Launcelot should be against me, for now I am sure the noble fellowship of the Round Table is broken for ever, for with him will many a noble knight hold. And now it is fallen so,' said the King, 'that I may not with my worship but my Queen must suffer death,' and was sore amoved.

So then there was made great ordinance in this ire and the Queen must needs be judged to the death. And the law was such in those days that whatsoever they were, of what estate or degree, if they were found guilty of treason there should be none other remedy but death, and either the menour or the taking with the deed should be causer of their hasty judgement. And right so was it ordained for Queen Guenevere. Because Sir Mordred was escaped sore wounded and the death of thirteen knights of the Round Table—these proofs and experiences caused King Arthur to command the Queen to the fire and there to be burnt. Then spoke Sir Gawain and said,

'My lord, Arthur, I would counsel you not to be overhasty, but that you would put it in respite, this judgement of my lady, the Queen, for many causes. One is this: though it were so that Sir Launcelot were found in the Queen's chamber, yet it might be so that he came thither for none evil. For you know, my lord,' said Sir Gawain, 'that my lady, the Queen, has oftentimes been greatly beholden unto Sir Launcelot, more than to any other knight, for oftentimes he has saved her life and done battle for her when all the court refused the Queen. And peradventure she sent for him for goodness and for none evil, to reward him for his good deeds that he had done to her in times past. And peradventure my lady, the Queen, sent for him to that intent, that Sir Launcelot should have come privily to her, weening that it had been best in eschewing of slander—for oftentimes we do many things that we ween for the best be, and yet peradventure it turns to the worst. For I dare say,' said Sir Gawain, 'my lady, your queen, is to you both good and true. And, as for Sir Launcelot, I dare say he will make it good upon any knight living that will put upon him villainy or shame, and in like wise he will make good for my lady, the Queen.'

'That I believe well,' said King Arthur, 'but I will not that way work with Sir Launcelot, for he trusts so much upon

his hands and his might that he doubts no man. And therefore for my queen he shall nevermore fight, for she shall have
the law. And if I may get Sir Launcelot, wit you well, he
shall have as shameful a death.'

'Jesu defend me,' said Sir Gawain, 'that I never see it nor
know it!'

'Why say you so?' said King Arthur. 'For, parde, you
have no cause to love him! For this night last past he slew
your brother, Sir Aggravaine, a full good knight, and almost
he had slain your other brother, Sir Mordred. And, also,
there he slew thirteen noble knights. And, also, remember
you, Sir Gawain, he slew two sons of yours, Sir Florence and
Sir Lovell.'

'My lord,' said Sir Gawain, 'of all this I have a knowledge,
which of their deaths sore repents me. But insomuch as I
gave them warning and told my brother and my sons beforehand what would fall on the end, and insomuch as they
would not do by my counsel, I will not meddle me thereof,
nor revenge me nothing of their deaths, for I told them there
was no boot to strive with Sir Launcelot. Howbeit I am sorry
of the death of my brother and of my two sons, but they are
the causers of their own death, for oftentimes I warned my
brother Sir Aggravaine and I told him of the perils.'

[XX.8] Then said King Arthur unto Sir Gawain, 'Make
you ready, I pray you, in your best armour, with your
brethren, Sir Gaheris and Sir [Gareth], to bring my Queen
to the fire and there to have her judgement.'

'Nay! my most noble King,' said Sir Gawain, 'that will I
never do, for wit you well I will never be in that place where
so noble a Queen as is my lady, Dame Guenevere, shall take
such a shameful end. For, wit you well,' said Sir Gawain, 'my
heart will not serve me for to see her die, and it shall never be
said that ever I was of your counsel for her death.'

'Then,' said the King unto Sir Gawain, 'suffer your
brethren, Sir Gaheris and Sir Gareth, to be there.'

'My lord,' said Sir Gawain, 'wit you well, they will be loath to be there present because of many adventures that is like to fall, but they are young and full unable to say you nay.'

Then spoke Sir Gaheris and the good knight, Sir Gareth, unto King Arthur, 'Sir, you may well command us to be there, but, wit you well, it shall be sore against our will. But, and we be there by your strait commandment, you shall plainly hold us there excused. We will be there in peaceable wise and bear none harness of war upon us.'

'In the name of God,' said the King, 'then make you ready, for she shall have soon her judgement!'

'Alas!' said Sir Gawain, 'that ever I should endure to see this woeful day!'

So Sir Gawain turned him and wept heartily, and so he went into his chamber. And so the Queen was led forth without Carlisle, and anon she was despoiled into her smock. And then her ghostly father was brought to her to be shriven of her misdeeds. Then was there weeping and wailing and wringing of hands of many lords and ladies. But there were but few in comparison that would bear any armour for to strengthen the death of the Queen.

Then was there one that Sir Launcelot had sent unto [that place] which weened to espy what time the Queen should go unto her death. And anon as he saw the Queen despoiled into her smock and shriven, then he gave Sir Launcelot warning anon. Then was there but spurring and plucking up of horse and right so they came unto the fire. And who that stood against them there were they slain, full many a noble knight. For there was slain Sir Bellyaunce le Orgulus, Sir Segwarides, Sir Gryfflet, Sir Braundiles, Sir Agglovale, Sir Torre, Sir Gauter, Sir Gyllymere, Sir Raynold, three brothers, and Sir Damas, Sir Priamus, Sir Kay d'Estraunges, Sir Dryaunt, Sir Lambegus, Sir Hermynde, Sir Pertolope, Sir Perymones, two brethren which were called the Green Knight and the Red Knight.

And so, in this rushing and hurling, as Sir Launcelot thrange here and there, it misfortuned him to slay Sir Gaheris and Sir Gareth, the noble knight, for they were unarmed and unawares. As the French book says, Sir Launcelot smote Sir Gaheris and Sir Gareth upon the brainpans, wherethrough that they were slain in the field. Howbeit, in very truth, Sir Launcelot saw them [not]. And so were they found dead among the thickest of the press.

Then Sir Launcelot, when he had thus done and slain and put to flight all that would withstand him, then he rode straight unto Queen Guenevere and made cast a kirtle and a gown upon her. And then he made her to be set behind him and prayed her to be of good cheer. Now, wit you well, the Queen was glad that she was at that time escaped from the death, and then she thanked God and Sir Launcelot.

And so he rode his way with the Queen, as the French book says, unto Joyous Garde, and there he kept her as a noble knight should. And many great lords and many good knights were sent him, and many full noble knights drew unto him. When they heard that King Arthur and Sir Launcelot were at debate many knights were glad and many were sorry of their debate.

[XX.9] Now turn we again unto King Arthur, that, when it was told him how and in what manner the Queen was taken away from the fire, and when he heard of the death of his noble knights, and, in especial, Sir Gaheris and Sir Gareth, then he swooned for very pure sorrow. And when he awoke of his swoon, then he said,

'Alas! that ever I bore crown upon my head. For now have I lost the fairest fellowship of noble knights that ever held Christian king together. Alas! my good knights be slain and gone away from me, that now within these two days I have lost nigh forty knights and also the noble fellowship of Sir Launcelot and his blood, for now I may nevermore hold them together with my worship. Now, alas, that ever this

war began! Now, fair fellows,' said the King, 'I charge you
that no man tell Sir Gawain of the death of his two brethren,
for I am sure,' said the King, 'when he hears tell that Sir
Gareth is dead he will go nigh out of his mind. Mercy! Jesu,'
said the King, 'why slew he Sir Gaheris and Sir Gareth? For
I dare say, as for Sir Gareth, he loved Sir Launcelot of all
men earthly.'

'That is truth,' said some knights, 'but they were slain in
the hurling as Sir Launcelot thrange in the thickest of the
press. And, as they were unarmed, he smote them and wist
not whom that he smote. And so, unhappily, they were
slain.'

'Well,' said Arthur, 'the death of them will cause the
greatest mortal war that ever was, for I am sure that when
Sir Gawain knows hereof that Sir Gareth is slain, I shall never
have rest of him till I have destroyed Sir Launcelot's kin and
himself both, or else he to destroy me. And, therefore,' said
the King, 'wit you well, my heart was never so heavy as it is
now. And much more I am sorrier for my good knights' loss
than for the loss of my fair Queen, for queens I might have
enough, but such a fellowship of good knights shall never be
together in no company. And now I dare say,' said King
Arthur, 'there was never Christian King that ever held such
a fellowship together. And, alas, that ever Sir Launcelot and
I should be at debate! Ah! Aggravaine, Aggravaine!' said
the King, 'Jesu forgive it thy soul, for thine evil will that
thou haddest and Sir Mordred, thy brother, unto Sir
Launcelot, has caused all this sorrow.'

And ever among these complaints the King wept and
swooned. Then came there one to Sir Gawain and told how
the Queen was led away with Sir Launcelot and nigh a four-
and-twenty knights slain.

'Ah! Jesu, save me my two brethren!' said Sir Gawain.
'For full well wist I,' said Sir Gawain, 'that Sir Launcelot
would rescue her or else he would die in that field. And, to

say the truth, he were not of worship but if he had rescued
the Queen, insomuch as she should have been burnt for his
sake. And as in that,' said Sir Gawain, 'he has done but
knightly, and as I would have done myself and I had stood in
like case. But where are my brethren?' said Sir Gawain. 'I
marvel that I see not of them.'

Then said that man, 'Truly, Sir Gaheris and Sir Gareth
are slain.'

'Jesu defend!' said Sir Gawain. 'For all this world I would
not that they were slain, and, in especial, my good brother,
Sir Gareth.'

'Sir,' said the man, 'he is slain, and that is great pity.'

'Who slew him?' said Sir Gawain.

'Sir Launcelot,' said the man, 'slew them both.'

'That may I not believe,' said Sir Gawain, 'that ever he
slew my good brother, Sir Gareth, for, I dare say, my
brother loved him better than me and all his brethren and
the King, both. Also I dare say, an Sir Launcelot had desired
my brother, Sir Gareth, with him, he would have been with
him against the King and us all. And therefore I may never
believe that Sir Launcelot slew my brethren.'

'Verily, sir,' said the man, 'it is noised that he slew him.'

[XX.10] 'Alas!' said Sir Gawain, 'now is my joy gone.'

And then he fell down and swooned, and long he lay there
as he had been dead. And when he arose out of his swoon he
cried out sorrowfully and said, 'Alas!' And forthwith he ran
unto the King, crying and weeping, and said, 'Ah! mine
uncle King Arthur! My good brother, Sir Gareth, is slain
and so is my brother, Sir Gaheris, which were two noble
knights.'

Then the King wept and he, both, and so they fell
aswooning. And when they were revived, then spoke Sir
Gawain and said, 'Sir, I will go and see my brother, Sir
Gareth.'

'Sir, you may not see him,' said the King, 'for I caused him to be interred and Sir Gaheris, both, for I well understood that you would make overmuch sorrow, and the sight of Sir Gareth should have caused your double sorrow.'

'Alas! my lord,' said Sir Gawain, 'how slew he my brother, Sir Gareth? I pray you tell me.'

'Truly,' said the King, 'I shall tell you as it has been told me: Sir Launcelot slew him and Sir Gaheris, both.'

'Alas!' said Sir Gawain, 'they bore none arms against him, neither of them both.'

'I wot not how it was,' said the King, 'but, as it is said, Sir Launcelot slew them in the thick press and knew them not. And therefore let us shape a remedy for to revenge their deaths.'

'My King, my lord and mine uncle,' said Sir Gawain, 'wit you well, now I shall make you a promise which I shall hold by my knighthood, that, from this day forward, I shall never fail Sir Launcelot until that one of us have slain that other. And therefore I require you, my lord and King, dress you unto the war, for, wit you well, I will be revenged upon Sir Launcelot. And, therefore, as you will have my service and my love, now haste you thereto and assay your friends. For I promise unto God,' said Sir Gawain, 'for the death of my brother, Sir Gareth, I shall seek Sir Launcelot throughout seven kings' realms, but I shall slay him or else he shall slay me.' . . .

King Arthur and Gawain besiege Launcelot in Joyous Garde. Launcelot says he is sorry he killed Gawain's brothers and affirms that Guenevere is 'true and good'. The French book says Arthur 'would have taken his Queen again' but Gawain would not let him, Launcelot having reminded Gawain that, whereas he slew Gareth and Gaheris mistakenly, Gawain and his brothers murdered Lamorak. The Pope arranges for Arthur to receive Guenevere again, and again Launcelot maintains her innocence, arguing that, when he fought at her chamber door, 'had not the might of God been with me I might never have endured with fourteen knights.'

H

Launcelot offers to perform vast acts of penitence for killing the
brothers, but Gawain insists he be banished.

[XX.17] . . . Then Sir Launcelot sighed and therewith
the tears fell on his cheeks, and then he said thus, 'Most
noblest Christian realm, whom I have loved above all other
realms, and in thee I have got a great part of my worship!
And now that I shall depart in this wise, truly me repents
that ever I came in this realm that I should be thus shamefully banished, undeserved and causeless. But fortune is so
variant and the wheel so mutable that there is no constant
abiding. And that may be proved by many old chronicles as
of noble Hector of Troy and Alexander, the mighty conqueror, and many more others—when they were most in their
royalty they alighted passing low. And so fares it by me,'
said Sir Launcelot, 'for in this realm I had worship, and by
me and mine all the whole Round Table has been increased
more in worship, by me and mine, than ever it was by any of
you all.

'And therefore, wit thou well, Sir Gawain, I may live upon
my lands as well as any knight that here is. And if you, my
most redoubted King, will come upon my lands with Sir
Gawain to war upon me, I must endure you as well as I may.
But, as to you, Sir Gawain, if that you come there, I pray you
charge me not with treason nor felony, for, and you do, I
must answer you.'

'Do thou thy best,' said Sir Gawain, 'and, therefore, hie
thee fast that thou were gone! And, wit thou well, we shall
soon come after and break the strongest castle that thou hast
upon thy head!'

'It shall not need that,' said Sir Launcelot, 'for, and I were
as orgulous set as you are, wit you well, I should meet you in
midst of the field.'

'Make thou no more language,' said Sir Gawain, 'but
deliver the Queen from thee and pick thee lightly out of this
court.'

'Well,' said Sir Launcelot, 'and I had wist of this short-coming I would have advised me twice ere that I had come here. For, and the Queen had been so dear unto me as you noise her, I durst have kept her from the fellowship of the best knights under heaven.'

And then Sir Launcelot said unto Queen Guenevere in hearing of the King and them all, 'Madam, now I must depart from you and this noble fellowship for ever. And sithen it is so, I beseech you to pray for me, and I shall pray for you. And tell you me, and if you are hard bested by any false tongues, but, lightly, my good lady, send me word—and if any knight's hand under the heaven may deliver you by battle I shall deliver you.'

And therewithal Sir Launcelot kissed the Queen and then he said all openly, 'Now let see whatsoever he be in this place that dare say the Queen is not true unto my lord, Arthur, let see who will speak, and he dare speak!'

And therewith he brought the Queen to the King, and then Sir Launcelot took his leave and departed. And there neither king, duke, earl, baron nor knight, lady nor gentle-woman, but all they wept as people out of mind, except Sir Gawain. And when this noble knight, Sir Launcelot, took his horse to ride out of Carlisle, there was sobbing and weeping for pure dole of his departing. And so he took his way to Joyous Garde, and then ever after he called it 'The Dolorous Tower.'

And thus departed Sir Launcelot from the court for ever. . . .

Saying there will be nothing but strife in Arthur's realm now the Round Table is broken, many knights leave with Launcelot for France, his own country, where he rewards them, and especially his relations, with lands. Arthur puts England and his Queen under the rule of Mordred and sets out with Gawain against Launcelot. He besieges him at Benwick but Launcelot offers peace which all Arthur's lords would accept except Gawain, who prosecutes his

revenge. When he fights Launcelot, his strength increases until
noon when it begins to wane. On both occasions, however, Launcelot will not kill Gawain but asks Arthur to 'remember you of old
kindness'. Arthur deplores the war, 'for ever Sir Launcelot fore-
bears me in all places, and in like wise my kin, and that is seen well
this day what courtesy he showed my nephew Sir Gawain'. Meanwhile Mordred is crowned King of England and plans to marry
Guenevere, his father's wife. She secures herself in the Tower of
London.

[XXI.1] . . . Then came there word unto Sir Mordred
that King Arthur had araised the siege from Sir Launcelot
and was coming homeward with a great host to be avenged
upon Sir Mordred. Wherefore Sir Mordred made writs unto
all the barony of this land and much people drew unto him,
for then was the common voice among them that with King
Arthur was never other life but war and strife, and with Sir
Mordred was great joy and bliss. Thus was King Arthur
depraved and evil said of, and many there were that King
Arthur had brought up of nought and given them lands, that
might not then say him a good word.

Lo! you, all Englishmen. See you not what a mischief
here was? For he that was the most king and noblest knight
of the world and most loved the fellowship of noble knights
and by him they all were upholden, and yet might not these
Englishmen hold them content with him. Lo! thus was the
old custom and usages of this land, and men say that we of
this land have not yet lost that custom. Alas! this is a great
default of us Englishmen, for there may nothing us please
no term.

And so fared the people at that time—they were better
pleased with Sir Mordred than they were with the noble
King Arthur, and much people drew unto Sir Mordred and
said they would abide with him for better and for worse.
And so Sir Mordred drew with a great host to Dover, for
there he heard say that King Arthur would arrive, and so he

thought to beat his own father from his own lands. And the most part of all England held with Sir Mordred, for the people were so newfangled.

[XXI.2] And so, as Sir Mordred was at Dover with his host, so came King Arthur with a great navy of ships and galleys and carracks, and there was Sir Mordred ready awaiting upon his landing to let his own father to land upon the land that he was king over.

Then there was launching of great boats and small and full of noble men-of-arms, and there was much slaughter of gentle knights and many a full bold baron was laid full low on both parties. But King Arthur was so courageous that there might no manner of knight let him to land, and his knights fiercely followed him. And so they landed, magre Sir Mordred's head and all his power, and put Sir Mordred aback and all his people.

So when this battle was done, King Arthur let search his people that were hurt and dead. And then was noble Sir Gawain found in a great boat, lying more than half dead. When King Arthur knew that he was laid so low he went unto him and so found him. And there the King made great sorrow out of measure and took Sir Gawain in his arms and thrice he there swooned. And then, when he was waked, King Arthur said, 'Alas! Sir Gawain, my sister's son, here now thou liest, the man in the world that I loved most. And now is my joy gone! For now, my nephew, Sir Gawain, I will discover me unto you, that in your person and in Sir Launcelot I most had my joy and mine affiance. And now have I lost my joy of you both, wherefore all mine earthly joy is gone from me!'

'Ah! mine uncle,' said Sir Gawain, 'now I will that you wit that my death-days are come! And all I may wite mine own hastiness and my wilfulness, for through my wilfulness I was causer of mine own death, for I was this day hurt and smitten upon mine old wound that Sir Launcelot gave me,

and I feel myself that I must needs be dead by the hour of
noon. And through me and ⟨my⟩ pride you have all this
shame and disease, for had that noble knight, Sir Launcelot,
been with you, as he was and would have been, this unhappy
war had never been begun, for he, through his noble knighthood and his noble blood, held all your cankered enemies in
subjection and danger. And now,' said Sir Gawain, 'you
shall miss Sir Launcelot. But, alas, that I would not accord
with him! And, there[fore], fair uncle, I pray you that I may
have paper, pen and ink, that I may write unto Sir Launcelot
a letter written with mine own hand.' . . .

> The letter begs Launcelot to return and help Arthur and pray for
> Gawain at his tomb. He dies and in a dream warns Arthur he should
> not fight tomorrow because he will be killed, but should await
> Launcelot's coming.

[XXI.4] . . . Then were they condiscended that King
Arthur and Sir Mordred should meet betwixt both their
hosts and every of them should bring fourteen persons. And
so they came with this word unto Arthur. Then said he, 'I
am glad that this is done,' and so he went into the field.

And when King Arthur should depart he warned all his
[host] that, and they see any sword drawn, 'look you come on
fiercely and slay that traitor, Sir Mordred, for [I] in no wise
trust him'. In like wise Sir Mordred warned his host, 'that,
and you see any manner of sword drawn, look that you come
on fiercely and so slay all that ever before you stands, for in
no wise I will not trust for this tretise'. And in the same wise
said Sir Mordred unto his host, 'for I know well my father
will be avenged upon me'.

And so they met as their appointment was and were
agreed and accorded thoroughly. And wine was fetched and
[they] drank together. Right so came out an adder of a little
heath-bush and it stung a knight in the foot. And so, when
the knight felt him so stung, he looked down and saw the

adder, and anon he drew his sword to slay the adder and
thought none other harm. And when the host on both parties
saw that sword drawn, then they blew beames, trumpets and
horns and shouted grimly. And so both hosts dressed them
together. And King Arthur took his horse and said, 'Alas!
this unhappy day!' And so rode to his party and Sir Mordred
in like wise.

And never since was there never seen a more dolefuller
battle in no Christian land, for there was but rushing and
riding, foining and striking, and many a grim word was there
spoken of either to other, and many a deadly stroke. But ever
King Arthur rode throughout the battle of Sir Mordred
many times and did full nobly, as a noble king should do,
and at all times he fainted never. And Sir Mordred did his
devoir that day and put himself in great peril.

And thus they fought all the long day and never stinted
till the noble knights were laid to the cold earth. And ever
they fought still till it was near night, and by then was there
an hundred thousand laid dead upon the earth. Then was
King Arthur wood wroth out of measure when he saw his
people so slain from him. And so he looked about him and
could see no more of all his host and good knights left, no
more alive but two knights—the one was Sir Lucan de Butler
and his brother, Sir Bedyvere—and yet they were full sore
wounded.

'Jesu, mercy!' said the King. 'Where are all my noble
knights become? Alas, that ever I should see this doleful day!
For now,' said King Arthur, 'I am come to mine end. But
would to God,' said he, 'that I wist now where were that
traitor, Sir Mordred, that has caused all this mischief!'

Then King Arthur looked about and was aware where
stood Sir Mordred leaning upon his sword among a great
heap of dead men. 'Now, give me my spear,' said King
Arthur unto Sir Lucan, 'for yonder I have espied the traitor
that all this woe has wrought.'

'Sir, let him be,' said Sir Lucan, 'for he is unhappy. And if you pass this unhappy day you shall be right well revenged. And, [good lord, remember you of your night's dream and] what the spirit of Sir Gawain told you tonight. And yet God of his great goodness has preserved you hitherto. And for God's sake, my lord, leave off this! For, blessed be God! you have won the field, for yet we are here three alive, and with Sir Mordred is not one alive. And, therefore, if you leave off now, this wicked day of Destiny is past.'

'Now, tide me death, tide me life,' said the King, 'now I see him yonder alone, he shall never escape mine hands, for at a better avail shall I never have him.'

'God speed you well!' said Sir Bedyvere.

Then the King got his spear in both his hands and ran towards Sir Mordred, crying and saying, 'Traitor! now is thy death-day come!'

And when Sir Mordred saw King Arthur he ran to him with his sword drawn in his hand, and there King Arthur smote Sir Mordred under the shield with a foin of his spear throughout the body more than a fathom. And when Sir Mordred felt that he had his death's wound he thrust himself with the might that he had up to the burre of King Arthur's spear, and right so he smote his father, King Arthur, with his sword, holding in both his hands, upon the side of the head, that the sword pierced the helmet and the tay of the brain. And therewith Mordred dashed down stark dead to the earth.

And noble King Arthur fell in a swoon to the earth, and there he swooned oftentimes, and Sir Lucan and Sir Bedyvere oft-times heaved him up. And so weakly betwixt them they led him to a little chapel not far from the sea, and, when the King was there, him thought him reasonably eased. Then heard they people cry in the field.

'Now go, thou, Sir Lucan,' said the King, 'and do me to wit what betokens that noise in the field.'

So Sir Lucan departed, for he was grievously wounded in many places. And so, as he yode, he saw and hearkened by the moonlight how that pillours and robbers were come into the field to pille and to rob many a full noble knight of brooches and byes and of many a good ring and many a rich jewel. And who that were not dead all out, there they slew them for their harness and their riches. When Sir Lucan understood this work, he came to the King as soon as he might, and told him all what he had heard and seen.

'Therefore, by my rede,' said Sir Lucan, 'it is best that we bring you to some town.'

[XXI.5] 'I would it were so,' said the King, 'but I may not stand, my head works so. Ah! Sir Launcelot,' said King Arthur, 'this day have I sore missed thee! And, alas! that ever I was against thee. For now have I my death, whereof Sir Gawain me warned in my dream.'

Then Sir Lucan took up the King, the one party, and Sir Bedyvere, the other party, and in the lifting up the King swooned, and in the lifting Sir Lucan fell in a swoon that part of his guts fell out of his body, and therewith the noble knight's heart brast. And when the King awoke he beheld Sir Lucan, how he lay foaming at the mouth and part of his guts lay at his feet.

'Alas!' said the King, 'this is to me a full heavy sight to see this noble duke so die for my sake, for he would have helped me that had more need of help than I. Alas! that he would not complain him, for his heart was so set to help me. Now, Jesu, have mercy upon his soul!'

Then Sir Bedyvere wept for the death of his brother. 'Now leave this mourning and weeping, gentle knight,' said the King, 'for all this will not avail me. For, wit thou well, and I might live myself, the death of Sir Lucan would grieve me evermore. But my time passes on fast,' said the King. 'Therefore,' said King Arthur unto Sir Bedyvere, 'take thou here Excaliber, my good sword, and go with it to yonder water's side. And when thou comest there, I charge thee, throw my sword in that water and come again and tell me what thou seest there!'

'My lord,' said Sir Bedyvere, 'your commandment shall be done, and lightly bring you word again.'

So Sir Bedyvere departed. And by the way he beheld that noble sword, and the pommel and the haft was all precious stones. And then he said to himself, 'If I throw this rich sword in the water, thereof shall never come good but harm and loss.' And then Sir Bedyvere hid Excaliber under a tree, and so, as soon as he might, he came again unto the King and said he had been at the water and had thrown the sword into the water.

'What saw thou there?' said the King.

'Sir,' he said, '[I] saw nothing but waves and winds.'

'That is untruly said of thee,' said the King, 'and, therefore, go thou lightly again and do my commandment. As thou art to me lief and dear, spare not but throw it in!'

Then Sir Bedyvere returned again and took the sword in his hand. And yet him thought sin and shame to throw away that noble sword. And so, eft, he hid the sword and returned again and told the King that he had been at the water and done his commandment.

'What sawest thou there?' said the King.

'Sir,' he said, 'I saw nothing but waters wap and waves wan.'

'Ah! traitor unto me and untrue,' said King Arthur, 'now hast thou betrayed me twice! Who would ween that thou that has been to me so lief and dear, and also named so noble a knight, that thou would betray me for the riches of this sword? But now go again lightly, for thy long tarrying puts me in great jeopardy of my life for I have taken cold. And, but if thou do now as I bid thee, if ever I may see thee I shall slay thee ⟨with⟩ mine own hands, for thou wouldest for my rich sword see me dead.'

Then Sir Bedyvere departed and went to the sword and lightly took it up, and so he went unto the water's side. And there he bound the girdle about the hilts and threw the sword as far into the water as he might. And there came an arm and an hand above the water and took it and cleight it and shook it thrice and brandished and then vanished with the sword into the water. So Sir Bedyvere came again to the King and told him what he saw.

'Alas!' said the King, 'help me hence, for I dread me I have tarried overlong.'

Then Sir Bedyvere took the King upon his back and so went with him to the water's side. And when they were there, even fast by the bank hoved a little barge with many fair ladies in it, and among them all was a queen, and all they had black hoods, and all they wept and shrieked when they saw King Arthur.

'Now put me into that barge,' said the King. And so he did softly. And there received him three ladies with great mourning. And so they set them down and in one of their laps King Arthur laid his head. And then the queen said, 'Ah! my dear brother, why have you tarried so long from me? Alas! this wound on your head has caught over-much cold!'

And anon they rowed fromward the land and Sir Bedyvere beheld all those ladies go from him. Then Sir Bedyvere cried and said, 'Ah! my lord, Arthur, what shall become of me now you go from me and leave me here alone among mine enemies?'

'Comfort thyself,' said the King, 'and do as well as thou mayest, for in me is no trust for to trust in. For I must into the Vale of Avalon to heal me of my grievous wound. And if thou hear nevermore of me, pray for my soul!'

But ever the queen and ladies wept and shrieked that it was pity to hear. And as soon as Sir Bedyvere had lost the sight of the barge he wept and wailed, and so took the forest and went all that night. And in the morning he was aware, betwixt two holtis hore, of a chapel and an hermitage. [XXI.6] Then was Sir Bedyvere fain and thither he went, and when he came into the chapel he saw where lay an hermit grovelling on all fours fast thereby a tomb was new-graven. When the hermit saw Sir Bedyvere he knew him well, for he was but little before Bishop of Canterbury that Sir Mordred flemed.

'Sir,' said Sir Bedyvere, 'what man is there here interred that you pray so fast for?'

'Fair son,' said the hermit, 'I wot not verily but by deeming. But this same night, at midnight, here came a number of ladies and brought here a dead corpse and prayed me to inter him. And here they offered an hundred tapers and they gave me a thousand bezants.'

'Alas!' said Sir Bedyvere, 'that was my lord, King Arthur, which lies here graven in this chapel.'

Then Sir Bedyvere swooned, and when he awoke he prayed the hermit that he might abide with him still, there to live with fasting and prayers, 'for from hence will I never go,' said Sir Bedyvere, 'by my will, but all the days of my life here to pray for my lord, Arthur.'

'Sir, you are welcome to me,' said the hermit, 'for I know you better than you ween that I do, for you are Sir Bedyvere the Bold, and the full noble Duke, Sir Lucan de Butler, was your brother.'

Then Sir Bedyvere told the hermit all as you have heard before and so he beleft with the hermit that was beforehand Bishop of Canterbury. And there Sir Bedyvere put upon him poor clothes and served the hermit full lowly in fasting and in prayers.

Thus of Arthur I find no more written in books that are auctorised, neither more of the very certainty of his death heard I never rede, but thus was he led away in a ship wherein were three queens. That one was King Arthur's

sister, Queen Morgan le Fay, the other was the Queen of
North Wales, and the third was the Queen of the Waste
Lands. Also there was Dame Nineve, the chief Lady of the
Lake, which had wedded Sir Pelleas, the good knight, and
this lady had done much for King Arthur. And this Dame
Nineve would never suffer Sir Pelleas to be in no place where
he should be in danger of his life, and so he lived unto the
uttermost of his days with her in great rest. Now more of the
death of King Arthur could I never find, but that these ladies
brought him to his grave, and such one was interred there
which [the] hermit bore witness, that sometime was Bishop
of Canterbury. But yet the hermit knew not in certainty that
he was verily the body of King Arthur, for this tale Sir
Bedyvere, a knight of the Table Round, made it to be
written.

[XXI.7] Yet some men say in many parts of England
that King Arthur is not dead but had by the will of our Lord
Jesu into another place. And men say that he shall come
again and he shall win the Holy Cross. Yet I will not say that
it shall be so, but rather I would say, here in this world he
changed his life. And many men say that there is written
upon the tomb this:

'Hic jacet Arthurus, Rex quondam Rexque futurus.'

And thus leave I here Sir Bedyvere with the hermit that
dwelt that time in a chapel beside Glastonbury, and there
was his hermitage. And so they lived in prayers and fastings
and great abstinaunce.

And when Queen Guenevere understood that King
Arthur was dead and all the noble knights, Sir Mordred and
all the remnant, then she stole away with five ladies with her
and so she went to Amesbury. And there she let make
herself a nun and wore white clothes and black, and great
penance she took upon her as ever did sinful woman in this
land. And never creature could make her merry but ever she

lived in fasting, prayers and alms-deeds, that all manner of people marvelled how virtuously she was changed.

Now leave we the Queen in Amesbury, a nun in white clothes and black, and there she was abbess and ruler as reason would. And now turn we from her and speak we of Sir Launcelot du Lake, that [XXI.8] when he heard in his country that Sir Mordred was crowned King in England and made war against King Arthur, his own father, and would let him to land in his own land (also it was told him how Sir Mordred had laid a siege about the Tower of London because the Queen would not wed him) then was Sir Launcelot wroth out of measure and said to his kinsmen,

'Alas! that double traitor, Sir Mordred! Now me repents that ever he escaped my hands, for much shame has he done unto my lord, Arthur. For I feel by this doleful letter that Sir Gawain sent me (on whose soul, Jesu have mercy!) that my lord, Arthur, is full hard bested. Alas!' said Sir Launcelot, 'that ever I should live to hear of that most noble King that made me knight thus to be overset with his subject in his own realm! And this doleful letter that my lord, Sir Gawain, has sent me before his death, praying me to see his tomb – wit you well, his doleful words shall never go from my heart. For he was a full noble knight as ever was born. And in an unhappy hour was I born that ever I should have that mishap to slay first Sir Gawain, Sir Gaheris, the good knight, and mine own friend, Sir Gareth, that was a full noble knight. Now, alas, I may say I am unhappy that ever I should do thus. And yet, alas, might I never have hap to slay that traitor, Sir Mordred.'

'Now leave your complaints,' said Sir Bors, 'and first revenge you of the death of Sir Gawain, on whose soul, Jesu have mercy! And it will be well done that you see his tomb and secondly that you revenge my lord, Arthur, and my lady, Queen Guenevere.'

'I thank you,' said Sir Launcelot, 'for ever you will my worship.'

Then they made them ready in all haste that might be with ships and galleys with him and his host to pass into England. And so, at the last, he came to Dover, and there he landed with seven kings and the number was hideous to behold. Then Sir Launcelot spirred of men of Dover where was the King become. And anon the people told him how he was slain and Sir Mordred, too, with an hundred thousand that died upon a day, and how Sir Mordred gave King Arthur the first battle there at his landing, and there was Sir Gawain slain. 'And, upon the morn, Sir Mordred fought with the King on Barham Down, and there the King put Sir Mordred to the worse.'

'Alas!' said Sir Launcelot, 'this is the heaviest tidings that ever came to my heart. Now, fair sirs,' said Sir Launcelot, 'show me the tomb of Sir Gawain.'

And anon he was brought into the Castle of Dover, and so they showed him the tomb. Then Sir Launcelot kneeled down by the tomb and wept and prayed heartily for his soul. And that night he let make a dole, [and] all that would come, of the town or of the country, they had as much flesh and fish and wine and ale, and every man and woman he dealt to twelvepence, come whoso would. Thus with his own hand dealt he this money in a mourning gown. And ever he wept heartily and prayed the people to pray for the soul of Sir Gawain. And, on the morn, all the priests and clerks that might be got in the country and in the town were there, and sang masses of requiem. And there offered first Sir Launcelot, and he offered an hundred pound, and then the seven kings offered, and every of them offered forty pounds. Also there was a thousand knights and every of them offered a pound. And the offering dured from the morn to night. And there Sir Launcelot lay two nights upon his tomb in prayers and in doleful weeping. Then, on the third day, Sir Launcelot called the kings, dukes and earls with the barons and all his noble knights and said thus:

'My fair lords! I thank you all of your coming into this country with me. But, wit you well, all, we are come too late, and that shall repent me while I live. But against death may no man rebel. But sithen it is so,' said Sir Launcelot, 'I will myself ride and seek my lady, Queen Guenevere, for, as I hear say, she has had great pain and much disease, and I hear say that she is fled into the west. And therefore you all shall abide me here, and, but if I come again within these fifteen days, take your ships and your fellowship and depart into your country, for I will do as I say you.'

[XXI.9] Then came Sir Bors and said, 'My lord, Sir Launcelot, what think you for to do, now for to ride in this realm? Wit you well you shall do find few friends!'

'Be as be may, as for that!' said Sir Launcelot. 'Keep you still here, for I will forth on my journey and no man nor child shall go with me.'

So it was no boot to strive, but he departed and rode westerly. And there he sought a seven or eight days. And at the last he came to a nunnery, and anon Queen Guenevere was aware of Sir Launcelot as she walked in the cloister. And, anon as she saw him there, she swooned thrice, that all ladies and gentlewomen had work enough to hold the Queen from the earth. So when she might speak she called her ladies and gentlewomen to her and then she said thus: 'You marvel, fair ladies, why I make this fare. Truly,' she said, 'it is for the sight of yonder knight that yonder stands. Wherefore, I pray you, call him hither to me.'

Then Sir Launcelot was brought before her. Then the Queen said to all those ladies: 'Through this same man and me has all this war been wrought and the death of the most noblest knights of the world. For through our love that we have loved together is my most noble lord slain. Therefore, Sir Launcelot, wit thou well, I am set in such a plight to get

my soul health. And yet, I trust, through God's grace and
through his Passion of his wounds wide, that after my death
I may have,a sight of the blessed face of Christ Jesu, and on
Doomsday to sit on his right side, for as sinful as ever I was
now are saints in Heaven. And, therefore, Sir Launcelot, I
require thee and beseech thee heartily, for all the love that
ever was betwixt us, that thou never see me no more in the
visage. And I command thee, on God's behalf, that thou
forsake my company. And to thy kingdom look thou turn
again, and keep well thy realm from war and wrake, for, as
well as I have loved thee heretofore, mine heart will not serve
now to see thee, for through thee and me is the flower of
kings and [knights] destroyed. And, therefore, go thou to
thy realm and there take you a wife and live with her with joy
and bliss. And I pray thee heartily to pray for me to the
Everlasting Lord that I may amend my misliving.'

'Now, my sweet madam,' said Sir Launcelot, 'would you
that I should turn again unto my country and there to wed a
lady? Nay! madam, wit you well, that shall I never do, for I
shall never be so false unto you in that I have promised. But
the self destiny that you have taken you to I will take me to,
for the pleasure of Jesu, and ever for you I cast me specially
to pray.'

'Ah! Sir Launcelot, if you will do so and hold thy promise!
But I may never believe you,' said the Queen, 'but that you
will turn to the world again.'

'Well, madam,' said he, 'you say as it pleases you, for yet
wist you me never false of my promise, and God defend but
that I should forsake the world as you have done. For, in the
quest of the Sankgreall, I had that time forsaken the vanities
of the world, had not your love been. And, if I had done so
at that time with my heart, will and thought, I had passed all
the knights that ever were in the Sankgreall, except Sir
Galahad, my son. And, therefore, lady sithen you have taken
you to perfection, I must needs take me to perfection, of

right. For I take record of God, in you I have had mine
earthly joy, and, if I had found you now so disposed, I had
cast me to have had you into mine own realm. [XXI.10] But,
sithen I find you thus disposed, I assure you, faithfully, I will
ever take me to penance and pray while my life lasts, if that I
may find any hermit, either grey or white, that will receive me.
Wherefore, madam, I pray you kiss me and never no more.'

'Nay!' said the Queen, 'that shall I never do, but abstain
you from such works.'

And they departed. But there was never so hard an
hearted man but he would have wept to see the dolour that
they made, for there was lamentation as they had been stung
with spears, and many times they swooned. And the ladies
bore the Queen to her chamber. And Sir Launcelot awoke
and went and took his horse and rode all that day and all
night in a forest, weeping. And at last he was aware of an
hermitage and a chapel stood betwixt two cliffs, and then
he heard a little bell ring to mass. And thither he rode and
alighted and tied his horse to the gate and heard mass.

And he that sang mass was the Bishop of Canterbury.
Both the Bishop and Sir Bedyvere knew Sir Launcelot and
they spoke together after mass. But when Sir Bedyvere had
told his tale all whole, Sir Launcelot's heart almost brast for
sorrow and Sir Launcelot threw his arms abroad and said,
'Alas! Who may trust this world?'

And then he kneeled down on his knee and prayed the
Bishop to shrive him and absolve him. And then he besought
the Bishop that he might be his brother. Then the Bishop
said, 'I will gladly.' And there he put an habit upon Sir
Launcelot, and there he served God day and night with
prayers and fastings.

Thus the great host abode at Dover. And then Sir Lionel
took fifteen lords with him and rode to London to seek Sir
Launcelot. And there Sir Lionel was slain and many of his
lords. Then Sir Bors de Ganys made the great host for to go

home again, and Sir Bors, Sir Ector de Maris, Sir Blamour, Sir Bleoberis, with more other of Sir Launcelot's kin, took on them to ride all England overthwart and endlong to seek Sir Launcelot.

So Sir Bors by fortune rode so long till he came to the same chapel where Sir Launcelot was. And so Sir Bors heard a little bell knell that rang to mass, and there he alighted and heard mass. And when mass was done, the Bishop, Sir Launcelot and Sir Bedyvere came to Sir Bors, and, when Sir Bors saw Sir Launcelot in that manner clothing, then he prayed the Bishop that he might be in the same suit. And so there was an habit put upon him and there he lived in prayers and fasting. And within half a year there was come Sir Galihud, Sir Galyhodyn, Sir Blamour, Sir Bleoberis, Sir Vyllars, Sir Clarrus and Sir Gahalantine. So all these seven noble knights there abode still. And, when they saw Sir Launcelot had taken him to such perfection, they had no lust to depart but took such an habit as he had. Thus they endured in great penance six years. And then Sir Launcelot took the habit of priesthood of the Bishop and a twelvemonth he sang mass. And there was none of these other knights but they read in books and helped for to sing mass and rang bells and did lowly all manner of service. And so their horses went where they would for they took no regard of no worldly riches, for, when they saw Sir Launcelot endure such penance in prayers and fastings, they took no force what pain they endured, for to see the noblest knight of the world take such abstinence that he waxed full lean.

And thus upon a night there came a vision to Sir Launcelot and charged him, in remission of his sins, to haste him unto Amesbury, 'and, by then thou come there, thou shalt find Queen Guenevere dead. And, therefore, take thy fellows with thee and purvey them of an horse-bere and fetch thou the corpse of her and bury her by her husband, the noble King Arthur.'

So this vision came to Launcelot thrice in one night.
[XXI.11] Then Sir Launcelot rose up ere day and told the
hermit.

'It were well done,' said the hermit, 'that you made you
ready and that you disobey not the vision.'

Then Sir Launcelot took his seven fellows with him and
on foot they yode from Glastonbury to Amesbury, the which
is little more than thirty miles, and thither they came within
two days for they were weak and feeble to go. And when Sir
Launcelot was come to Amesbury within the nunnery,
Queen Guenevere died but half an hour before. And the
ladies told Sir Launcelot that Queen Guenevere told them
all, ere she passed, that Sir Launcelot had been priest near a
twelvemonth, 'and hither he comes as fast as he may to fetch
my corpse, and beside my lord, King Arthur, he shall bury
me'. Wherefore the Queen said in hearing of them all, 'I
beseech Almighty God that I may never have power to see
Sir Launcelot with my worldly eyes.'

'And thus,' said all the ladies, 'was ever her prayer these
two days till she was dead.'

Then Sir Launcelot saw her visage, but he wept not
greatly but sighed. And so he did all the observance of the
service himself, both the dirige and, on the morn, he sang
mass. And there was ordained an horse-bere, and so ⟨they
went⟩ with an hundred torches ever burning about the
corpse of the Queen. And ever Sir Launcelot and his eight
fellows went about the horse-bere, singing and reading many
an holy orison, and frankincense upon the corpse incensed.
Thus Sir Launcelot and his eight fellows went on foot from
Amesbury unto Glastonbury, and when they were come to
the chapel and the hermitage there she had a dirige with
great devotion. And, on the morn, the hermit that sometime
was Bishop of Canterbury sang the mass of requiem with
great devotion, and Sir Launcelot was the first that offered,
and then, also, his eight fellows. And then she was wrapped

in cered cloth of Rennes from the top to the toe in thirtyfold, and, after, she was put in a webbe of lead and then in a coffin of marble. And when she was put in the earth Sir Launcelot swooned and lay long still, while the hermit came and awaked him and said, 'You are to blame, for you displease God with such manner of sorrow-making.'

'Truly,' said Sir Launcelot, 'I trust I do not displease God, for he knows mine intent. For my sorrow was not, nor is not, for any rejoicing of sin, but my sorrow may never have end. For, when I remember of her beauty and of her nobless, that was both with her King and with her, so, when I saw his corpse and her corpse so lie together, truly mine heart would not serve to sustain my careful body. Also, when I remember me how, by my default and mine orgule and my pride that they were both laid full low, that were peerless that ever was living of Christian people, wit you well,' said Sir Launcelot, 'this remembered, of their kindness and mine unkindness, sank so to mine heart that I might not sustain myself.' So the French book makes mention.

[XXI.12] Then Sir Launcelot never after ate but little meat, nor drank, till he was dead, for then he sickened more and more and dried and dwined away. For the Bishop nor none of his fellows might not make him to eat, and little he drank, that he was waxen by a cubit shorter than he was, that the people could not know him. For evermore, day and night, he prayed, but sometimes he slumbered a broken sleep. Ever he was lying grovelling on the tomb of King Arthur and Queen Guenevere, and there was no comfort that the Bishop nor Sir Bors nor none of his fellows could make him. It availed not. So, within six weeks after, Sir Launcelot fell sick and lay in his bed. And then he sent for the Bishop that there was hermit, and all his true fellows. Then Sir Launcelot said with dreary stevin, 'Sir Bishop, I pray you give to me all my rights that long to a Christian man.'

'It shall not need you,' said the hermit and all his fellows.

'It is but heaviness of your blood. You shall be well mended by the grace of God tomorn.'

'My fair lords,' said Sir Launcelot, 'wit you well, my careful body will into the earth. I have warning more than now I will say. Therefore give me my rights.'

So, when he was houseled and eneled and had all that a Christian man ought to have, he prayed the Bishop that his fellows might bear his body to Joyous Garde. (Some men say it was Alnwick, and some may say it was Bamborough.)

'Howbeit,' said Sir Launcelot, 'me repents sore, but I made mine avow sometime that in Joyous Garde I would be buried, and, because of breaking of mine avow, I pray you all, lead me thither!'

Then there was weeping and wringing of hands among his fellows. So at a season of the night they all went to their beds, for they all lay in one chamber. And so, after midnight, against day, the Bishop that was hermit, as he lay in his bed asleep, he fell upon a great laughter. And therewith all the fellowship awoke and came to the Bishop and asked him what he ailed.

'Ah! Jesu, mercy!' said the Bishop, 'why did you awake me? I was never in all my life so merry and so well at ease.'

'Wherefore?' said Sir Bors.

'Truly,' said the Bishop, 'here was Sir Launcelot with me, with more angels than ever I saw men in one day. And I saw the angels heave up Sir Launcelot unto Heaven, and the gates of Heaven opened against him.'

'It is but dretching of swevens,' said Sir Bors, 'for I doubt not Sir Launcelot ails nothing but good.'

'It may well be,' said the Bishop. 'Go you to his bed and then shall you prove the sooth.'

So when Sir Bors and his fellows came to his bed they found him stark dead, and he lay as he had smiled, and the sweetest savour about him that ever they felt. Then was there weeping and wringing of hands and the greatest dole they made that ever made men. And, on the morn, the Bishop did his mass of requiem and, after, the Bishop and all the nine knights put Sir Launcelot in the same horse-bere that Queen Guenevere was laid in before that she was buried. And so the Bishop and they all together went with the body of Sir Launcelot daily till they came to Joyous Garde. And ever they had an hundred torches burning about him.

And so within fifteen days they came to Joyous Garde, and there they laid his corpse in the body of the choir and sang and read many psalters and prayers over him and about him. And ever his visage was laid open and naked that all folks might behold him, for such was the custom in those days that all men of worship should so lie with open visage till that they were buried.

And right thus, as they were at their service, there came Sir Ector de Maris that had seven years sought all England, Scotland and Wales, seeking his brother, Sir Launcelot. [XXI.13] And when Sir Ector heard such noise and light in the choir of Joyous Garde he alighted and put his horse from him and came into the choir. And there he saw men sing and weep and all they knew Sir Ector but he knew not them.

Then went Sir Bors unto Sir Ector and told him how there lay his brother, Sir Launcelot, dead. And then Sir Ector threw his shield, sword and helm from him, and when he beheld Sir Launcelot's visage he fell down in a swoon. And when he waked it were hard any tongue to tell the doleful complaints that he made for his brother.

'Ah! Launcelot,' he said, 'thou were head of all Christian knights! And now I dare say,' said Sir Ector, 'thou, Sir Launcelot, there thou liest, that thou were never matched of earthly knight's hand. And thou were the curtest knight that ever bore shield, and thou were the truest friend to thy lover that bestrode horse, and thou were the truest lover of a sinful man that ever loved woman, and thou were the kindest man that ever struck with sword, and thou were the goodliest person that ever came among press of knights, and thou was the meekest man and the gentlest that ever ate in hall among ladies, and thou were the sternest knight to thy mortal foe that ever put spear in the rest.'

Then there was weeping and dolour out of measure.

Thus they kept Sir Launcelot's corpse aloft fifteen days and then they buried it with great devotion. And then at leisure they went all with the Bishop of Canterbury to his hermitage and there they were together more than a month.

Then Sir Constantyne, that was Sir Cador's son of Cornwall, was chosen King of England, and he was a full noble knight and worshipfully he ruled this realm. And then this King Constantyne sent for the Bishop of Canterbury, for he heard say where he was. And so he was restored unto his bishopric and left that hermitage. And Sir Bedyvere was there ever still hermit to his life's end.

Then Sir Bors de Ganys, Sir Ector de Maris, Sir Gahalantine, Sir Galihud, Sir Galyhodyn, Sir Blamour, Sir Bleoberis, Sir Vyllars the Valiaunte, Sir Clarrus of Cleremount, all these knights drew them to their countries. Howbeit, King Constantyne would have had them with him, but they would not abide in this realm. And there they all lived in their countries as holy men. And some English books make mention that they went never out of England after the death of Sir Launcelot. But that was but favour of makers! For the French book makes mention, and is auctorised, that Sir Bors, Sir Ector, Sir Blamour and Sir Bleoberis went into the Holy Land thereas Jesu Christ was quick and dead. And, anon as they had stablished their lands—for, the book says, so Sir Launcelot commanded them for to do ere ever he passed out of this world—these four knights did many battles upon the miscreants or Turks. And there they [died] upon a Good Friday for God's sake.

Here is the end of the whole book of King Arthur and of his noble knights of the Round Table, that, when they were whole together, there was ever an hundred and forty. And here is the end of the 'Death of Arthur'.

I pray you all, gentlemen and gentlewomen, that read this book of Arthur and his knights from the beginning to the ending, pray for me while I am alive that God send me good deliverance, and, when I am dead, I pray you all, pray for my soul!

For this book was ended the ninth year of the reign of King Edward the Fourth by Sir Thomas Malory, Knight, as Jesu help him for his great might, as he is the servant of Jesu both day and night.

Caxton's Epilogue

Thus ends this noble and joyous book entitled *Le Morte Darthur*, notwithstanding it treats of the birth, life and acts of the said King Arthur, of his noble knights of the Round Table, their marvellous inquests and adventures, the achieving of the Sankgreall, and, in the end, the dolorous death and departing out of this world of them all. Which book was reduced into English by Sir Thomas Malory, Knight, as before is said, and by me divided into twenty-one books, chaptered, and imprinted and finished in the Abbey of Westminster, the last day of July, the year of our Lord, 1485. Caxton me fieri fecit.

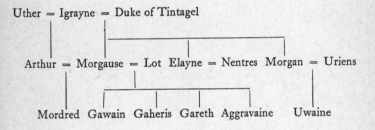

Uther = Igrayne = Duke of Tintagel

Arthur = Morgause = Lot Elayne = Nentres Morgan = Uriens

Mordred Gawain Gaheris Gareth Aggravaine Uwaine

Explanatory Notes

⁌⁊

27   *histories . . . doctrine:* 1. about or for religious meditation e.g. *Golden Legend* (saints' lives and homilies, 1483); 2. acts of great conquerors e.g. *Histories of Troy* (1475), *Godfrey of Boulogne* (1481); 3. examples and doctrine e.g. *Catho* (a 'book (that) may well be called the regiment or governance of the body and soul', 1483).

27   *nine worthy:* a commonplace of the later Middle Ages, characteristically medieval in its grouping into three threes. See, for example, G. Cary, *The medieval Alexander*, ed. D. J. A. Ross (Cambridge, 1956), p. 247 and n. 146.

28   *in him . . . might be aretted:* 'to him might be imputed'.

28   *Polychronicon:* 'the description of the universal world . . . and also the historial acts and wonderful deeds since the first making of heaven and earth', by Ranulf Higden of Chester Abbey (14c.), translated by John Trevisa and printed by Caxton in 1482. Boccaccio's Latin *De Casibus Virorum Illustrium* ('The downfall of famous men'), written between 1355 and 1360, appeared in an English version by John Lydgate (15c.) as the *Fall of Princes*. *Geoffrey* (of Monmouth): see pp. 24–5. *Brutish book* because it traced the descent of the Kings of Britain from Brutus of Troy.

29   *Patricius . . . imperator:* 'Arthur, the nobleman, Emperor of Britain, France, Germany and Dacia'.

29   *no man . . . own country:* e.g. John iv. 44.

33   *shall be your . . . avail:* 'will honour you and be of benefit to the child'.

page

34   *Morgause . . . Elayne . . . Morgan:* Malory omits to explain
why these ladies are mentioned here. They are the daughters of
Igrayne by her previous husband (see p. 253).

37   *made . . . life:* i.e. made their confessions and were absolved.

40   *Twelfth Day:* the Epiphany, 6 January.

44   *made do cry:* had announced.

62   *And some there were . . . passed:* difficult to punctuate – 'some
who were only just knights, (who) increased in honour (and) surpassed' etc.(?) or 'some who were only just knights (who had)
increased in honour, who surpassed' etc.(?)

64   *else hast . . . [grace]:* 'otherwise thou wilt enjoy the best fate',
that is, if your striking the basin does not bring the expected
disastrous response.

67   *yours:* i.e. on your champion, by fighting him.

85   *needed him:* he needed.

93   *make . . . parties:* 'take recompense from everyone'(?)

106   Title of Book Five: cf. Caxton Book X beginning chapter 50.

106   *measures of blowing . . . vermins:* the belief that Tristram
invented the terms of the hunt seems to be an English tradition;
but which book is referred to is uncertain. (See F. Remigereau,
'Tristan, maître de vénerie dans la tradition anglaise et dans le
roman de Thomas'. *Romania* lviii (1932), pp. 218–37.)

171   *I may not do withal:* I cannot help it.

174   *mass-penny:* money offering made at the Offertory during mass
throughout medieval Europe, at the altar-rail, often in order of
social precedence.

176   *all herbs and trees renew a man and woman:* I do not know
what this means. Mr. B. F. Nellist tentatively suggests that *a* may
be a mistake in copying made by the scribe for abbreviation of
and, in which case read *all herbs and trees renew, and man and
woman*.

178   *no maner . . . arms:* 'no kind of display of their own heraldic
arms'.

201   *the cross of Sir Tristram:* presumably the cross at his grave.

222   *that ever held . . . together:* 'that ever Christian king held
together'.

226   *fortune . . . low:* The impermanence of the world and man's

life in it, awareness of which haunted medieval people, was symbolized in the continual turning of her wheel—on which all were placed—by the Goddess Fortune, blindfold and unregarding any worth, so that at one time a king might be ascending and reign, but at the next must topple down. To make the general commonplace reference and then to cite stock examples is another common medieval mode.

237   *Hic . . . futurus:* 'Here lies Arthur, the once and future king'.

245   *my sorrow . . . sin:* i.e. not because I can no longer enjoy the sinful pleasure of love now Guenevere is dead.

246   *because of breaking:* 'so that I may not break'.

250   *Caxton me fieri fecit*: 'Caxton had me (i.e. this book) made'.

Textual Notes

❧

See note on p. 25 about the text.
C = Caxton's edition, W = Winchester MS.

page

42 And therewith Merlin: *from this point on the text is based on the Winchester MS.*

50 fetched (fette): *so* C, sette W.

54 the: *so* C, sir W.

55 of their: *so* C, other W.

55 succour: *cf.* C, . . . gentylwymmen socour vpon payne of dethe.

56 on her lands (londis): *so* C, W *may read* lordis.

64 here nigh-hand: *so* C, nize here honde W.

64 bole: *Vinaver's emendation;* body W, hoole C.

64 grace: *so* C, knyght W.

67 hold: *cf.* C, . . . ye hold me a promyse.

71 towers: holes C, *which Vinaver prefers because a French source has* fenestres.

71 said Sir Madore de la Porte: *so* C, *omitted* W *which has* (*what* C *omits*) and seyde *between* Arthur's *and* Yonder.

81 done: *so* C, dome W.

92 smote him that: W *has expuncted* with *between* him *and* that, s.h. within the hand t. C.

93 deaths: *so* C, dedys W.

99 the Castle Perilous: this C.P. W *and* C.

112 W *and* C *do not make sense to me and I have therefore transposed the names of the ladies.* W *reads* made (*for* told, *as in* C) *and Vinaver amends*, bade.

112 as he issued: *so* C, and a. h. i. W.

113 none but . . . lusts: *so* C, none noþer with clyppynge and kyssynge as for fleyshely lustys W. *Despite the implications of the second*

259

page

point which the French book is reported as mentioning, I am by no
means certain I am right in amending *W* in the light of *C*.

115 'Ah!' said Sir Launcelot, 'Sir Lamorak: A syre Lamorak *C*,
A seyde sir lamorak *W*.

120 hoved: *so C*, heved *W*.

125 am: *so C*, is *W*.

128 censer: *so C*, sawser *W*.

130 lived: *so C*, loved *W*.

131 night.' Then: *between* night *and* Then *C & W insert* And so Sir
Launcelot . . . departed *as in next paragraph, where both have
these words also.*

134 loud the: *so C*, l. that t. *W*.

142 Tristram: *so C*, launcelot *W*.

149 any realm: *so C*, ony co realme *W*.

152 fromward: toward *W & C*.

154 six: *so C*, vii *W*.

154 Pescheours: *so C*, Petecherz *W*.

155 horse: *so C*, crosse *W*.

159 though: *so C*, thou *W*.

160 him: hit *C*, them *W*.

161 'What have you seen . . . have seen,': *so C*, Why have ye sene *W*.

162 four-and-twenty years/days: *so C*, iiii y./d. *W*.

162 a: *so C*, no *W*.

163 palace: place *C*, pallesy *W*.

167 your: youre *C*, youe *W*.

170 said she, 'have: have *C*, said she woll ye be my paramoure have *W*.

170 you, I shall: *so C*, you and I shall *W*.

175 man: *so C*, men *W*.

176 we: *so C*, he *W*.

178 gift of King: *so C*, gyffte of the kynge *W*.

187 horse that is slain: hors slayne that ys slayne *W*, hors that was
slayne *C*.

189 When the . . . they: But whan the . . . And than they *W*, thenne
whanne the . . . they *C*.

192 So then it: so that it *W*, Soo it *C*.

194 Sir Lavaine, 'my: *so C*, Sir Launcelot Lavayne my *W*.

196 that: *so C*, of *W*.

page

200 request . . . knights of: rekeyste where they were at the hyze feste as knyghts of *W*, request made hem alle that were there at that hyz feest as of the knyztes of *C*.

204 of a hundred: a hundred *W*, of honderd *C*.

205 *W. continues without any distinction, immediately after* Aggravaine: And here on the other side followeth the most piteous tale of the Morte Arthur Saunz Guerdon par le Shyvalere Sir Thomas Malleorre Knyght. Jesu ayedé ly pur voutre bone mercy, Amen. *After a space of one inch the tale, that in this edition begins on p.* 206, *then follows on the same page. The scribe must have copied without thinking. C. has:* And here after foloweth the moost pytous history of the morte of kynge Arthur the whiche is the XX book.

207 Do you . . . Aggravaine: doo as ye . . . Agrauayne *C*, but do ye . . . Gawayne *W*.

211 never live: *so C*, lyve longe *W*.

214 adretched: dretched *C*, adremed *W*. *Should W be kept?* = 'had such dreams'(?)

215 ere (or): *so C*, for *W*.

215 doubt for, who that: done/doue for who who that *W*, sayd before who *C*.

217 there destroy: *so C*, there destroy there *W*.

217 for by: *so C*, to do for by *W*.

220 Gareth: *so C*, Gawayne *W*.

223 wept and swooned: *so C*, wept amonge and sowned *W*.

227 Tower: gard *C*.

234 I: *so C*, he *W*.

239 and: *so C*, of *W*.

241 were in the Sånkgreall: *here the version in the Winchester MS. ends.*

248 died: ded *C*.

Glossary

&

abraided, started (up)

abstinaunce, self-denial, fasting

accord, reconcile, agree

ado, had little a., did not much care

adretched, disturbed

advantage, boasting; *do my a.*, seize my advantage, help myself; *at such a.*, at such a disadvantage; *of a great a.*, most advantageously

adventure, chance, accident

adventurous, perilous

advise (sometimes reflexive), consider, think, look at, inform; be advised, take thought, be cautious, reluctant; be advised to do, beware of doing

advoutrer, adulterer

affiance, trust

affray, at a great a., in a great commotion

again, in front of

against him, at his coming

ailed, what he a., what was the matter

aligeaunce, alleviation

alight, fell

alighted, illumined

amated, confused

amoved, angry

an(d), if

anon, at once; *a. as*, as soon as

apointed, resolved

appeal, accuse

appertinence, privileges belonging

arace, tear away, obliterate

araged, enraged, frenzied

array, state of affairs

arson, raised front or back of a saddle

assotted (upon), infatuated (with)

astoned, dazed, stunned, astounded

auctorised, authoritative

avail, advantage

avoid, dismount from, dismiss, go away from

await, watch, attend; *have greatly in a.*, watch most suspiciously

ballad, 'verse'

barget, small boat
basnet, helmet
bate, quarrel
battle, army
bawdy, dirty
beames, trumpets
bedaished, bedecked, adorned
beeke, warm
begone, covered
behest, promise
beleft, remained
bente, open grassy place
bere, litter
bere, took their b., behaved?
bereve, take from
beseem, seem, be fitting
besene, equipped, dressed; *well-b.*,
   good-looking
beset, bestow
besparkled, bespattered
betake, entrust to
betaught, commended
bewared, bestowed
bezant, gold coin
boot, remedy, 'help', use
borow, pledge
bought, evil b., fully avenged (?)
bounty, worth, favour
box, blow
brachet, bitch-hound
brast(e), see *to-brast(e)*
Bretayne, Britain, Brittany
brewte, fame
browes, broth
buishment, ambush
burre, ring on spear to guard
   hand
buskes him, hastens

but (if), unless
bye, ring, bracelet
cankered, malignant
careful, sorrowful
carle, churl
carpe, speak
cast (reflexive), intend, plan
cered, waxed
certes, indeed
chariot, cart
chivalry, knights, knighthood,
   appropriate act of a knight
   especially prowess in knightly
   warfare, knightly code
clatter, chatter
clean(ly), bare, bright, excel-
   lent(ly), complete(ly), full(y)
clearness, brightness, splendour
cleight, clasped
clerk, scholar
clip, embrace
coif, close-fitting cap
complished, filled
conceit, judgement
condiscended, agreed
conditions, character, disposition
coronal, circlet (about the helmet?)
countenance, appearance, look
courage, spirit, desire, vigour
courtesy, courteous, ideal conduct
   of knights and ladies; refined,
   kind and generous behaviour
crupper(s), hind-quarters of
   horse, strap preventing saddle
   slipping forward
cunning, skill
curtest, most courteous

danger, captivity, power

deal, part, bit

debate, strife

deeming, suspicion, guessing

defamed, spoken of

default, *in my/your d.*, through my/your failure

defend, forbid

defoul, put to shame, defile

deliverly, quickly, adroitly

departition, departure, separation

deprave, disparage

depreve, convict

despite, insult, wrong, resentment, defiance, contempt

device, will

devoid, remove

devoir, duty, utmost effort

dight, prepared, furnished

dint, blow

dirige, service for the dead

disease, discomfort, trouble

diseased, weary, ill

disherit, deprive, dispossess

disparbeled, dispersed

display, draw

divers, various, several

do, interfere; put (e.g. on); *d. made/set*, caused to be made/set; *d. me/you to wit*, cause me/you to know

doctrine, instruction

dole, distribution of gifts

done, gift, boon

doubt, fear

draught, recess

draw, render, translate, derive

dress (sometimes reflexive), set in position, prepare, arrange, rise, get ready, advance

dretching, trouble

dryed, suffered, dried

duke, leader, ruler (in particular of a duchy)

durable, indefatigable

dure, exist, last

dwell, delay

dwined, wasted, pined

dyked, defended with ditch

eagerly, swiftly

eft, again

endite, write

endlong, from end to end, along

eneled, anointed in extreme unction

enforce, force, ravish

enprised, undertaken

entromedled, mingled

environ, round about

estate, rank, pomp

estures, rooms

even, straight, close

even-infourmed, well-directed

fain, willing(ly), glad(ly)

fare, fuss

faren withal, dealt with

farme, fixed tax

fathom, unit of measurement, length of the forearm (?)

fear, frighten

feawtir, (noun) support for spear on saddle; (verb) to put spear in support

felony, perfidy

fiaunce, promise

fiercely, with high-spirit

flaket, flask

flemed, put to flight

foin, thrust

for why, because

forbled, weak for loss of blood

force, no f., that does not matter; *take/took no f. (of)*, do/did not mind (about)

forfare, destroy

forfend, deny, banish from

forhewen, cut to pieces

forthink (reflexive), grieve, regret

forward, ready

foyled, defiled, trodden down

freike, man

freshly, eagerly, gaily

gan, began, did (i.e. mere auxiliary)

garnish, supply, equip

gates, ways

gaynest, quickest

gear, armour, weapons

genitrottes, genitals

gentle(ness), noble, gentle

gesseraunt, light coat of armour

geste, man

ghostly, spiritual

give, incline; *g. nought of*, care nothing for

glaive, spear

gloore, stare

good, make (it) g. (upon), enforce one's assertion, substantiate by fighting

grauntmercy, many thanks

gre, victory, prize for victory

Grekysshe, Greek

greve, trouble, feel anger, sorrow

gripe, grasp, seize

grounden, sharpened

gyserne, battle-axe

hailse, speak to

halfondele, half

handled, captured

hap, befall, happen

hardely, indeed

hardy(ness), brave, bold, audacious

harms, wrongs, sufferings

harness, armour, arms

harnessed, equipped, adorned

hart of grece, fat deer

haunt, resort

head, magre (mine/thine) h., in spite of (my/thy) self

helm, helmet, armed man

hight, was named

hight, on h., loudly, aloud, aloft

historial, of the nature of history, (pseudo-) historical

history, story (true or professedly true), chronological narrative of events

hole, window (?)

holtis hore, bare woods

houseled, shriven

hove, wait, float

howbeit, nevertheless, although

hurling, commotion

idight, prepared

iwis, indeed

journey, exploit

joust, fight on horseback, especially of two knights contending with lances and swords *keep*, guard, wish, care; *k. of*, care about

kind(ly), nature (al), family; *do their k.*, act according to their nature

knave, boy

kyd, famous

laine, conceal

langage, talk

large, broad

largely, fully, freely

latten, latten (brass or similar metal)

lay adown, allay

lazar-cote, leper-house

lechés les alere, let go

lendes, loins, buttocks

let, hindrance, hinder, prevent

let, cause

lever, rather, dearer

levest, dearest, most desirable

licourous, lecherous

lief, dear, willing

light, grow light, cheerful; alighted

lightly, quickly

like, please

likely, good-looking, looking capable

list, (it) pleases

livelode, possessions

lodged, tracked down (to his 'lodge')

long, be fitting, belong

luske, sluggard

lust, desire

lusty, handsome, pleasant, merry, full of desire, vigorous

magre, ill-will (and see *head*)

maker, poet, story-teller

mal engine, evil intention

marches, borders, country

maystry (make), (do) deed of power or skill; contest

mean(s), mediators, ambassadors, mediation, agency

measure, out of m., without limits, excessively, intemperately

meddle, mix, fight, have to do, interpose

menour, behaviour

merrily, pleasantly

mickle, much

misfortuned, unfortunate

most, greatest

move(ing), propose(ing), persuade

much, big

namely, especially

neish, soft

nere, not at all, never

nobless, nobility, nobleness

noise, rumour

notforthan, nevertheless

notoirly, notoriously

obeisance, rule

obley, wafer

of, with regard to, because of, about, from

open-mouthed, talkative

ordain, arrange, prepare, command

ordinance, decision, command

orgule, pride

orgulous, proud

oughte, felt towards, possessed, owed

outrage, violent wrong

overthwart (*at an*), across, cross-wise, (with a) crosswise (blow)?

pace, more than a p., a great p., at a good speed

pain, penalty, trouble; *do my p.*, do my utmost

paramour, lover, mistress

parde, indeed, assuredly

parters, umpires (?)

party, part, region; (*for*) *the most p.*, the greatest part

passage, way, road

passing, very

pavilion, large tent

paynim, heathen

paytrel, horse's breast-armour

peaceably, easily, without opposition

peril, on my p., I assure you

perilest, most dangerous, formidable

perowne, large block of stone

pick (reflexive), steal (thee) (?), go (?)

pille, plunder

pillour, plunderer

plain, open

plenour, with the full number

plucking, urging

points, at all p., in every respect

prime, first hour

providence, contriving, provision

purvey (sometimes reflexive), arrange, provide

pusil, chaste youth, virgin

put to the worse, defeat

put upon, accuse of

quest, trial

quick, alive

quite, repay, punish

race, pull, snatch

ransack, examine

rase, cut, slash

rasure, scraping, shaving

ravish, fetch

rear-main, back-hander

rebuke(d) (*put to a*), defeated, shamed

recomfort yourself, take courage again

record, witness

recover, obtain, get

recrayed, cowardly

recreant, surrendering

rede, advise, advice

redouted, distinguished, dreaded

reduce, render, translate

report (reflexive), appeal for confirmation

resorts, requests

respite, delay for consideration

reverence, at the r. of, in honour of

rews, me r. of, I'm sorry for

rights, at, unto all r., in all respects

rightwis, rightful

rome, go

rove, stabbed, tore

royalty, magnificence, pomp

rumour, noise, uproar

sadly, soundly, solidly, quickly

saint, holy

sakering, consecration

salew, greet, salute

samite, rich silk

scaffolds, platforms, stands

scripture, inscription

search, examine

sege, seat, place

self, same

sendel, fine silk or linen

sew, follow, practise

shaftemonde, hand-breadth

shapes, aims a blow

shent, injured, ruined

shondeship, shame, disgrace

shortcoming, falling short (?), failure (?), misadventure(?)

shunts, moves aside

side-boards, side-tables

siker(ly), certain(ly), sure(ly)

sith, since

sithen, then, since

slade, valley, glade

slake, abate

slight, skill, sleight

slipped, (=*O.E.D.* slipe v.¹?) sharpened (?), polished (?)

small, fine

so that, provided that

sodden, boiled

soft, steady

sowgh, swoon

sparde, barred

spirre, ask

stable (stability), constant, unchanging, firm

stand(with), side(with)

sterte, mount

stevin, occasion, voice

still(y), silent(ly)

stint, stop(ping), abate(ing), loss (?)

stir, row, steer

stoon, break, crush

strait, close(ly), strict(ly), narrow

strength, secure, bring about

stuff, furnish, supply

sufferance, will

surety (of), security, confidence, certainty of obtaining

sursingles, horse's girths

sweven, dream

tacches, habits, qualities

take, accept (as a champion); give

taught, guided

tay, outer membrane

tene, suffering

term, (space of) time

than, by t., by the time that

thinks, *thought*, me/him etc. t., it seems/seemed to me/him etc.

thirl, pierce, run

thrange, pressed

tide, befall

(to-) brast(e), broke(n) (in pieces)

to-crached, badly scratched

to-drive, burst to pieces

to-hew, cut to pieces

tomorn, tomorrow

tourney, take part in tournament, i.e. a contest between knights divided into two contending parties *trase*, tread

tray, pain

treason, treachery

trenchant, sharp

tretise, agreement, entreaty

trewage, tribute

trouth, faith

truncheon, piece, shaft (of spear)

undern, evening, about nine a.m.

undertake, afflict, seize

unhap, misfortune

unhappy, unfortunate, disastrous, harmful

unhilled, uncovered

unneth, scarcely

until, to

untrouth, infidelity

unwraiste, unfastened

upon loft, on horseback

utterance, fullest extent

vengeably, vindictively, cruelly

verily, really, fully

vilans, of a villain, base, vile, shameful

villain, low-born rustic, serf

villainy, conduct of a villain, vile wickedness, insult, disgrace, boorishness

visage, stare at

wagge, shake, totter

wait, observe, watch, be careful; w. *upon*, guard, attend

wait (with), treat (with)

wallop, gallop

waltered, tossed about

wanne, become dark

wap, lap

wardrobe, dressing-room

warly, warlike

warn, prevent

watch, lie awake, lie in wait, guard

ways, by w., on the way

webbe, sheet

ween, weened, think (thought), expect(ed)

welde, possess, rule

werlow, monster

whether, even if

while, until

wight, strong

wilsom, lonely, dreary

wite, blame

with (that), by, provided (that)

wood(ness), mad(ness)

worship, with *my w.*, (act) honourably, and keep one's honour

wrake, injury, hostility

wrath, injure

wroken, vented

wroth, twisted

yode, went

your althers, of you all

Further Reading

The Works of Sir Thomas Malory, ed. E. Vinaver (London: Oxford Standard Authors, 1954 etc.). 1 volume.

The Works of Sir Thomas Malory, ed. E. Vinaver (Oxford, 1947). 3 volumes. [The standard edition with full introductions, notes and textual variants. *]

The tale of the death of King Arthur by Sir Thomas Malory, ed. E. Vinaver (Oxford, 1955). [Book Eight with introduction and notes.]

[The next three books grew out of Vinaver's edition.]

Essays on Malory, ed. J. A. W. Bennett (Oxford, 1963). [*]

Malory's originality: a critical study of Le Morte Darthur, ed. R. M. Lumiansky (Baltimore, 1964).

C. Moorman. *The book of Kyng Arthur: the unity of Malory's 'Morte Darthur'* (University of Kentucky Press, 1965).

E. K. Chambers, 'Malory', in *English literature at the close of the Middle Ages* (Oxford, 1945).

H. S. Bennett, 'Fifteenth-century prose', in *Chaucer and the fifteenth century* (Oxford, 1947).

R. T. Davies, 'The worshipful way in Malory', in *Patterns of love and courtesy*, ed. J. Lawlor (London, 1966).

D. Everett, 'A characterization of the English medieval romances', in *Essays on Middle English literature* (Oxford, 1955).

R. S. Loomis. *The development of Arthurian romance* (London, 1963). [Short and readable.]

Arthurian literature in the Middle Ages: a collaborative history, ed. R. S. Loomis (Oxford, 1959). [The standard work. *]

Full bibliographical information is to be found in *The Cambridge Bibliography of English Literature* ed. F. W. Bateson (Cambridge, 1940) and the *Supplement* ed. G. Watson (Cambridge, 1957), together with those works above that are followed by an asterisk.